TRIALS OF UPPSALA

KEVIN TUREK

authorHOUSE®

AuthorHouse™ UK
1663 Liberty Drive
Bloomington, IN 47403 USA
www.authorhouse.co.uk
Phone: UK TFN: 0800 0148641 (Toll Free inside the UK)
      UK Local: (02) 0369 56322 (+44 20 3695 6322 from outside the UK)

This is a work of fiction. All of the characters, names, incidents, organizations, and dialogue
in this novel are either the products of the author's imagination or are used fictitiously.

Published by AuthorHouse 04/11/2022

ISBN: 978-1-6655-9798-2 (sc)
ISBN: 978-1-6655-9799-9 (e)

Print information available on the last page.

This book is printed on acid-free paper.

CHAPTER 1

VINCENT HAGLAZ

THE LIGHT OF THE MOON finally peered out from the overcast sky, bringing light and shadows to the landscape. The rock face of the cliff was the first to be illuminated. The cliff looked down on a large compound. Large walls stood strong around its borders, and a tower with a large spire made the centrepiece. Men in ebon armour stood as sentinels along the inner walls. They walked the many balconies that rose high above the cliff.

The light of the moon finally crept its way over the top of the cliff, revealing two silhouettes positioned just outside the treeline at its peak. They looked out at the tower with anxiety and ambition building.

The man of the pair, Vincent, knelt with a holy symbol in his hands. He was a man of thirty years, his hair brown with golden-blond streaks. His leather boots and dressings were worn loosely. A small black cape hanging just beyond his shoulders was finished with a crimson lining. Silver decoration in honour to God faced outward. A silver rapier and iron short sword decorated his belt. To combat his anticipation of the

1

coming test, he prayed to his God. He prayed not just for their victory but for his own.

The female, Ambrose, paced in circles around the kneeling Vincent. Her steps were high and swayed. She swung a silver rod around herself as she continued her strut. Ambrose, a woman of twenty-eight years, wore grey leather armour that hugged tightly around her Amazonian frame. She stood tall, with legs like oak trees. Her upper body was fit and toned. She was light enough to move with great agility but sturdy enough to take a hit.

"Your prayers will not win you this day, Vincent," Ambrose antagonized.

Vincent ignored her prodding.

"Fine. You can use your God to cover your shortcomings," she teased.

"Do not forget that God gives strength to you as well," Vincent finally replied. "Or am I mistaken and you do not channel his power through your staff?"

Ambrose stopped short in her strut in front of Vincent, her back to him. The cockiness in her voice was gone. "This power I use is my own. The magic I channel through this staff belongs to me and is mine—mine alone!"

"That's blasphemy," Vincent said calmly. This was an argument that had occurred many times in their training over the past ten years. It was circular and always started and ended the same.

"The alchemists of the west use their own power to power their magic without God," Ambrose began. "Who is to say that mine does not work the same?"

"Alchemists use the power that dwells from within the earth and nature to fuel their magic. We use faith and holy symbols of power for our own," Vincent corrected.

"Ah, but as you know, I do not use a holy symbol, nor do I pray to your *God*," she said with a snicker.

"Perhaps that relic you use is your holy symbol. I believe that we all work to serve God in our own way. Doing right by the world and bettering ourselves is a version of prayer." Vincent knew that he was not persuading her, but this was still what he believed.

Ambrose just stayed standing, silently rejecting Vincent's line of thinking, as she always had. "He's late," she stated. She referred to a man they were waiting to rendezvous with: the man who would decide their fate, a fate that had been a decade in the making.

Vincent laughed. "No, he's here."

The approaching man made no sound, even though he had moved through heavy wood before exiting the treeline. He was not seen until the whites of his dark eyes glistened in the moonlight.

Vincent, who was still kneeling with his eyes closed, did not need to see or hear the man. He could detect the usual pungent odour of the man's pipe. Whatever blend of herbs it contained, there was an identifiable aroma. It was a smell Vincent knew better than anyone else. After all, this man was his father, Umbra Teiwaz. Haglaz was Vincent's mother's maiden name.

As he stepped into the light, the man, in black furs with stark, black, slick hair, cast his heavy gaze on the two. He looked to be in his fifties, with tanned hide and a gaze that seemed to penetrate through their beings and for a thousand miles more.

Ambrose stood at attention. Vincent stayed unmoved.

"Ambrose, run down our mission objective," Umbra quietly barked.

"We are here to kill Lord Broch, a lord in open rebellion with the theocracy of Sylvania," she stated. "He wishes to upset the peace they have with the kingdom of Avalon. He uses his men to ransack churches with men dressed as Avalon knights and alchemists."

"Right," Umbra spat out. "Vincent, what have I been training you all for?"

Over the past ten years, Umbra had taken on ninety-six pupils. These pupils were chosen based on prowess and accolades in battle, skill with magic, and refined minds. They were told that they had been selected to assemble an elite team to fight the heretics of Sylvania. For five years, they were taught battle tactics, politics, language, and religion—and they sparred. Most dropped out or were selected out. Some died.

After the five years, there were ten. Those ten were then told the real purpose of their training: Both the theocracy of Sylvania and the kingdom of Avalon were run by a shadow government. The pope of the theocracy and the king of Avalon were figureheads. The true leaders were bred and trained to lead. The ruler of Sylvania was due to be replaced, and these ten would be tested to decide who was worthy to replace him. After hard missions, personal breakdowns, and failings, two remained.

"This will be the deciding test on who you believe should take control," Vincent said flatly.

"Don't sound so excited," Umbra chuckled. "I want you both to know that I won't play favourites here. This will be a very objective test. Whoever kills Lord Broch will move on in training. You both have shown competency in your classes and in battle. There were many who coveted this position. I would gladly put this country in the hands of either of you. However, should one of you die, that will make the decision even easier," he added with a cynical smile.

He walked to the cliff edge and scoffed. "There are over two hundred men in there, no doubt with skilled warriors and mages. Good luck." He spoke with what almost sounded like sarcasm.

As the two watched him walk into the treeline, he seemed to just vanish.

"Vincent," Ambrose began, "I have nothing against you, even after all these years of being pitted against each other. I may not agree with you, or this country, on many things. However, I respect you."

Vincent was silent, not sure how to respond to this almost uncharacteristic praise.

"That doesn't change the fact that I can't let you win!" Ambrose declared.

She bounded down the cliffside like an ibex down a mountain.

This was a burst of emotion that, again, Vincent had come to not expect from her. Of course, those who had made it to the final ten were not exactly friends, most not being incredibly sociable.

Vincent knew he'd better get a move on if he wanted any chance of reaching the target first. He walked right to the edge of the cliff and let himself fall over.

The rush of freefall always brought elation to Vincent. There were few things that brought him joy, but the exhilarating kiss of air overtaking him felt like the first time every time.

Vincent's cape opened, and he made good use of the magic he had learned in many years of training. Hot air rushed under the cape. Vincent had the ability to control flames. Using this to his advantage, he had learned how to gain such control and let just a trickle of hot air rush from his palms.

He had to be careful to fly low when coming down. Avoiding the eyes of the sentinels was paramount. He glided safely to the ground just outside the compound of Lord Broch.

Vincent had an affinity for flame magic; he also enjoyed its study. An element with the ability to create with equal destructive capabilities resonated well with him. Vincent made his way to the large walls by ducking in and out of shadows. Guards were about in every direction. Two stood directly in front of the way in.

Vincent waved his hand at the torches near the doorway. Everything went dark in that corner. The guards were stumbling to get the torches back on. While one of them tried to light a torch, Vincent cast his magic to "help" the ignition process. The torch flared up and scorched the guard's face. The guard dropped the torch and grabbed his face, screaming in pain.

In the dark and among the confusion, Vincent picked the pocket of a guard and moved swiftly into Broch's manor. He had to be quick while making it to the tower's base. Those torches would be on again soon.

As he snuck around the base of the tower, from above came the thud of a body dropping to earth. Vincent, hand on his sword, was ready to square off. However, this body was already dead. No doubt that was courtesy of Ambrose from somewhere in the tower above.

"Damn, is she trying to get us noticed?" Vincent whispered to himself angrily.

A door directly to Vincent's left swung open. A guard peered out, no doubt having heard the crash of his compatriot. Upon seeing the body, he jumped back in surprise and was going to let out a cry, but before sound could leave his mouth, a hand was clasped around it. As he looked down, he saw the gleaming tip of a silver rapier poking out from his chest. He barely let out a small gasp before death stole his life.

Vincent felt the hands of the guard grasp his hand and reach toward his face before falling silently dead. When the body hit the ground, Vincent saw that the guard was in fact a young woman. Vincent only felt sorrow that this poor soul was being manipulated by such an evil man.

Vincent moved into the tower. The doorway opened directly to a wooden stairway. It seemed like this was just a pathway for guards, not the proper entry to the tower. Vincent ascended the stairs, moving with care not to make a sound.

The stairway let out into one of the lower balconies. To his right, Vincent spotted two guards armed with crossbows looking out. To his left was a door. In front of him was a stairwell moving up to the next balcony. Vincent could see the glow of a torch coming down the stairwell in front of him, making the door the more enticing option.

He crept through the doorway, which led into an armoury with racks full of weapons—crossbows, swords, ebon uniforms, spears, shields, and notably to Vincent, barrels of oil for lamps. Vincent moved towards a door at the other end of this armoury but stopped in his tracks when he saw the flicker of a torch light up the seams of the door in front of him.

Two guards opened the door to the armoury. "This is going to take all bloody night!" one of the guards complained.

"Hush. Moaning about it won't help," the other retorted.

"*We need those weapons cleaned and sharpened for tomorrow's drills,*" the first said in a mocking tone, flicking his wrist to imitate whoever had given this order.

The second laughed. "Just find ones that look shabby and used, and this shouldn't take too long."

"Whatever," the first huffed. He moved down the rows of weapons, just briefly looking them over with little care.

The two split up, moving up and down the racks, until the first one stopped, noticing that one of the swords did not look like the others.

"Blimey, how long have we had such a posh sabre?" He picked up a silver rapier he had found placed on the rack where a standard broadsword should be.

The second chuckled. "Is that sarcasm? All these swords are rubbish."

There was no answer.

"Oi? Oi!?"

Again there was no response.

He moved towards the torch where his fellow was positioned. "What are you on about?"

As he turned the corner of the rack, he saw the torch on the ground with a trail of blood leading away. He was about to yell, but then the entire room went dark as the torches were extinguished, along with his life.

AMBROSE GAINS

Ambrose had made her way through the various levels of the tower. She had scaled the stone walls on the compound's outer walls. She'd then made it to a balcony that encircled the tower. She had quickly dispatched some guards in her way, though one of them gave her some trouble when he charged her. She had used his own momentum to send him over the railing of the balcony. She was strong, but she wasn't going to out-muscle a huge man.

She had found an armoury on this level and took the advantage of absconding with a uniform. Her silver staff would stand out as not being a standard-issue weapon, so she took a uniform that looked fit for a mage. Using this disguise, she moved up the levels of the tower, not making eye contact with guards. She was not exactly sure where she would find Lord Broch, but she figured that he would be somewhere near the top of the spire.

She had made it up about seven levels before she heard an alarm bell sound. She froze, hoping that she had not been discovered. The guards rushing past tipped her off that she was not fingered as an intruder. Had Vincent been found? More likely the bodies she had left in her wake had been discovered.

She started to move with urgency to blend in with the guards fumbling to get into position. This was not going quite to plan. She had hoped that she would have at least found Broch before all hell broke loose.

She noticed a group of guards ascending the levels instead of descending like the rest of them. She decided that she would group in with them. When she caught up with them, Ambrose asked one of them what was happening.

"There's been units found dead at their posts. Also, rumours are that there is an intruder at the second level," the guard replied.

"Just one?" Ambrose exclaimed, trying to maintain the ruse.

"Mage, why aren't you at your post?" asked what seemed to be a guard with some authority.

Ambrose cursed and bit her lip. "I'm going to speak with Lord Broch. He may need my protection," Ambrose replied, hoping that would be an acceptable answer. She gripped her staff, ready to fight.

"Fine," the leader retorted. "We could use a mage to back us up. Just keep it under control. I don't need any friendly fire."

"Understood!" Ambrose affirmed, quite pleased with her deception.

The squad of six made it to the tenth level—almost to the top. Then the captain of the squad held up a hand and gave a signal. *Damn.* This wasn't known to Ambrose. But in the end, it hardly mattered. The squad instantly had her surrounded with weapons drawn.

"What gave me away?" Ambrose asked.

"The mages here are of higher rank than any soldier," the captain responded. "They wouldn't take orders from us. So drop the staff and come quietly," the captain demanded.

Ambrose had a hand on her weapon, ready to jump into action. It was then that she heard from below the screams of guards yelling, *"Fire! The tower is on fire!"*

The guards surrounding Ambrose shifted their gaze towards the sound for just an instant, but that was all she needed. She quickly spun her staff around with all the speed and strength she could muster. She had guards at her twelve, two, four, six, eight, and ten o'clock, with the captain being at twelve. The swords held by the guards were knocked away from Ambrose but were still in their owners' hands.

Ambrose thrust the staff forward directly into the guard at her two o'clock. It pierced both the guard's armour and flesh. The guard looked down in horror as blood erupted from his gut. But how did a mere staff stab through him? Ambrose channelled her magic into her staff, which could then project a magic light that took the form of any weapon Ambrose could imagine. In this instance, she had erected a spike of physical magic light on the end of the staff, functionally making a spear.

She removed her spear from the guard by tossing him over into the captain. She then spun around to her left. She could anticipate that the guard at her four would thrust his sword at her. Her instincts not failing her, an easy block was made by knocking it away with the rod of the staff. She continued her momentum and thrust the tip of the spear behind her, where it pierced through the guard.

The incoming guard, coming in an overhead swing, did not see Ambrose change the spear head to a battle axe. She swung upward, hacking off the arm of the guard and clipping his jaw. The next two came in fast, so she quickly switched to a double-ended sword. She spun quickly, with one end going low, the other high. The low end clipped the leg of the guard to her left, the one on her right blocking the high end. This left him open for Ambrose to sweep his legs.

"No, *wait!*" the guard screamed.

Ambrose would be lying to herself if she said that diving the blade into his heart brought her no satisfaction—not because of a lust for blood, but for the joy of demonstrating her superior abilities.

There was still an injured guard behind her, and the captain was back to his feet in front of her. Smoke was starting to rise. *Is Vincent trying to burn down this whole tower?* she wondered.

"Damn you, bitch," the captain cursed.

"Where's Lord Broch?" Ambrose asked. "I still need to speak with him after all," she added with a wink.

"Two floors up. Can't miss the room," he growled.

"That was easy," Ambrose stated, genuinely confused.

"If you've come for his life, you'll be disappointed. He is a high-class mage; he'll kill you for sure. Anyway, I'm getting out of here before this tower goes up in smoke. That is, if you let me pass. I doubt you have time to deal with me," the captain said.

Ambrose didn't like letting him go, but he had a point: she had to get Broch. If he simply died in the fire, the victory would technically be Vincent's.

The captain collected his man with the wounded leg, and they made their way down. Ambrose continued her way up. She could hear crashes and flashes of light from the levels below. *Sounds like Vincent is having his own trouble.*

VINCENT HAGLAZ

Vincent tucked and rolled, narrowly dodging a bolt of lightning. He had found a quite competent mage, one who was keener on fighting than fleeing the flames Vincent had started via the oil in the armoury.

"A lucky dodge, worm," the mage taunted, "but let's see how long you wriggle before you fry!"

Vincent shot flames at the mage, but they were easily avoided. The enemy mage kept up the pressure, firing bolt after bolt. Vincent had no time to counter this barrage, nor did he have the time to wait till this mage's mana depleted.

"You're boring me, worm," the mage teased again. "You know, I don't find boring men very attractive."

This gave Vincent an idea. He cast a flare of fire, with the flames coming nowhere near his quarry. It did, however, obstruct his enemy's vision just long enough for him to lose Vincent.

"Oh?" the mage exclaimed. "That's more like it, honey. I love a man of mystery".

Vincent came charging, swords in hand, from the enemy's right flank. He was spotted quickly.

"Oh, nice try, dear, but I found you!" he exclaimed, hurling another bolt of lightning at Vincent.

The bolt would fry Vincent if it found its mark, but at the last moment, Vincent tossed his iron sword to his left, making the bolt arch in its direction just long enough for Vincent to sidestep and keep charging. His silver rapier pierced the enemy mage.

"Sorry, but you're not my type," Vincent snarked. To Vincent's surprise, the man had a look of pure ecstasy. "Creep," Vincent scoffed. The enemy mage fell dead, with a smile on his face no less.

The tower was in complete chaos; the fire was growing stronger. Vincent was on the fifth floor now. The flames seemed to have reached the fourth floor. Guards were running about, fleeing, or trying futilely to extinguish the flames. Vincent continued to climb higher. He knew Ambrose had to be close to the target, and he had come too far to let her win.

AMBROSE GAINS

Ambrose found the room the captain had described. Double doors stood in front of her—the only thing standing between her and all she had ever wanted. This was not just the climax of ten years of training; no, it went far beyond that. Anger, fear, confidence, and satisfaction were all boiling up inside her. It was hard for her to fight back tears. *Not yet.* She wasn't done. The only thing left to do was remove this man who stood in her way.

She opened the door and strutted into the room, her staff in its base form so as to not give away her abilities. She saw him, Lord Broch, packing a case. He was a tall slender man wearing a fine black robe. He oddly wore chains around his body and a whip around his waist, no doubt as a means of combat. He moved with haste but not panic, despite the fact that the building was on fire. He didn't seem to notice her.

She got ready to pounce and began to rush in. Immediately, two chains erupted forth, springing to life. Ambrose, able to separate her staff into two pieces, did so. The piece in her left hand becoming a shield of light, the other a sword.

She swatted one of the chains away with her sword and blocked the other with the shield. She could see that the one she blocked was trying to wrap around her arm and immediately sliced at it, knocking it down. But then her sword wrist was slapped and caught by the whip. The pain was immense, and the whip was somehow tightening. The rope in the whip was also behaving strangely, as it went completely erect, with no slack.

Ambrose let out a scream of pain. The whip had forced her to drop the sword from her hand. One of the chains had wrapped around her legs. Broch swung the whip, which forced Ambrose to the ground. She dropped the other half of her staff.

"Well now, that was amusing," Broch mused.

"I'm going to fucking kill you!" Ambrose yelled.

The whip was tightening down on her wrist even more. She could feel it was cutting off circulation and soon would crush her bones.

"Clearly," he scoffed. "You're no doubt one of Umbra's peons."

Ambrose was stunned that he would know such a thing.

"Surprised?" he asked. "Oh yes, I'm aware of Umbra and his intentions. I know there is another running around this tower right now trying to kill me too."

"How could you know that?" Ambrose asked.

Broch looked down. He almost appeared sad. "The cycle never ends. Not until someone breaks it," he said almost to himself.

Ambrose began punching at the whip. Her knuckles began to bleed. She tried biting at it, but it was tough as stone. Her mouth bled. The chains still bound her legs tightly. This was bad. She had come so close, only to be thwarted here. No, there had to be more.

"Where is your God to help you, huh?" he mocked.

"Screw you, bastard! I don't need a God. I can handle you myself," Ambrose yelled, blood drops flinging from her lips, one landing on Broch.

Broch wiped it away in disgust. "Strange that a non-believer would fight so hard for a country centred around religion," he said. "Oh well, guess you lose this one. Hopefully your friend puts up a better fight. But now I really must repay you for ruining my beloved home."

He raised a hand, and another chain, this one with a spike on the end, lifted from the ground.

Suddenly, flames erupted from the ground beneath Broch. He jumped back, but not before those flames singed half his face. He dropped the whip.

Vincent emerged from below. Ambrose felt the release of the whip from her wrist. The chains had also gone limp. She was able to get up and secure her staff's two parts. But her right wrist was still in a bad way.

She put half the staff through her belt and projected a sword in her left hand. This put her at a disadvantage, but it was much better than her previous position. There was still hope.

"Damn, still alive? I got here too early then," Vincent jested with a wink.

"I still can't let you win, Vincent," Ambrose remarked.

"I know, but we must work together to beat him."

Ambrose nodded and yet again began her attack. She came at Broch from the right side. Again, a volley of chain fired at her. She rolled under the first and swatted away the second. A third one came belting toward her, but flames shot it down.

Vincent was charging in now too. Broch was not going to be able to deflect or avoid this one. So Ambrose charged directly in the way of Vincent's path, throwing off his attack.

"Are you serious, Ambrose? We had him!" Vincent protested.

"No, *you* had him. I told you, I'm not letting you win."

This time, it was Broch charging in, with chains poised and ready for attack. The two, Ambrose and Vincent, were not going to be able to counterattack in time. But as Broch came forth, one of the boards beneath him gave out, and he fell to the floor and fire below.

Broch could be heard screaming down below. Ambrose readied to go down and finish the job. Vincent grabbed her shoulder.

"Are you kidding? Don't be daft. We need to get out of here. This place is coming down!" Vincent yelled.

Ambrose looked down towards Broch, her hopes and dreams slipping away just like that. But she knew going down there was certain death.

"Damn it!" Ambrose cried.

Vincent opened a set of doors leading to the balcony. "Grab on!" he yelled.

Ambrose gave one last look towards Broch, who was still crying out in agony, being burned alive. "Ambrose!" Vincent repeated.

She reached out, holding onto Vincent. Vincent opened his cape. They jumped out, the tower crumbling behind them. They were coming in hard. Vincent was not used to having a passenger. "Brace yourself!" he yelled.

They crashed down onto the grass, yet again finding themselves on the cliff edge.

"Well done," they heard a familiar voice say. "Congratulations, Vincent, you've made it to the next stage," Umbra said through a toothy grin.

CHAPTER 2

VINCENT HAGLAZ

VINCENT STOOD TALL WITH PRIDE, his holy symbol clutched tightly in his hands, as he thanked God that he had been guided to this point. Joy was one of many emotions within Vincent, but it was mainly pride and satisfaction that filled his heart. After years of training, studying, fighting, and killing, he took a long-awaited cathartic breath.

Sadly, with the sweet came the bitter. Vincent realized that Ambrose had been denied her victory this day. He glanced over at her. She wasn't facing the two of them; she was simply looking out at the crumpling inferno that was the tower of Lord Broch, poetically watching her aspirations go up in flames.

Vincent felt for her. He had felt something every time another rival dropped from the program. This might be one of the more impactful. He knew she had wanted this—more than most, for reasons that were not known to him. While he empathized with Ambrose, he still had not lost any of his own convictions. He had his own dreams and visions of what he would like to see in this country.

"Come, Vincent," Umbra commanded. "We are heading back to Uppsala."

Uppsala was the campus and home base in which they had been trained. Ten years earlier, Victor had arrived at its doorstep just one of ninety-six highly competent candidates. The halls and living quarters used to be bustling. However, as the years passed, those numbers had dwindled. The place was still staffed with maintenance crews and training personnel, but there was no one to share in the trials and tribulations.

Something didn't sit right with Vincent about returning to this place alone. "Father, wait," he protested.

"That's *Master Teiwaz*," Umbra interrupted. "You are not ruler just yet. Not for a while."

"Master Teiwaz," Vincent corrected begrudgingly. "I could not have gotten so far without Ambrose—" he started to say.

"She knew exactly what was on the line and what she had to do," Umbra again interrupted. "We went over this at the very beginning of this encounter, if you remember. Or do you simply wish to hand your victory over to her?"

"All I was proposing is to let her come back with us. Let her continue to push me forward," Vincent suggested strongly.

Umbra turned around and simply said, "Do as you wish. You will regret it in time." With that, he disappeared into the treeline.

There was a long moment of silence. The moon had hidden itself yet again behind the clouds. The only noises that remained were the crackle of the fire, the yelling of Broch's men, and the quiet rustle of branches in the wind. They stood facing away from one another, Ambrose looking into the depths of the cliff contemplating the appeal of escape, Vincent looking into the darkness of the treeline. Just like his future, it held many mysteries.

"Want to keep me at that place to hold your victory over me?" Ambrose asked, finally breaking the silence.

"No, that's not it," Vincent began.

"Is it pity then? Because I don't need it, nor do I want it," she said with tears finding their way to her eyes. "Not from you," she concluded.

"I know what this meant to you," he said. "What this meant to all of

15

us. Every time one of us didn't make the cut, every death we endured, every single person left a mark on us. I know every single time I could just have easily been the one cut. There is still a journey ahead of me. While I fill the role I won, why not find a way to carve your own path?" Vincent explained.

Ambrose looked back. She had composed herself, although these were surprising words to hear from Vincent. "What happened to the man who only needed God?" she asked. "You never seemed to care much for the rest of us before."

"God is all I need," Vincent stated. "However, He has presented me with many gifts and friends to help me shape the world in the way He wants. I simply use the gifts He has granted me," Vincent said with a theatrical bow.

"I don't know about all that," Ambrose said, rolling her eyes. Then she smiled and punched Vincent on the shoulder. "Let's go home," she said.

Vincent stood and looked her in the eyes. "No longer do we have to see each other as competitors. Now we can behave as allies. I like this thought. I should hope you like it too."

"You're still a rival," she told him, "and if you ever falter in this path, I will take it from you."

"Fine by me," Vincent said.

The two made their way through the woods to the horses they had come in on. Umbra had already left on his own. Vincent had never seen his father's magic. The man never needed it to win a fight, most times not even drawing a weapon. Vincent sometimes wondered if his father's magic had something to do with transportation, as he always seemed to appear from nowhere.

They made the day's journey back to Uppsala, which was hidden well by mountains surrounding it on all side. The two of them tied up the horses and went back to their individual rooms in the living quarters for a much-needed rest. They knew the drill at this point. They would wait for an undetermined amount of time before Master Teiwaz summoned them for the next assignment.

AMBROSE GAINS

Ambrose had held strong for the journey home. However, now that she was alone in her room, all her doubts and harsh feelings about herself invaded her mind. She sat down on her bed and gripped her knees tightly. She hated crying; she hated being so weak as to give in to emotion like this. She truly felt alone in this moment, more so than she had felt in a long time.

She gripped tighter at her knees, sending a wave of pain through her wrist, which had been broken. She had made a bandage for herself and was stabilizing it with twigs she had found on the way back.

She and Vincent had said little to each other on the way back. She had lost. After all this time, to come so far and have it taken from her—it wasn't fair. How could it be?

She remembered what Vincent had said to her: *I know what this meant to you.* This just made her mad—unreasonably so.

Clutching her right wrist, she stood up and moved to her desk, which looked out into one of the courtyards. On it she saw the notes, scrolls, tomes, and texts she had collected over the years. The notes had many underlines and detailed diagrams. The texts had many flagged pages, with passages circled and so forth. This was a mass collection of her work over ten years. It began to almost fill her with nostalgia … until the rage came back and she remembered that this was ten years wasted.

Ambrose swept everything off the desk angrily with her left arm, grasping at certain pages and crumpling them, throwing them. She let out a yell of frustration as she continued to flail about, knocking this pristine workplace amok. Her right wrist slamming into her nightstand was promptly followed by the sound of glass shattering.

Ambrose winced and clutched at her wrist, the pain sobering her rage. She then looked at the floor. The crash of glass had come from a framed painting of her family. "Come on," she said, angry at herself for losing it like this. The painting showed her mother, father, older sister, and herself. Her father's face had been cut out—this being an edit she personally made. The memories and significance of this painting was not helping her fight back tears of sadness and rage.

There was a knock at the door.

"Not now, Vincent!" Ambrose said.

The door opened anyway.

"I said *not now*, Vincent—" Ambrose began to yell, but she stopped when she saw that it wasn't Vincent but someone she hadn't expected: Hamilton Thero, a personal butler at Uppsala. He helped with the day-to-day tasks at the manor but also was an instructor to these pupils. Hamilton taught both tactics and combat. Of course, he also possessed skills in magic, though none of the students knew what kind.

"Yes, but I'm not Vincent," Hamilton replied with a wink. He was dressed very finely, as one would expect of a butler. With his black hair slicked back and his glasses perched on a long nose, he looked both old and spry. "I heard of the goings-on the other day, and I wanted to see if you needed anything," Hamilton said in a more professional tone.

"No need to put on airs for me, Hamilton. As I'm sure you know, I'm no longer a student here. I failed." That last statement finalized the defeat for her.

"I did not come here to serve one of the candidates of Uppsala," Hamilton quickly interjected. This confused Ambrose. "I came to see if a long-standing friend of mine needed someone on her side," he added, his tone softening.

Ambrose chuckled. She ran up and hugged Hamilton.

"Oh, and to serve a guest of Master Teiwaz, of course," Hamilton said, back in his professional tone.

"Thank you, Hamilton," Ambrose said. The two shared a quiet moment. Hamilton noticed the painting she was holding. "Thinking of your sister?" Hamilton asked, trying not to sound sad.

Ambrose turned around and set the painting down on the nightstand. "No," she lied.

"You haven't failed her, you know," Hamilton said. "You still have a future and can still accomplish great things."

Ambrose looked out the window into the bleak courtyard. "I'm not so sure," she replied.

AMBROSE GAINS

12 years ago

Ambrose was gasping for air. Sweat dripping from her face, the sun stinging her skin, she looked up to see her sister, Marya, three years her senior, standing opposite from her. Marya was patiently waiting for Ambrose to ready herself.

"Marya, stop playing around and finish it," Ambrose could hear her father barking.

Ambrose and her sister were in a makeshift arena. In the middle of the woods, there was a small circle of dirt in what would usually be grass. This circle was outlined with stones marking the boundaries. Ambrose's father, Andar Grey, stood just on the outside of this circle, looking in with discontent. "She won't improve if you continue to coddle her," Andar stated.

Marya closed her eyes and sighed. She then charged in at her sister, who she knew would not be ready for this attack. Marya had a small pole she channelled her magic through to form weapons. This was identical to Ambrose's weapon. These each were two halves of the weapon that Ambrose used in the current day.

Marya, forming a dull blade, came in with a feint to the left. Ambrose fell for the feint and raised her own blade to parry but was now off balance. Marya quickly spun around and ducked low, kicking out her leg. This swept Ambrose off her feet.

Ambrose's eyes shut when she hit the ground, and when she opened them, she was met with a blade an inch from her face.

Ambrose threw her arms up in defeat. Marya offered a hand to help her up, but Ambrose declined it. She got up, brushed herself off, and stormed off into the woods. Marya watched her leave.

Ambrose ran all the way to a stream where she had spent a lot of time when she needed to let off steam. She channelled her magic into her half of the weapon and started pounding on large boulders. These boulders had many scars from the many times she had come here in similar fashion.

When Ambrose had finally exhausted her stamina and mana, she collapsed, lying on the bank. She closed her eyes. Again, when she opened her eyes, she found her sister standing over her.

"I am sorry about earlier," Marya said.

Ambrose sat up. "Why would you be?" she huffed. "You're not the failure." It stung Ambrose that she never beat her sister. All she wanted to do was to win one time to prove to her father that she was not useless.

Ambrose had never once beaten Marya in sparring. She had similar skill with her weapon, but she always got too hot-headed and made mistakes. Also, Marya was physically stronger and faster, having had three extra years of muscle training.

"You are getting better," Marya countered. "You just need to relax and focus. If you do that, I surely would be no match for you," Marya embellished.

"Don't patronize me," Ambrose barked.

"I'm not," Marya replied, now annoyed. "I am giving you advice so that next time, you can show Father what you are capable of." She knew the thoughts of her little sister. She could tell by the look on Ambrose's face and in her actions that she wanted nothing but their father's approval. She recognized these things in Ambrose because they were the exact thoughts she used to have.

Marya regathered her composure. It wasn't really Ambrose she was upset with anyway. "Why do you want to please Father so much?" she asked, staring off downstream. She knew the response that this question would trigger.

"Because I want to be father's successor!" Ambrose yelled, now on her feet. Andar was a man of great importance in the area. He was an influential priest for the town and a mage of significant power. He taught the other priests of the town in the ways of God and magic. The whole town thought of him as a successful and kind man. He gave sermons that lifted the spirits of hundreds who lived rather ordinary lives.

Ambrose's mother had left the family when Ambrose was very young. The memories of her mother were fond ones, but at the time, it had been hard for Ambrose to accept.

"I will show him that I am worthy of the gifts that he and God have blessed me with," Ambrose ranted with tears in her eyes. "I will bring honour to myself and the town when I become head priestess. I only wish that I can be as worthy a servant of God as he has been," she finished, more composed.

Marya continued to stare off in the distance. It made her sad to hear how utterly blindly her sister devoted herself to the faith. Not only that, but to their father as well. "If those are your goals, then you can have it," Marya said, still distant.

"What?!" Ambrose asked, again losing her composure.

"Lately, I have distanced myself from the faith, and I have no interest in taking up Father's mantle," Marya said.

"Heresy!" Ambrose screamed. "You are so ungrateful! To Father a-and to God!" Ambrose had to fight for her words through tears and anger. "All of these gifts you've been given. You have food, shelter, power, and you could have the respect of the entire town, but you choose to throw all that away? How selfish and disrespectful!" Ambrose continued to rave.

"I am grateful for my comforts in life," Marya said. She tried not to sound too angry, but she could not help it after being insulted. "I see Father and the faith for what they are, and I do not wish to have any part in it."

Marya had witnessed hideous acts done by the Church. Women who disobeyed their husbands would be shunned by the Church, and therefore the town. Women caught in adultery were banished from the town, while the men simply were put in the stocks for a day for all the town to shun. There were even some stories of children being abused by some of the priests—her father in amongst some of those rumours.

Marya knew the Church was a crutch for many people and provided a lot of good. It helped defend the town from bandits and invaders with its many competent mages. Its creeds and tenets also provided a good moral structure for the masses to follow. However, Marya could not simply look past its dark side.

As for Andar, he pushed his daughters to their breaking points. They did not have a life outside of training, no friends to talk to and share their thoughts with, only each other. If they were not sparring or practicing their magic, they were in church praying.

Marya had looked up their father when she was young, just as Ambrose did now, but lately, she wanted nothing more than to leave this life. She wanted no part in being her father's pupil and definitely did not want to end up like him. However, she could not bring herself to leave Ambrose as their mother had, and Ambrose was still so devoted to him.

"You don't know what you're talking about," Ambrose finally countered. She stood up and yet again ran off.

Marya stood up and looked back into the treeline. She met eyes with Andar, who had witnessed the entire exchange. The two traded a long and hateful stare. Marya finally broke it by walking away.

For the next several months, training continued as usual—survival exercises, magic training, and praying to the faith. However, the two sisters were not put through sparring drills like usual. Their father, for some reason, was keeping the two from fighting.

Yet the distance between the two sisters was growing. Marya had been skipping out on some services at the church. This usually would bring her name shame throughout the town and the wrath of her father. However, her father covered for her by telling any curious souls that Marya had been ill as of late.

Andar and Marya barely spoke, and there was obvious disdain between the two. He wouldn't bring up her absences in church but only spoke to give her his orders for training. Ambrose was growing closer to her father and was upset by her sister's continued progress in skill, even while being rebellious to God.

The day came when Andar announced that there would be another match between the two tomorrow. Ambrose was nervous, as she knew she was not much better than she was the last time. She did not want to disappoint Father or God by losing to her heretic sister.

Once again they squared off in the arena. Each manifested a blade just as before. This time, though, Andar stepped forward and cast a spell on the arena. The circle, which had been outlined by stones, was now enclosed by a physical transparent barrier. The two sisters looked confused.

"This time, you fight till the other can no longer continue. There will be no easy way out this time," he said with a toothy smile.

"Bastard," Marya said under her breath. She knew that if they were to get out of this, she would have to thoroughly beat her sister. The thought of doing such harm to Ambrose hurt her.

Ambrose gulped and felt the pressure go straight to her stomach. She could tell Father was interested in seriously testing her. To fail here would bring not only pain but humiliation and shame.

"Start!" Andar yelled.

The sisters exchanged looks for a while, each of them waiting for the other to move first. Then finally, Ambrose grew impatient and moved in. The two were locked in a fierce battle, with Ambrose on the offensive. She would strike at what she believed were openings but were only gaps that Marya left open to bait her.

Marya was fighting very defensively, blocking all of Ambrose's incoming attacks, throwing out an occasional thrust to keep Ambrose off her rhythm. She knew that sooner or later, Ambrose would get too impatient and do something risky. Also, Ambrose would soon wear herself out.

Ambrose was starting to get angry. However, even though she was mad at her sister for her insolence, she knew Marya had given her sound advice. She needed to remain calm and level-headed. She kept up her assault, keeping Marya on the defensive, but still found no openings.

Finally, just as Marya predicted, Ambrose tried to go for a big strike and attack Marya's legs, but this was an obvious feint. Marya called the bluff and was well prepared to parry the big swing she knew was coming high. Yet again, Ambrose was thrown off balance, and Marya swept Ambrose off her feet.

Ambrose, filled with rage, knew her sister would quickly have her in checkmate. She let out a scream and gripped her weapon tight. She manifested the weapon into a spear and thrust it upward. Then she felt a warm splash on her face, which quickly sobered her rage. She looked up to see her sister skewered by her lance. The look on her sister's face was at first one of shock, but it soon changed to a smile.

"N-no," Ambrose muttered weakly. In her rage, Ambrose had let go of her concentration that kept the blade dull. Her anger sharpened the point of the spear.

She let go of her weapon, which made it go back to its original form of a small pole. She held her sister and continued to just repeat "No, no, no, no." Her sister had a very absent stare, but she was almost smiling, and her face was not contorted in anger or pain.

"You finally beat me," Marya said weakly.

"Shut up!" Ambrose screamed. "Father, help her!" she pleaded with tears filling her eyes.

"Next time, you will not get such a lucky hit," Marya joked. "Be who you want to be, Ambrose, not what he wants you to be," she used her remaining strength to utter.

The barrier around the two faded. Ambrose was trying desperately to put pressure on the wound. Although she had no gift for healing magic, she knew that her father possessed some talent for it. "Father, please, she's dying," Ambrose begged.

Andar stepped forward and casually said, "I'm sorry, but this is as God wills. There's nothing I can do." He put a hand on his youngest daughter. "Rejoice! Your faith has been rewarded. See how God punishes heretics and aids those who are devoted to him," Andar said, trying to comfort Ambrose and find some justification for this.

Ambrose was frozen in a flurry of emotion. She knew that Marya and her father were at odds with one another, but how could he so casually dismiss his eldest daughter? This also felt like anything but a reward from God. Ambrose felt like she was the one being punished. Marya was her only friend in this world. The two had been rivals for as long as they could stand and fought constantly. Recently, they'd had different views of the Church and of their own father. Still, they never truly hated one another. Without her sister, Ambrose's life would be hollow.

"Come, Ambrose," her father ordered. "We must celebrate your victory. You have made me proud today. Leave the heretic there. I will send for her body to be dealt with later."

Ambrose began to shake with anger. She now saw her father's abuses of them for what they were. All this time, Ambrose simply took it as trials to make them stronger. She thought that he had done this for some tough love to prepare them. However, if he could so easily throw them away, then this wasn't love.

She watched the light finally leave her sister's eyes and Marya's body go completely limp. Her tears did not stop. She stood up, now with both halves of the weapon in her hand.

"Oh, how splendid. You shall make her past strength your own," her father praised.

Ambrose manifested two swords, just like she was used to. She walked up to her father. He went to put his hand on her shoulder to praise her. However, his hand was severed before he could.

Andar was caught off guard, and he screamed out in agony. Ambrose, no longer able to bury her feelings, unleashed a flurry of slashes, cutting the man to ribbons. She jumped on the man's lifeless corpse and continued stabbing him until there was just an undistinguishable mess of blood and flesh. Her own hands bled from how tightly she grasped the weapon.

She then remembered who her father was. If she was discovered, she would be tortured and killed by the town and the Church. So she ran, as far as she could. She was no longer Ambrose Grey. She would take her mother's maiden name.

For almost a year, she wandered from place to place, living off the land as she had been trained to do for all those years. She had completely thrown away her devotion to God. She was the only one she could rely on. She did not re-enter society for fear that she would face retribution. She talked only to her weapon, who she began calling Marya.

Then one day, a man in a butler's attire approached her. It was Hamilton. He explained that there was a great mage in this country who was looking for skilled warriors to create an elite team. They would be hunting heretics, which was of no interest to Ambrose, but

Hamilton explained that these individuals would have great influential power and could change much for the state of the country.

This was what piqued her interest. If she could create change that would prevent anything like she went through, then maybe she could honour her late sister. She could make the world one that would make her sister happy. She would no longer be a pawn of the Church. This is what she believed Marya would have wanted.

CHAPTER 3

VINCENT HAGLAZ

VINCENT HAD PASSED THE LAST few days as he always had at Uppsala. He spent his mornings and nights in the chapel. Sometimes, he would be joined by some of the staff that kept Uppsala running. He prayed to a statue that resembled the small holy symbol he kept on his necklace. The symbol was a cross with a half circle that arced over the shorter half of the cross.

The holy symbol on his necklace helped him channel the gifts that God had graced him with. Without it, he could produce a flame the width of a garden hose and propel it for about 50 yards. With the holy symbol, he could project flame twice the distance and with four times the girth and intensity.

When Vincent was very young, he had lived with his mother, Chesa Haglaz. Umbra was not around a lot. Some days, he would drop in to check on them—especially to check on how Vincent was getting on. Vincent would forget what his father looked like between the visits but would always remember the smell of the smoke that followed him.

Chesa hated that smell, while Vincent enjoyed it. This smell would bring happy memories of times spent with his father.

His father would bring him presents from around the world and would help Vincent learn swordplay. However, Umbra never stayed long. He always left just as quickly as he had come.

When Vincent was 10 years old, Chesa fell ill and passed away. Umbra came for the funeral service. Though sad about his mother's death, Vincent believed that he would now get to travel with his father. He would no longer have to wait around and wonder when his father would be coming home, because they would be together. Vincent could not wait to learn how his father lived, seeing new places and learning sword fighting.

However, Umbra, though smelled like Vincent's father, was not the same man. The spark of happiness that had been within Umbra was no longer there. The father Vincent loved hanging out with was no more. Umbra forbade Vincent to come with him, saying that instead he would be handed over to the church, where they would teach him how to be a priest. He would study religion and learn the ways of magic to defend the people.

Umbra did leave Vincent with one parting gift: the holy symbol, known as the tree of life. The believers were the roots of the tree, and when they passed, their souls would provide a leaf on one of its many branches. This was the religion of this country, the tree of life, and God was its caretaker.

Vincent would not see his father for another ten years. During this time, he did just as his father had instructed, and he discovered he had a strong connection to flame magic. Whenever Vincent had free time, he would practice with his rapier and short sword. These had been gifts from when Umbra had been teaching him swordplay. He would constantly practice the drills that Umbra had taught him.

Vincent had also made a name for himself as one of the more competent priests. He had many scores of kills of bandits within his first three years. Not only that, the town loved his sermons whenever it was his week to deliver one.

Vincent had even made a friend when he was at the clergy—John Bracken, also a very competent priest. John had grown up at this church all his life. He had been orphaned at birth, and since then had lived at the church. The two of them had started their priest training at around the same time.

Then the day came when Umbra was looking for recruits to train at Uppsala. Umbra came personally to pick his son to be a candidate. John would also be selected for the training. The two spent their years in training as friends, but of course, they were also each other's competition.

✦✦✦✦✦✦

After the first five years had passed, John and Vincent were in the top ten. The rivalry grew even more when they learned the truth of what was at stake. However, the two still looked out for each other.

Then, as the years dragged on, John started spending more time with one of the other candidates, Meredith Blair. The two became inseparable, and eventually a love sparked between the two. Vincent tried to warn John that getting too attached to Meredith could ruin what they had strived for. But John grew angry with this and saw it as jealousy on Vincent's part.

Just as Vincent had feared, when Umbra found out, he expelled the both. This was six years into the program. John protested, and when he knew he was gaining no ground, he asked if Meredith could stay if he dropped out. His request was denied, and they were both forced to leave. John and Vincent did not speak a word to one another at that time, and had not since. Of course, now Vincent was the final candidate in this whole ordeal.

Vincent liked to tell himself he had grown and changed as a man, but in this present day, he still felt like that impressionable boy who was always waiting for his father to come home and help him move forward. These thoughts and reflections found Vincent often in his prayers.

✦✦✦✦✦✦

Finally one morning, during Vincent's morning prayers, Hamilton entered the chapel and said, "Pardon me, Vincent. Master Teiwaz has summoned you."

"Thank you, Hamilton," Vincent replied. "I presume I am to report to the briefing room as usual?"

"Of course," Hamilton confirmed. "Oh, and also, Vincent ..." Hamilton began.

"Yes?" Vincent asked.

"Congratulations," Hamilton said, smiling a genuine proud smile, just as a parent would at a child's achievements.

"Thank you," Vincent said.

Hamilton escorted Vincent through the halls of Uppsala to arrive at the briefing room. When Vincent came through the door, he was met by Umbra and Ambrose. Seems Umbra had summoned her there as well. *That's good*, Vincent thought. He had wondered what would happen to her.

"Master Teiwaz," Vincent acknowledged.

"Sit down, both of you," Umbra said.

The two sat opposite each other at a long wooden table, while Umbra sat at the end, which was about five seats over. This briefing room was made to hold all the original candidates, so there were many long tables. It felt hollow and empty now that it was just the three of them. Hamilton stood by the door they had entered through.

Vincent and Ambrose met eyes momentarily, then quickly looked back to Umbra, as they did not know what to say to one another.

Umbra took a last puff of his pipe and stood up. "I have found a mission that will serve as your final test," Umbra stated.

Vincent had known that he had further training to come before he would take his role as ruler of Sylvania, but he was surprised that his father still had a test for him. However, he guessed that this was to be expected.

"There have been rumours of either a group or an individual seeking an ancient relic known as the Well," Umbra stated. "The Well has enough magical power that even a single person could be a threat to countries, or even the world. Your job will be to put a stop to them," he finished.

"How do you know someone is after this 'Well'?" Vincent asked.

Umbra smiled. "As you know, I have connections all over this world. These are trustworthy sources."

"So, our foe is going after a relic strong enough to threaten the world. You don't think this might call for a stronger force than just myself and Ambrose?" Vincent asked.

"This is why it will act as a final test," Umbra said. "It will be your task to assemble whatever force you believe necessary to handle this threat. When you take up your new position, it will be your duty to identify and eliminate threats to your country."

Vincent was never quite sure what his father's position in this world was, but he knew he worked for this shadow government in some facet. Did the government give them this mission, or was it his father specifically?

"We do not know where the enemy operates out of, but we do know where the Well is," Umbra said. "It is in the Kingdom of Avalon, hidden on the peak of Mount Bors."

Vincent was uncertain about going to Avalon. He knew that there was a peace between the two nations, but still, they were a godless people. That might give him issues. Vincent was unsure of what force he would be able to raise, but he believed that they would have enough skill and experience to hunt down and kill some heretics.

"As I'm sure you're aware, you will be foreigner in Avalon, and I hope you do nothing to threaten the peace we have with them," Umbra reminded.

Vincent now fully understood why it was the perfect test. He must act as a leader and put together a group to hunt down a mysterious threat to the world. While doing this, he must act with discretion so as to not start panic and give away secrets. Also, his force could not disturb the political situation that was always hanging in the balance.

Umbra stood up and began to walk towards the door.

"Is that everything?" Vincent asked.

"Yes. As stated, this one is all your responsibility. Time for you to spread your wings and fly."

"Well then, sir, I would like to request your help for this mission," Vincent said bluntly.

Umbra laughed. "Sorry, kid, but it doesn't work like that. You won't get any help from me. I won't have you leaning on me when times get tough. You'll just have to find those willing to follow you. I have already compromised by allowing Ambrose to stay here. If she chooses to follow you, that is her own choice. You have resourcefulness and talent. Now use it."

Umbra began to walk out of the door, then stopped dead in his tracks. "Oh yeah, I wouldn't go hunting down those you knew during your time here. Most are not the same as you remember them," he said, taking a puff of his pipe.

The door closed behind him, and all was silent in the room. Vincent had not thought about it, but it made sense that his father, and whoever he worked for, would be keeping tabs on those selected out of the program. They were, of course, some of the most capable, intelligent, and powerful individuals around. Their fate was something Vincent had wondered about from time to time. However, he had been distracted by the constant challenges this place threw at him.

Vincent and Ambrose didn't look at each other for the longest time. Finally, it was Ambrose who broke the silence.

"So, what are you going to do?" she asked.

Vincent wasn't quite sure. He needed time to consider where he would be able to find those willing to put their lives on the line for him. He'd had no contact with others for ten years, and he had no friends or allies ready to rally behind him.

Hamilton moved forward to the table. He cleared his throat. "I would be more than willing to accompany you, sir," he proposed while bowing his head.

This was a shock to Vincent. Hamilton had always been kind to him and the students of Uppsala, but he didn't expect Hamilton to give up his job.

"What of your job, Hamilton?" Vincent asked.

"My job is to tend to the needs of those residing at Uppsala. This seems to fit the description aptly. Don't you agree, Master Haglaz?" Hamilton asked with a wink.

Vincent laughed.

"You know I won't let you fail," Ambrose stated. "As I said before, if you ever falter in this path, I will take it from you."

Vincent had felt isolated for a long time. He had God, and that had been enough for him up to this point. Those who he'd had around him had coveted the same position as he and were willing to kill for it. But now, he had actual allies who were willing to follow him into the dark of the unknown, most likely to their deaths.

"So, where do you plan do find recruits?" Hamilton asked.

"Let me sleep on it," Vincent answered. "I have some ideas, but I need time to consider."

"Of course, sir. I shall go prepare some meals," Hamilton said with a bow. "Also, I shall prepare some more rooms in the living quarters."

"Thank you, Hamilton. I couldn't do this without you," Vincent replied.

Yet again, Vincent and Ambrose shared a long quiet moment, Vincent thinking about what he was going to do and what was to come, Ambrose still contemplating what all this meant for her. She was not in charge here; she would be following the orders of Vincent. That's what she felt she always did: she took orders from someone above her. First it was her father, then Umbra, now Vincent.

Ambrose wanted to be in Vincent's position more than anything, but she also was at a loss for what to do here. In the end, the two left without saying a word.

<hr />

Vincent returned to the chapel. His prayers were more like questions as to what his next move should be. He wondered how he could become the leader he was destined to be.

Hamilton and Ambrose were counting on him. Their lives depended on the steps he took. In his reflections and prayers, he could tell that he was faltering. How did Umbra do this?

He thought of what his father would do. The man was always so stern, so decisive in his actions and decisions. *That's what I must do*, Vincent thought. If he was to be successful, he had to show his father that he didn't need any coddling and hand-holding. So he promised to himself and to God that he wouldn't be so weak and indecisive.

AMBROSE GAINS

Later that evening, Ambrose was in one of the training arenas. She looked at the obstacle ahead of her. She had run this course over a hundred times—so many times that running it had become second nature.

She rubbed at her right wrist, which had been injured in the previous mission. She had gone to the infirmary here at Uppsala to have it taken care of. They had staff skilled in healing arts that helped speed up the healing process. This was something that came in handy when students ran dangerous missions day in and day out.

Ambrose took in a large breath of air, then charged down the decline. She hopped side to side on platforms that increased in height a little bit every time. On the highest platform were a series of ropes to swing from to make it across a pool of water. She quickly swung from rope to rope, wasting no movement.

Upon making it across, she ran straight ahead on a very thin strip of platform. Spinning poles came low and high, trying to knock her off the path, but she leaped and slid past them like she had practiced time and time again. She had to maintain her momentum as the platform ended to make the leap to the net that she had to ascend.

Once that was done, there was just the log that dangled on a descending rope. She leaped on it, having to keep her grip strong as the log flew down the rope before finally ending just ten feet from the ground. Right before it reached that point, she released her grip and hit the ground with a roll. She let out a breath of air and smiled.

Her composure was broken when she heard clapping. She stood up quickly and stared at the source. It was Vincent. She was upset and embarrassed. "Guess you were watching the whole time," she snapped.

"Hey now, that was a great run. I'm impressed. No need to get upset," he said.

She turned away and sat down on a bench. "It wasn't the fastest run, either. He's still got the fastest time," Ambrose huffed angrily. She was referring to another one of the final ten candidates who'd run the fastest on this course—and just about all of them.

"Yeah, speaking of Trevor." Vincent sat down next to Ambrose.

"I think we should bring him on with us," he said, knowing what the reaction would be.

"Are you kidding me!?" Ambrose yelled, jumping to her feet.

"We need him," Vincent replied calmly. He was not even looking at Ambrose. He just calmly looked down at his feet.

"No, we don't! Ambrose yelled. "Besides, you heard what Umbra said: those we knew here are not the same people we knew then. And even if they were," Ambrose began clenching her fists, "he was nothing but trash when we knew him." She was clearly upset.

"I remember what Father said," Vincent agreed, intentionally not referring to him as *Master Teiwaz*. "He said that this was on *me*. I'm the one calling the shots now. God has set this path in front of *me*, not him, and not you," Vincent said in finality. He needed to remind her of the roles they played on this mission.

Ambrose was moved to anger by that statement. She slapped Vincent across the face.

Vincent stood up and made direct eye contact with her. She gave thought to her actions and realized that he was right: he was the one in charge now, and she was yet again a subordinate. She wasn't happy about it and especially hated having it waved in her face. But she calmed herself down.

"Anything else, Vincent?" she asked.

"Yes, but it can wait till tomorrow morning's briefing. Nine a.m., don't be late," Vincent said. He began to walk away, then stopped in his tracks. "Oh yes, and it probably would be best if you started to refer to me as *sir*," he added, and then actually did walk away.

When he was gone, Ambrose just looked toward the doorway he'd walked through. How quickly he had taken to this new position of power. She began to wonder if following him was the right thing to do. She manifested a large hammer with her weapon, Marya, and smashed a training dummy. This would be the first of many.

✦✦✦✦✦✦

In the morning, Ambrose met with Vincent and Hamilton in the briefing room. It was now Hamilton and Ambrose who sat opposite from one another, with Vincent sitting in the captain's chair at the end of the table.

Vincent stood up and addressed them. "I have come to a decision on what we can do to bolster our forces. We will need to accomplish two things: First, we need to increase our sheer numbers. To do this, I will go to the pope and request the aid of some priests and soldiers. These will serve as our main force. Next, we need to increase the numbers within our leadership. Ambrose and Hamilton, you will serve as my captains. However, I believe we still need some extra strength. We will request the aid of one of the previous students of Uppsala, Trevor Blackwell," Vincent reported.

Hamilton looking shocked by this decision. Trevor, while being one of the more skilled students, was also one of the more unpredictable and hard-to-control. Trevor's dismissal from Uppsala was not due to any failures but the fact that he had attacked Hamilton just to see if he could best him. Hamilton would not be here if Trevor had been successful.

Hamilton cleared his throat and said, "Um, pardon me, sir. I do believe Master Teiwaz warned against hiring students who previously were residents here. No doubt Trevor's skills would benefit us greatly, but I just don't know if we can trust him."

"Thank you for the insight, Hamilton. Yes, I am aware of those concerns. Trevor would not have been my first choice either. However, he is the only one we know the location of. If we can get him to join our cause, then that's an asset that would certainly be welcome."

"That's just it," Ambrose chimed in. "Sir," she added begrudgingly. "How do you know we can get him to join our cause? He has no love for God, or even for this country. He just does whatever benefits himself. Not exactly a team player."

Vincent nodded. "You are correct that Trevor has no love of God or country, but I don't think your second assessment is quite right. Trevor is always trying to prove his ability, whether or not it benefits him. That's why he takes the risks that he takes. If we spin it that way, then perhaps he just feels up to the challenge."

"And just how do we do that?" Ambrose asked. "Sir," she added sassily.

"Glad you asked," Vincent replied with just as much sass. "We know that when Trevor left here, he went back to the life he had before. He is in the slums of Arithia, a city just south of here. My first assignment for you and Hamilton will be to go down there and recruit him."

"You're joking," Ambrose replied. "Why don't you go?"

"I must make my way to the capital city, Parth. There I will speak to the pope about getting some priests to join us. You must see why speaking to the pope is something more suited to me," Vincent said.

Ambrose agreed, but in silent protest. She did not like this plan; however, she had no other options to offer. Hamilton, while also having reservations about this idea, simply nodded his head. He would obey the orders he was given without fuss.

"If there are no more questions, then we are dismissed. We all will depart to our separate destinations tomorrow morning," Vincent concluded.

All went their separate ways, again with no words said among the lot of them. Things were off to a very rocky start.

CHAPTER 4

VINCENT HAGLAZ

VINCENT LEFT UPPSALA RIGHT AFTER he completed his morning prayers. He set out north for Sylvania's capital, Parth. Vincent had only met with the pope one other time before this. It was during his time as a priest in the small town of Grund, where he grew up. Parth was just about a day's ride north, so he brought enough food to make it there and back.

On the ride over, he was thinking about what he would say to the pope. Since being at Uppsala, he had learned that the pope was just acting as a figurehead. Vincent wondered how much the pope knew about the shadow government and how involved he was. Again, Vincent knew that he was going to have to handle this conversation very carefully. He didn't want to divulge more information than the pope already knew, but he needed to get enough across to him to justify this crusade.

Vincent began to think about the party that was trying to reach the Well, just as he was. What would happen if Vincent were to fail here? Would the world as he knew it cease to exist? These pressures were leading Vincent to doubt himself. It was also what drove him to continue and lead with all the strength he had. He had his allies, but it was God he felt was his greatest source of strength.

--- ✦✦✦✦✦ ---

He arrived at the capital of Parth by day's end. He had to wait in a line leading into the city gates. Guards were standing by and questioning all who were entering and leaving.

Now, this was new. Vincent didn't remember there being such high security the last time he was in the city. He wondered what was causing the extra precautions. Perhaps it had something to do with the threat of someone finding the Well. This didn't make much sense to him, though. He believed that the pope would be trying to keep panic low and not draw questions.

When he was the next to be questioned, he dismounted his horse. "Hello, friend," Vincent began, trying to seem harmless.

"State your business, traveller," the guard interrupted abruptly.

Vincent was taken aback by this hostility. This definitely wasn't the same Parth he remembered from the past. "Umm … I am a priest to see Pope Charles," Vincent said, stumbling through his sentence.

"A priest? So well-armed, and to see his holiness? I think not," the guard said. "Turn around," he barked.

"Sir, I assure you that I am a priest. I also can assure you that my business with Pope Charles is of utmost importance," Vincent protested, now done with being polite.

"No papers or seals to back you up, I can presume?" the guard badgered.

Vincent was starting to feel backed into a corner. He needed to get through, but he didn't want to force his way in either.

"Perhaps I can be of assistance," came a voice from behind the guard. By the robes, the man appeared to be a priest. "You say you are a priest, yes?" the man asked.

"Yes," Vincent answered.

Vincent did not recognize the man. The priest was clearly of higher status to these guards, as the guards were now looking to him to call the shots.

"Which church are you from, brother?" the priest asked.

"I come from the small village of Grund," Vincent answered.

The priest nodded. "That it is not too far from here. I can send word over there to see if they know who you are. Which, by the way, what is your name?" the priest asked.

"I am Vincent Haglaz," Vincent stated. "I haven't been with the church there for ten years. However, they should still recognize the name."

The priest's eyes opened wide. "Well then, there is no need, for I know who you are," the priest replied. "You are the son of Umbra Teiwaz, yes?"

Now Vincent was very confused. How could this priest know of his father? Well, he figured it shouldn't surprise him. His father was a mystery even to Vincent. He nodded in agreement.

"Well then, welcome to Parth," the priest said with a bow. "Also, our chapel has some spare beds for you, should you wish to stay there this night."

"Thank you, brother," Vincent replied. The two walked to the priests' chapel. Along the way, the priest explained to Vincent that he was one of Umbra's many eyes and ears. This all made sense to Vincent now. This was how Umbra was aware of the others who had left Uppsala. He was grateful for it in this case, as it solved a potential problem. It just made him yet again wonder: how far did his father's web stretch?

"I would be happy to announce you to his holiness in the morning," the priest said to Vincent, while showing him to the bedrooms.

"Thank you. That would be most helpful," Vincent said.

"I'll have two of my fellow brothers waiting to escort you to his holiness's throne room in the cathedral," he said.

"Thank you, my brother. I do apologize, as I have not caught your name," Vincent realized.

"My name is Father Darrel," he replied. With that, Father Darrel left Vincent to get some rest.

AMBROSE GAINS

Ambrose had not been looking forward to the task ahead. She was almost positive that no matter what situation they were in, Trevor Blackwell was not the answer. Nevertheless, she and Hamilton set out for Arithia.

"You don't agree with Vincent on this one, do you?" Hamilton asked.

"Do you?" Ambrose countered.

"It isn't really my place to say," Hamilton replied.

"You more than anyone shouldn't trust Trevor," Ambrose said.

"No, I can't say I'm particularly fond of him. However, I do trust Vincent. He has made it this far on his good instincts," Hamilton said.

"He would have you believe that it's been God guiding him," Ambrose spat.

"Perhaps it has been. No matter the reason, Vincent is capable and is in charge," Hamilton said.

"I think that's the problem," Ambrose posed.

Hamilton looked over at Ambrose. "You are aware his judgement is why you are still here, yes?" Hamilton asked.

"He's arrogant, Hamilton. His belief in God driving him causes him to not second-guess himself," she argued.

"Then you must be there to keep him in check," Hamilton stated.

"How can I do that when he feels so entitled? His new 'God-given' station has already corrupted him. He listens to no one but God," Ambrose said, sounding defeated.

"Then you must show him that you are a valuable advisor, not just a weapon," Hamilton said. "There will be times when he makes the wrong call, and you must simply present your opinion to him without fighting him. When he sees that he makes the wrong call and you had it right, that's when he will start to heed your advice," Hamilton advised.

"So that's what your game has been? You play for the long con?" Ambrose asked.

Hamilton simply smiled.

"Let's just hope that day comes before his mistakes cost us everything," Ambrose threw in.

They finally arrived in Arithia. This city was not so notable as to have guards stationed around the perimeter. All the buildings were made of stone and sand and were all at least half a century old. Some of the buildings had scars from wars and ransackings of the past.

They began their search in the streets, which were cold and barren. The only people they could see were either drunks or vagabonds. It might be after dark, but Ambrose still anticipated there to be some foot traffic of the citizens at least.

"So, where do we start?" Ambrose asked.

"Perhaps we should just find a decent place to stay for the time being," Hamilton answered.

"No, I don't want to stay here. We should just find him and get out of here as soon as we can," Ambrose countered.

"I believe it may be quicker for him to find us, than us to find him. Seeing as this place doesn't seem to get a lot of visitors, news of our arrival will spread quickly," Hamilton said.

The two eventually found one of the only inns that didn't look like a bar for villains and lowlifes to thrive. Still, their entry was noted by the patrons. They were by far the best-dressed individuals in this place, and clearly not from town. All the stares were cold and clearly hostile.

Ambrose and Hamilton made their way to the owner of the inn and rented a room with two beds. Then they turned to find a large man in a hood standing before them.

"You shouldn't be here," the man said.

"Oh yeah?" Ambrose replied, her hand on Marya. "Says who?"

"My God," Hamilton said. "John? John, is that you?"

Ambrose took another look at the man. Surely Hamilton could not be referring to the John who used to train at Uppsala. But upon second examination, she could just faintly recognize him.

John was a large man in both height and stature, and this hadn't changed from when they last saw him. But that was about the only thing. His face was scarred and almost looked burned. His hair was a mess, not at all resembling the once clean and organized man she knew.

Why was he here, of all places? She would have assumed he went off with Meredith, back to his hometown.

"You should not have come," John said. His voice was less threatening than just sad.

"John, what are you doing here?" Ambrose asked.

"I'm where all the unwanted go. This is where people go when society doesn't want to look at them, and when we don't want society to look at us," John answered. He sat down at a table nearby, a bottle in his hand.

"I thought you didn't drink," Ambrose said. John had once been a priest, just like Vincent. He was always against poisoning himself with drink or other vices. This was certainly not the man she remembered.

"I didn't," John replied.

Hamilton cleared his throat, "We are ..." he began.

"Yes, Trevor is around here," John interrupted. "Where's Vincent?"

"Not here," Ambrose answered.

"Of course not," John answered.

"John, we need Trevor to come back to Uppsala," Hamilton said, trying to guide the conversation back on track. "However, maybe you would like to come back too?"

"What's in Uppsala for us?" John asked.

"A new mission," Hamilton replied.

"A chance for a new life," Ambrose threw in.

John took a long swig from the bottle he had been nursing. "What's Umbra got you doing now?" he asked.

"We actually are under the orders of Vincent now," Hamilton answered.

"So, in the end, he wins it all. Daddy's playing favourites, is that it?" John asked.

"Will you not come with us then?" Ambrose asked.

"That depends on what Trevor has to say," he said.

"What, you're with Trevor now? What about Meredith?" Ambrose asked.

"Dead. Trevor is the only one I can trust now," John said.

This confused both Hamilton and Ambrose. What could have happened to make John like this? Why was Trevor the only one he could trust?

"Follow me," John said. They followed him through the inn and to a back room where they found Trevor aggressively sharpening a knife.

"Well, well, look what the cat dragged in," Trevor said, almost laughing. "An old man and a failure."

Trevor was average in size but well-muscled. He had brown hair and pale skin; the most remarkable thing about him was his bright blue eyes. He also was wearing tight leather armour with knives from head to toe. Ambrose could not even discern how many he had and where they might be concealed. He stood up and began pacing about the room, knife in hand.

Ambrose readied Marya. Hamilton put his arm in front of her. He was trying to avoid a nasty turn of events here.

"Aw, you don't want a round two, old man?" Trevor asked.

"I remember round one not going so well for you," Hamilton reminded him.

Trevor just scoffed.

"Trevor, they want us to come back to help Vincent," John piped in.

"Vincent, huh? What's the job?" Trevor asked.

"That, we will discuss when we get to Uppsala," Hamilton replied.

"What does it pay?" Trevor asked.

"Yet again, we will discuss that when we get there."

"So, a mystery job with no promise of pay?" Trevor asked, sounding sceptical.

"You will receive payment, I promise you that," Hamilton replied.

"Someone is after an artefact that could give them the power to rule this world," Ambrose interjected. She knew that this conversation was going to end quickly if the two men had no interest in this battle.

This definitely perked up the ears of both Trevor and John.

"Such an artefact exists?" John asked.

"Indeed it does. Our nations have kept it secret to prevent any catastrophes, but now it's in danger," Hamilton explained. "We need capable individuals to keep it from falling into the wrong hands."

"You know that I would rather see you rot in this hellhole," Ambrose added, "but unfortunately, Vincent sees you as a valuable asset that we can't do without. So, for his sake, we need you to come with us, please."

"Ah, now I get it," Trevor said with a smile. "You don't *want* our help, you *need* it. Oh, how happy this makes me. Of *course*, we'll give you our help. I just wanted to hear you beg for it, sweetheart."

"You piece of garbage!" Ambrose yelled, manifesting Marya into a pair of swords. Again, Hamilton got in front of her.

"Thank you, both of you," Hamilton growled. "We shall meet up with you in the morning, when we will depart together. Until then, I bid you gentlemen goodnight."

Hamilton and Ambrose turned around to leave. Hamilton immediately raised his left hand and caught the knife Trevor had been so aggressively sharpening. The look on Hamilton's face was no longer the cool and calm one Ambrose knew. Instead, he had a look of rage she had not seen before. This face was a clear sign that if Trevor wanted to pursue this course of action, Hamilton would certainly respond in kind.

"Sleep tight," Trevor teased.

The two parties went to their separate rooms, Ambrose hating the idea of this whole thing even more than she had already.

VINCENT HAGLAZ

Vincent arose the next morning and was greeted by two other priests. They guided him through the city to the castle where the pope resided. Along the way to the castle, Vincent took in the scene that was Parth. The city was bustling with people and sounds—merchants yelling and haggling, criers spreading the news and rumours about the town. The architecture of the buildings was far grander than what he was used to from his old hometown. However, there were still far more guards and military personnel than there should have been.

Finally, they made it to the castle. This was the most spectacular building of all—a very gothic style, with ornate decorations and scenic painted glass.

Vincent climbed the steps and made his way through the large doors. Inside was even more lavish and decorative architecture. Most of the scenes depicted priests planting and praying to trees.

Many nuns were about the castle cleaning murals and decorations. Vincent was led to the throne room, where he found Pope Charles praying to the holy symbol. This was the same symbol that Vincent wore around his neck: a cross meant to look like a tree. The other priests left Vincent and the pope to talk in private.

Vincent went down on his knees. Pope Charles turned to him and began laughing. "Rise, my child. Soon it might be I who is bowing to you, I hear."

"I don't believe I——" Vincent began.

"It's all right, its all right. We are alone here and can speak freely," Charles said.

Vincent stood up and looked Charles in the eye. The two shared a knowing glance.

"So you have come for a purpose, I suppose," Charles said frankly.

"Yes, but before that, I would like to ask you something."

Charles looked at Vincent quizzically and then opened his arms as if to say, "Fire away."

"What do you know about those really in charge? Surely they must have contact with you. I want to know what I'm getting myself into here. How does my father fit into all this?" Vincent started rattling off.

Charles put his hand out as if to slow the young man down. "You have been told that you will be the ruler of this country. That much is true. However, there are more who help keep up the curtain. There is a council of trustees that works with the rulers of our two countries. Your father is simply one of those council members—may I say one of the more terrifying members. They make their decisions and simply pass them on to me. I'm the salesman who pitches these ideas to the people," he concluded.

This was a lot for Vincent to take in. He had known his father was involved, but to find out he was on some council that runs both countries? That was insane to think about. What would he be getting himself into here?

"So, have you come all this way just to seek my wisdom?" Charles asked.

"No, I need your aid," Vincent said.

"I'm sorry, dear Vincent, but I can't simply leave my post here," Charles began.

"No," Vincent interrupted. "Sorry. I need troops and supplies to carry out the mission my father has given me," Vincent said.

"Oh, and what mission would that be?" Charles asked.

"For my final mission, my father has tasked me with finding those who seek the Well," Vincent told him.

"The Well?" Charles asked.

"Yes. Have you not heard of the Well on Mount Bors?"

"Oh, yes, *that* Well," Charles said.

It seemed odd to Vincent that someone of such importance would forget about such a powerful relic.

"As for the support you need," Charles went on, "I can spare about 20 priests and 20 soldiers to your cause. I can't spare more than that."

"That's another thing I've been meaning to ask you about," pondered Vincent. "Why all the extra security? I thought we were at peace. If the two countries are all led by the same people, then why would there be a threat of war? Surely you can't be this scared of bandits robbing the town."

"It's as you say, Vincent. There are those who seek the Well. If they get it, they will be hard to stop. I need my people here guarding the city in case the worst should come and you fail in this mission. However, I have the utmost faith that the chosen of Uppsala will rise up and defend us all," Charles said.

Vincent wasn't so convinced by the pope's words. "How long until the force is able to march?"

"I shall send them to Uppsala in three days' time. You are welcome to stay here while you wait for me to assemble them."

"That's all right." Vincent responded. "I must go ahead of them back to Uppsala. I have people who expect me back quickly."

"Very well then, my son," Charles said.

Vincent took his leave of the castle, and of Parth. He knew that the others would be arriving back at Uppsala shortly, and he wanted to be there to put out any fires.

CHAPTER 5

VINCENT HAGLAZ

WHEN VINCENT RETURNED TO UPPSALA, the others had already made it back. Hamilton was there to meet him at the door. "How did it go?" Vincent asked.

"I think you will need to see for yourself, sir," Hamilton replied.

Vincent was unsure what Hamilton meant by this, so he went inside to investigate. He passed by the training courtyard, where he saw Ambrose hard at work, practicing sword and shield techniques. Their eyes met briefly, and Ambrose's glare was not friendly.

She motioned her head to the left—towards the briefing room. He entered and found Trevor sitting in the captain's chair, feet up on the table.

"So, the puppet master finally makes his way to the stage," Trevor teased.

Vincent, only mildly amused by this, motioned his hand for Trevor to stand up. "Trevor, you've had your fun, but come on," Vincent said.

"Oh, and after we have been waiting here for you so patiently, you're going to take my seat?" Trevor said in a falsely sad tone.

"We?" Vincent asked.

The door closed behind Vincent. He spun around to see a man he used to know standing by the door. It was John. Vincent hardly recognized him but did know him by his frame and what remained of his face.

"John, where have—?" Vincent began.

"He's been with me," Trevor cut in. "I know, a man of the cloth hanging out with a lowlife like me. Strange world we live in, but I guess when you get cast out by all those you knew in life, the misfits band together." He laughed.

"But what about—"

"*Let's,*" Trevor interjected, "not bring her up right now. Big man still gets a little touchy."

Vincent looked at John, who only looked down at the ground. John might have been there physically but by no means was his mind.

"I hear you have a little job for us to do, isn't that right, old pal?" Trevor asked.

Vincent gathered the others to the briefing room. He explained the mission again, this time for John and Trevor. He promised Trevor and John compensation when the job was done. With his new title, he would certainly be able to find funds and stations for them.

They would set out in two days' time when the reinforcements made it to Uppsala. Until then, they were dismissed and told to prepare however they needed to.

Trevor had a smile on his face. *No doubt he's excited by the prospect of a conflict where he will be able to kill powerful foes*, thought Vincent.

Ambrose left the briefing immediately after it was over. She went straight to her room.

Hamilton told them he would have the staff prepare meals to be brought to their rooms. Vincent wanted to speak with John, but he just couldn't find the right words. So they left the room, saying nothing more to one another.

TREVOR BLACKWELL

That night, Trevor stared up at the sky, looking into the moon. He pointed his blade up at the moon, hoping to pierce the heavens.

However, the glass window kept his blade from God's heart. "Hmmph, what a tease you are, my dear," Trevor said, seemingly to no one.

He stood up and left the room. This was the same room he'd had during his previous stay here. Just like before, he was leaving this room for good. Just like before, he would be hurting friends to aim higher.

John was sitting outside his door with a bottle of liquor.

"Anything good?" Trevor asked.

John took a very long swig, killing the bottle.

Trevor gave an acknowledging nod. "I guess so. Knew that Hamilton kept some hidden away in here," Trevor said.

John held up the bottle up in the air. "To old friends," he said.

"You still good to do this?" Trevor asked.

"Think I can't handle my liquor?" John replied.

"I have no doubt you could kill two more of those. But what about two friends?" Trevor asked with a grin.

"I don't have friends," John replied quickly.

"That hurts, John. After everything we've been through."

John stood up and dropped the bottle. "I would never have a bastard like you for a friend," he snarled. Then he put his hand on Trevor's shoulder. "Just too bad you had to go and become my brother," he added, almost smiling.

The two shared one last look, and then John made his way through the living quarters on his way to the chapel. Trevor stood there for a moment, John's words rattling around in his mind. "Good luck to you," Trevor said, even though John was far beyond hearing those words.

Trevor turned in the opposite direction from John. He looked down at the end of the hall to see Hamilton standing illuminated by the light of the moon peering in through the windows. Hamilton was wearing the same look of rage that Trevor remembered from Arithia.

Trevor laughed. "That's it, that's perfect. That's the look I wanted."

"You and John have five minutes to gather your belongings and leave Uppsala," Hamilton growled.

"What gave me away, old man?" Trevor asked.

"For as deceitful as you may think you are, you can't lie to me. Your bloodlust is almost palpable," Hamilton proudly stated. He had two scimitars on his hips, their gleam in the moonlight shining bright.

"Since you put on something nice, I guess I'll give a dance," Trevor jested.

"You are just a child who needs a reprimand. We've been down this road before. You know how it ends," Hamilton growled.

Trevor threw three daggers at Hamilton. The daggers found themselves harmlessly lodged in the wall behind where Hamilton once stood. Trevor didn't even see Hamilton move—and where could he have gone in a narrow hallway? This meant only one thing.

"Oh, goodie, you going to show me the tricks you've been hiding from us, old man?" Trevor said with glee. He was on edge, trying to hear any movement, see any change in the light. But he couldn't sense Hamilton at all.

Then he heard the bell—the alarm bell for Uppsala, used to signal an attack.

"You sly old fox," Trevor said.

Trevor ran down the hall, making his way to the bell tower. Somehow, Hamilton had used some trick to move himself to the bell tower in the blink of an eye. This both terrified and excited Trevor.

"So he's fast too? This is going to be fun," Trevor said to himself.

Around the corner, two of the staff members of Uppsala came out from their rooms, weapons in hand. They served as security guards for Uppsala. They only saw Trevor for an instant before they fell to the ground, throats slashed. His speed was fuelled by magic, and any normal human would be helpless to see his attack coming. With the pinpoint accuracy of his cuts, most wouldn't even realize what happened.

Trevor sped down the halls at blinding speed, headed for the bell tower. He saw it only a fraction of a second before it struck—the familiar gleam of a scimitar flying in from his left side. Trevor moved at top speed to dodge the attack, but it still grazed his left leg. Trevor swung out with his knife to meet his attacker. However, no one was there.

"You're spry for an old man," Trevor yelled. He was trying to bait a reaction out of Hamilton. He had to find a way counter whatever trick the old man had up his sleeve. Trevor wondered for just a moment if he was just too outmatched.

He kept moving down the halls at breakneck speed. If he slowed down, he feared he would be cut to ribbons. He couldn't hear Hamilton, couldn't see him, and there was no real trace of him. Was he using invisibility? No. Otherwise, Trevor wouldn't be able to see the flash of light from the blades.

Again, another flash. Trevor went to block, but again he was only able to stop the blade from cutting deep. This time, the cut was to his forearm. However, what was different this time was that he saw a quick blur blow past him from his right to his left. He could tell Hamilton was aiming for his legs. He wanted to slow Trevor down, take his speed.

Trevor changed course; he was now running for the lounge. He had to get out of this narrow hallway.

VINCENT HAGLAZ

Vincent sat in prayer, as he did most nights. He was searching for answers. He wanted to know if the steps he was taking were the right ones. Were they the ones his father would take? Were they the steps God wanted him to take? He hoped they were enough.

It was in the midst of his prayers that he heard the tolls of the bell. He jumped to his feet. *An intruder? Who would attack Uppsala? Could the foes they sought already be coming to attack them?* He turned around to make his way out the door.

Suddenly, the doors of the chapel flew open. And there, standing in the doorway, was John. His demeanour was dark. Vincent had never felt this aura coming off John before. The man's breaths were deep and heavy. He was almost shaking.

The two met eyes for the first time since those years ago when John was expelled from Uppsala. Before, Vincent had hardly recognized his old friend. But now, he couldn't believe that this was the John he'd known before. His eyes used to be soft and caring. Now they held pain and anger.

"John? What's going on?" Vincent asked slowly.

There was no response other than John taking a step forward.

Vincent put his hands on his weapons.

"John, do you know what's going on here?" Vincent asked again.

Vincent had all but figured it out. He just didn't want to believe he would have to fight an old friend.

John just kept walking forward slowly.

"John, stand down right!" Vincent commanded. He drew his rapier and lit fire in his left hand.

Vincent was familiar with John's fighting style. John's magic covered him in a layer of impenetrable armour. The armour was just a clear film, but it was all the same unbreakable by normal means. John used his invincibility paired with brutish strength to charge in and break his enemies. However, there was a limit to John's mana, and Vincent would just have to wear him out. It was only a matter of whether Vincent could launch a large enough barrage on John to break through before he himself was beaten and broken.

Flames erupted from Vincent's hand and blasted directly onto John. The flames flowed around John like a river flows around a stone. Though the ground was singed, John was unharmed.

John let out a roar before he charged like a bull straight towards Vincent, flames continuously blasting into his ultimate shield. He found the source of the flames and smashed down at Vincent, who ducked and spun around John, launching a flurry of thrusts into the armour. But Vincent's blows just bounced off harmlessly.

Vincent kept ducking and rolling out of the way of huge swings, one of which hit one of the pews in the chapel, splintering it. Vincent knew John was inhumanly strong, but he had never been this strong. Something was different.

Vincent, after several successful evasions and ripostes, finally got caught in the ribs by a deadly right hook that sent him rolling backwards. He felt several ribs had been broken. He glared up at John, who was slowly walking up to him.

"The look on your face is the most honest you've been with me since I got here," John said. "It hurts when your friends betray you doesn't it? Doesn't it?!" John yelled. He kicked Vincent in his already broken ribs, sending Vincent flying into the wall behind him.

Vincent gasped for breath. The air had been knocked from his chest. Most ribs were broken. Things were taking a turn for the worse.

"We spend over a decade studying together, eating together,

training together, sharing in each other's successes," John went on. "In our failures. But when I was cast out, you wouldn't stand up for me. No. You had to make sure you won in the end. Couldn't disappoint Father, now could you? I had to go at some point, right? Better to get rid of the competition then and there.

"Don't get me wrong," he continued, "it made sense, it was smart. It's just not what I would have done. But hey, I never was very bright. Not compared to the rest of you, anyway. I guess I'm the fool that would have stood up for a friend. If I couldn't do that, then I would have at least left with him." John had tears in his eyes. However, his anger had not dissipated.

Vincent was using every bit of strength to get to his feet. He had just the short sword, as his rapier was over by John. He thought about conjuring more fire, but this might just provoke John again. So Vincent tried to say something, but he still had trouble getting air.

"I should have never left home," John said, mainly to himself. "I should have never come here." Then he walked over to Vincent.

Vincent grasped John's face and let loose all the fire he could summon. He stabbed at him with the short sword, but this was all in vain. John picked him up by the neck, cutting off Vincent's ability to produce flame. Vincent felt his neck being crushed in John's hand, although John was holding back, just a bit. He had more to say.

"You don't know what's happened since then, do you? Do you care? No, you would have let me suffer. What was my crime, Vincent? Was it because I loved Meredith? Or was I just not good enough in your eyes? Was I holding you back? Of course—how does the well-being of a friend compare to the love of God? You were always the devout follower; guess I had to be punished for deviating. Well, I got my punishment. I've been through my hell. Guess it's time we shared that too," John finished.

Vincent felt John's grasp tightening. He knew it was over. He had come to this point just to fail right here. The blackness was coming over his eyes.

TREVOR BLACKWELL

Trevor had been bounding down hallways trying desperately to get to the lounge. Hamilton's attacks were coming fast and frequent. Trevor had started to adjust to the timing. Still, he was covered in cuts. None of the cuts was deep or life-threatening, but they were taking their toll.

Occasionally, guards would pop out, and Trevor wouldn't even slow down as he cut their strings to this life. He broke through the doors to the lounge.

For the first time, he stopped moving. He had two daggers at the ready. Where would Hamilton come from? He had yet to discover the trick to this. But he knew all mages reached their limit. Hamilton had to be using mana, and eventually, that mana would run out.

Still, it would be hard to gauge when that would be. Since none of the students ever actually saw him use his magic, they had no idea how much mana it used, or how much Hamilton had in him.

If it was teleportation or invisibility, it would drain Hamilton fast. If it was a simple speed amplifier like Trevor had, it could last much longer. Trevor was convinced there was more to it than just speed, though. If not, Trevor would have seen him coming.

That made Trevor think: how had Hamilton been attacking? He always came from the sides of the hallways, never attacking head-on or from behind. Which meant he wasn't rushing at Trevor from the ends of the hallways, just the sides. So could he move through walls? No, that wasn't it, but Trevor had an idea as to what it was.

The lounge had a few couches sitting around an inactive fireplace. There where a couple of large glass windows, some portraits, a bookshelf, vases, a decorative set of armour, and a mirror. The only light in the room came from the moon.

Trevor waited. He had a fairly good idea where the attack was coming from. He looked at the doorway. He knew the attack would not come from there, but he didn't want to give away his discovery.

Sure enough, out of the corner of his eye, he saw a glimmer from Hamilton's scimitar. Expecting this, Trevor leaped back, throwing three knives. One caught Hamilton in the leg, and the man fell, rolling to the ground.

"You know, you old bat, I didn't give your lessons enough credit," Trevor teased. "You always lectured ad nauseam never to show your opponent your secrets too many times. Otherwise, they might figure out how to counter it. Isn't that right?" Trevor mocked.

Hamilton pulled the dagger from his leg. It had gone deep. Hamilton feared it might have severed a tendon.

"You've been using reflections, haven't you? Quite impressive, old man," Trevor continued.

"It does please me, and surprise me, that you actually took my lectures to heart. However, you'll still die for your betrayal. Is your need for vengeance against me and Uppsala so great you'd—" Hamilton began.

Trevor lunged out at Hamilton, daggers out. Hamilton blocked them but was pinned against the wall.

"And here I thought you were this wise old man who could see behind the curtain. Pity. I looked up to you, did you know that?" Trevor said.

Hamilton was trying to get a read on what Trevor meant. What was he talking about? Hamilton had realized Trevor was going to betray them, what he couldn't figure out was why.

"Still can't figure it out? You really have dropped the ball. We were hired to do it," Trevor said with a smile of absolute pleasure. How it filled Trevor with elation to see the in-control persona of Hamilton wither away.

"By who?" Hamilton asked, trying to regain his composure.

"Oh no, no, no, that would be telling," Trevor teased.

Trevor kicked out, a knife stuck out from the front of his boot. He kicked forward, but his kick only found the wall. Hamilton had vanished again.

"Hiding in your reflection again, Hamilton?!" Trevor yelled. "I know your trick, geezer. You won't get the best of me this time."

Trevor looked around the room. He looked to the windows. Hamilton had been hiding in the reflections of the windows in the castle. That's how he had been attacking Trevor before. However, Trevor didn't see him in the window's reflections now.

That's when he remembered the mirror. He spun around, and he could see Hamilton standing in the mirror. In an instant, Hamilton vanished. He had now moved to one of the windows. He was jumping from reflection to reflection, trying to confuse Trevor and find an opening.

Trevor knew he was in trouble. If Hamilton was moving between reflections, that meant he was moving at the speed of light, something Trevor would not be able to keep up with, even with his own speed. Hamilton tried a couple more attacks. Trevor was able to dodge them, but they were close calls.

"I told you, I know your trick, old man!" Trevor yelled. He kept moving with his high speed as he dodged and kicked out the windows and broke the mirror. "What will you do now, you shrivelling fuck? You have no reflections to hide in," Trevor declared victoriously.

Trevor heard Hamilton's voice echoing in the room. "Oh, so simple-minded of you. You've played to my advantage," he chuckled.

"Shit," Trevor exclaimed. There were hundreds of little glass shards now lining the ground. In a flurry and storm of blades, Hamilton erupted from every direction. He could strike from the tiniest of shards of glass, or even the reflections of the vase and the decorative suit of armour.

Trevor tried to dodge, parry, and block, but nothing would help. He could hold off the assault at first, but then cut after cut got through, and Trevor was losing blood, and the fight, quickly. He started to slow, his mana draining away. This fight would be over soon.

Yet Trevor still tried his best to keep Hamilton at bay. He knew that Hamilton would soon go in for the killing blow. Up until this point, Hamilton had only been trying to wear him down.

Trevor could see the shifts in the glass on the ground as Hamilton would attack. This meant Hamilton had to step out of the reflections to attack. Also, if Trevor could see that, Hamilton was also slowing down. These truly were the final moments of this battle.

Trevor waited for the right moment—the moment in this fight he had been waiting for. He still had one last play to run. Watching and listening to the movements, he waited until he believed the final strike was coming. Then, when he saw the twin flashes of scimitars reflecting the light of the moon, Trevor pulled a cord around his waist. Small blades erupted from his armour. The blades were sharp and curved like hooks.

As Hamilton rushed by, he was caught by several of the hooks, and they dug deep. Without hesitation, Trevor ran Hamilton through.

Hamilton let out a gasp, and his swords dropped at his feet.

Trevor spun, which wrenched Hamilton off his hooks. Hamilton fell to a floor that was covered in glass and blood.

Trevor stood still, breathing hard. "Looks like round two goes to me. I really must thank you for all of those lessons over the years. Every enemy has a pattern to how they fight, even if subtle. You are no exception. All I had to do was learn it, and I could know where you would strike," Trevor coaxed.

Hamilton reached for one of his scimitars.

"Also, always have an ace in the hole," Trevor said. He kicked the scimitars away and sat on Hamilton. He cut into the back of the man's arm and tugged at a tendon with his knife before slicing it. "Won't be flexing that arm anymore. So, no more swordplay," he laughed.

Trevor cut open Hamilton's other sleeve and then sliced into his other arm the same way, cutting the same tendon. Hamilton let out a primal scream.

"Guess you have nothing up your sleeves," Trevor teased. "I am grateful for all the dangerous missions Uppsala sent us on. Plenty of bodies means plenty of cadavers. Be thankful. My first dissections were a bit more crude," Trevor said.

"You could have been something great," Hamilton said. "You have talent and a drive to overcome any obstacle. Yet you use this to make some quick coin. Your ambition trumps morality, friendships, duty, relationships …"

At that note, Trevor degloved the back of Hamilton's hand. Hamilton yelled, but his voice choked up.

"Watch your words. I can make this much more painful and slow. I told you this is a job. It would be the same way if I were to have joined up with your helpless band. You are just on the unfortunate side of the knife this time," Trevor said.

"So maybe there is a part of you that still feels," Hamilton rasped. "Did I finally get through your façade? Vincent believed in you. We told him you couldn't be trusted. Just a lowlife out for blood. I had hoped you'd prove me wrong, but you just lived up to all my expectations."

Hamilton's vision was getting blurry. He knew this was it. He had wanted to see how Vincent and Ambrose would change this world. He was sad that he could not protect them this last time.

There were sounds of crashing—as if the entire castle was crumbling. Tremors and shakes were rattling the place. Hamilton looked up, scared.

"Sounds like John's having some fun too," Trevor said ominously.

Trevor came off Hamilton and sat next to him. He no longer had the rage and bloodthirsty edge to his tone. He was much calmer now. "You lived up to my expectations too, old man. In fact, you surpassed them. Thank you," Trevor said sombrely.

"I'll be going now," Hamilton said. "Could you do me the honour of knowing who orchestrated this? Just to bring peace to my passing," Hamilton asked.

Trevor smiled, "Sure thing, old friend."

VINCENT HAGLAZ

Vincent's eyes opened again. He was on his knees, coughing to regain air in his lungs. He looked up to see John standing over him. Only then did Vincent see the blade of light piercing through John's abdomen. Blood was dripping onto Vincent's face.

"Vincent! Vincent!" he could hear faintly. He started to regain his senses.

"Vincent, come on!" He now realized it was Ambrose yelling.

Vincent got to his feet and stumbled away from John. He could now see that Ambrose had run through John with Marya. However, John stood still, as if this didn't bother him much.

"You were able to pierce my ultimate shield? Well done. Looks like I let my guard down," John said.

"Bullshit. You're running out of juice and you know it," Ambrose barked.

"Am I?" John smiled.

"Vincent, you wanna help here?" Ambrose asked snarkily.

"Right," Vincent said, snapping back to his senses fully now. He launched a wave of fire.

Ambrose backed off. Her blade was covered in blood. She knew she'd got him. Why wasn't he going down?

When the flames cleared, John was still standing there, unfazed. The hole in his abdomen was gone, though blood was still soaking his clothes.

"That's impossible," Ambrose said, sounding defeated. "I ran you through! How are you even alive?!" Ambrose yelled.

"Hmmph, *now* you care," John said. "*Now* you care what happened to me," John repeated. "*Now* you care how you made me this way!"

Vincent had no idea what John was talking about. *Made him this way?* Also, Vincent knew about John's ultimate shield, but John had never had the power to regenerate.

"John, just calm down. We're all listening to you now. Tell us what happened," Vincent said, sharing a worried look with Ambrose.

"When you expelled me from this place, I thought I could bear it. Thought I would just settle down somewhere, live the quiet life. However, it ruined Meredith. I knew she wanted revenge on this place for casting her out, but I didn't know how far she'd go. I thought if we ran away and had a family, we could be happy. I'd leave my life as a priest and marry.

"So we did. I had to give up being a priest, of course. We even had a child, Rose, and she was my world. I thought she was Meredith's too—until the night I found her using our child in a ritual to summon a demon she would send to attack Uppsala. I tried to stop her, but it was too late. Rose had been sacrificed, and when the demon came … it took me as a host!" John yelled.

It was then that John's body began to twist and turn, contorting into some unhuman form.

"Shit!" Vincent yelled. He began running to the door, casting fire upon John. No good; his shield still held strong.

On Vincent's way out, he swooped up the rapier he had dropped. Then he and Ambrose ran out of the chapel, into the hallway. John's form was growing into a 20-foot-tall beast with wings, horns, and a barbed tail. The clothes he was wearing ripped, exposing a fleshy muscled beast. It let out a roar, then smashed through the doorway and started chasing the two through the halls, wrecking the place. The ceiling and walls crumpled as it tore its way after Vincent and Ambrose.

"Now what?!" Ambrose yelled.

"Your blade can break through his shield. I don't know how strong it is now that it has to cover that whole body. Once you do that, I'll take care of the rest," Vincent said.

Ambrose realized that he didn't call it John, just *it*. So the true devoutness of Vincent was coming out. No longer was this a fight to subdue a man. This was an extermination.

Ambrose had no problem with this, as she knew this was how she was going to survive. It just saddened her to see how Vincent's beliefs guided him. A long-time friend strays from the path and must go, along with all other heretics. She wondered how much of an offense she would have to commit before she too would be hunted. Is this who should lead this country—another zealot?

The two ducked down another hallway, but this time Vincent was caught in the clutches of the monster. The beast beat its mighty wings, busting through the ceiling and flying into the air. Higher and higher it took him, and the height was certainly concerning to Vincent. He tried to slice at the hands with his short sword. The shield was holding, although Vincent could tell it was not as sturdy.

The beast opened its mouth to bite off Vincent's head. Vincent freed a hand and launched fire into the beast's mouth. It recoiled and dropped Vincent. He sheathed his blades, struggled to position himself, and began gliding with his cape.

Vincent struggled to keep stable with the winds. This was higher than he had ever been before. He couldn't believe how badly things had turned out. His new allies were already betraying him. Uppsala was crumbling around him. Now, he was just fighting to survive. He wondered how he could possibly get things back under control. He began descending quicker.

The beast had crashed through the bell tower, completely destroying it. The demon stood, trying to shake off the debris. Suddenly, it found a sword had been thrown in its chest and had penetrated the shield. It was half of Marya. The beast let out a huge roar.

Ambrose charged in with the other half of Marya. The beast lashed out its tail, and Ambrose manifested a shield to block it. She made another sword, jumped up, and thrust it into the beast's abdomen. Then, using this handhold, she swung herself up to grab her other sword.

She pulled it out, turned, and slashed open the beat's chest to the waist. Black blood began erupting from the abdomen. The wound seemed to be trying to close and repair itself. The beast let out a deafening roar.

Vincent, swooping in, fired a blast of flames into the beast's chest. The burning flames kept the wound open. Then Vincent plunged into the beast's chest with his rapier. This seemed to be the coup de grace. It began shaking violently. Vincent fell and tumbled off of it to the ground.

Again, the beast contorted and shifted—this time shrinking. Finally, the beast reverted to its humanoid form. Now, in the rubble of the bell tower, lay John with the rapier stuck through him, the other half of Marya lying at his side.

Vincent and Ambrose lay in the rubble, exhausted and drained. Marya was no longer in the shape of any weapon; it had returned to its unimpressive form of just two rods.

Finally, Vincent stood up and limped over to the rubble. He drew his short sword, his rage building. He climbed up the pile of rubble until he was standing over John. All of his rage reached a boil. Vincent's home had been destroyed, and his mission already seemed doomed to fail. He wanted nothing more than to act as a priest of Sylvania should and slay this demon and heretic.

However, when he was met with the face of his old friend, his rage was extinguished. John, still alive, was lying there tears in his eyes.

"There it goes. Finally, the demon is gone," John said, crying.

"Don't try and sell me that. That demon wasn't calling the shots. You were in control of your own actions," Vincent growled.

"I won't lie. I was at the helm of my actions. But I have been haunted by the demon within. Not the beast you saw, but the beast you see now. The beast that couldn't save his own child. Who couldn't achieve his goals. Who left everything and everyone he knew behind to become something he didn't recognize. Just left alone to rot and be eaten away at by a monster within," John went on.

Ambrose, who was standing behind Vincent, now chimed in. "So after all that, why would you make the mistake of joining a lowlife like Trevor? Why join him in a cause to destroy your friend?" Ambrose asked.

"Because when I was in that dark and tormented place, when everyone had forsaken me—Uppsala, the Church, even my own wife—Trevor found me. He didn't care what I had become, didn't care that I had given up. He took me in and got me back to my feet. When I was stronger, Trevor helped me track down Meredith and kill her. We became brothers. I finally had someone who cared for me again," John said.

"He was using you. Couldn't you see that?" Vincent asked.

"Does it matter? I was content to destroy myself. But the only one to find me at my lowest and give me a reason to go on, I'd do anything for him," John said.

"Even join him in a crusade to kill your friends? Just for his own sick revenge?" Vincent asked.

"It was a job," John corrected.

Ambrose and Vincent looked at one another in confusion. They realized that these two could have been hired by the very people Vincent was tasked to destroy. Which meant, those people already knew about Vincent's mission. This would destroy any hope of success.

"By who?" Vincent asked.

"She didn't give us her name. She showed up one day and offered to pay us handsomely if we eliminated Vincent and Hamilton," John said.

Ambrose's eyes opened wide. "No! Hamilton!" She ran off in search of Hamilton, realizing now why Trevor wasn't here.

Vincent was left alone with John, the two sharing in John's last moments quietly.

"I know you hate me. I know you hate Trevor. I know the devout in you has no love for me," John said.

"Goodbye, John," Vincent said finally. Vincent could not find the words he needed in this moment. He could not forgive his friend for what he had done. But he couldn't just forget the friendship they'd had for so long. So, with finality, Vincent removed the rapier from John, and he walked away to join Ambrose.

TREVOR BLACKWELL

Trevor had limped and dragged himself out to the horses. He had watched the final moments of the battle between John, Vincent, and Ambrose. He realized where the fight was going and knew he was not prepared for another battle, especially not one involving those two. He mounted his horse, took one last look back, and took off.

He couldn't help but feel something for his lost ally. Even more so that they had failed in this mission. Now he would have to lick his wounds and try again. That is, if he even survived the wounds inflicted by Hamilton.

CHAPTER 6

AMBROSE GAINS

A MBROSE HAD FOUND HAMILTON. OR at least, she had found his body. She fell to her knees next to him. She closed her eyes and tried to fight back tears. She lifted up his head to see that he was in fact dead.

Hamilton had been kind to her. She trusted very few people in her life, and Hamilton was one of them. He had helped her and wanted nothing in return. Even when she failed at being the champion of Uppsala, he still was kind of her—not because it was his job, but because he actually cared about the pain she had gone through.

She stood up and looked around for Trevor. "*Trevor! Trevor!* Where are you, you fucking coward! Damn you! Damn you!" she screamed.

Vincent had at that moment arrived on the scene. She turned her anger on him.

"You! This is your fault! You brought this evil upon us. We warned you. We pleaded with you not to do this," she shouted.

Vincent took the abuse for now. He knew that she needed to get this off her chest.

"But you wouldn't heed our warning. You know Hamilton believed in you? He trusted your judgement, even though he knew Trevor had bad intentions. He followed your orders faithfully!" she continued to yell.

"His weapons are gone," Vincent stated flatly.

Ambrose turned back to see. "Great, so now Trevor insults him by robbing his corpse," she said, throwing her hands in the air. "So what now, great leader? How will you screw us over even more?"

"This would have happened either way. You heard John: they were hired to kill us. They were coming for us anyway," Vincent tried to reason.

"Yes, except you *brought them into our home*. They had us with our guard down, and now Hamilton is gone and Trevor has escaped," Ambrose said, defeated.

"If he has run, it is because he is too injured to fight us," Vincent said.

"Good. I hope he bleeds to death," Ambrose proclaimed.

"I will make sure he does. This I swear upon God," Vincent stated.

"In case you forgot, we have a mission to carry out."

"Trevor stands in the way of that mission. If we don't track him down, he'll come again and strike us on the road, in our sleep, whenever we are weakest," Vincent reasoned.

"We are weakest *now*," Ambrose snapped. "Besides, Trevor being hired to kill us proves that whoever we're up against already knows we're coming. They will be making their move on the Well."

"Trevor is part of them, can't you see that?" Vincent asked. "Besides, he fraternizes with demons. This is an offense that can't be overlooked by a man of God. When the priests get here, we will track down Trevor and be done with him."

"And where did he go, huh? Any idea? How much time do you intend to waste on this? Until the Well is discovered by our enemies, and we lose our country? I won't have you damn us further by going after Trevor again," Ambrose persisted.

Vincent knew she was right but couldn't accept that Trevor would get away free—after destroying his home, his staff, his friend.

Ambrose could see the internal struggle Vincent was having. "Look, it's as you said. Trevor will come again. When he does, we'll be ready. Next time, he won't have a John to save him from us," Ambrose put in.

Vincent went along with this idea for now. They could do nothing anyway for the time being. The reinforcements would arrive tomorrow, and then they would be off to Avalon. Without Hamilton, things would be much more difficult. He looked at the ruined state of Uppsala. This place was nothing but a graveyard now.

"We need to give our people a proper send-off," Vincent said.

"You see any shovels around?" Ambrose countered.

Vincent simply lit a flame in his hand.

Ambrose and Vincent lined up all of the bodies they could salvage from the wreckage. Servants, cooks, security, Hamilton, John—all were dead. Vincent, one by one, set them ablaze so their souls could be at rest.

He hesitated when he came upon John's body. Did John deserve such a send-off? He decided that God would judge John either way, so he lit the body like the others.

Neither Vincent nor Ambrose slept this night. There was just too much to think about. They didn't say much more to one another. They had already spoken their hearts. No longer could they return to this place. No way to look back after setting off on this journey.

———— ⁘⁘⁘ ————

In the morning, the army arrived—a small army of forty, made up of twenty priests and twenty soldiers. The army looked quite surprised to find Uppsala in ruins.

One of the priests went up to Vincent. "What happened here?" he asked.

"It would seem that our enemies have struck first. This is what we're up against. I hope you all are ready," Vincent said.

Ambrose watched as all of the soldiers and priests rallied around Vincent, paying her no mind. These fools deserved each other. When the dust fell and Vincent ruled over them, he would lead them to ruin again, just as he had led her and Hamilton to ruin. That was if they even were to succeed in the trials to come.

TREVOR BLACKWELL

Trevor's horse walked for days as he slipped in and out of consciousness. He had applied first aid when he was just outside the gaze of Uppsala. But this didn't help with all of the blood he had lost. The horse began to tire, and somewhere between Uppsala and Arithia, he fell from his horse and lost all consciousness.

When he awoke, he was on a bed. This bed was unfamiliar to him. He was in a dark candlelit room. Again, he had never been there before. He had been tied to the bed and his armour and weapons removed.

A woman walked in with bandages in her arms and a bucket of warm water.

"Who the hell are you?" Trevor spat.

She jumped back, spilling the bucket, then ran back out the door.

"Hey, get back here and untie me, you useless bitch!" Trevor yelled. No response. "Damn it," Trevor mumbled to himself.

He wondered how long he had been here. He noticed that his wounds had been properly tended to and were beginning to heal. So the attack on Uppsala had been a couple days ago at this point.

Vincent must already be close to the border, he said to himself. He realized that he had failed in his mission. He was satisfied in his victory over Hamilton, but he hadn't thought they would actually beat John. He was unsure whether he could have pulled that off, and he knew about that monster.

Both Vincent and Ambrose had gotten so strong. Back in the days they were all in Uppsala, Trevor was sure he was the strongest—stronger even than John. Now, he was unsure where he stood.

"So, I see you're finally awake," a man's voice said. A man stepped through the doorway. He looked to be in his fifties, with a grey moustache, and he was wearing priest's robes.

"Oh fuck," Trevor said.

"What a foul mouth you have," the man said. "And after we took the time to nurse you back to health."

"Well, thank you, kind sir. Now I should really be getting going," Trevor said.

"It's Bishop Malloy, and why the rush?" the man said as he moved towards the bed. "After all, I have a couple of questions for you."

"Not interested," Trevor said.

"You seem to be under the impression that you will have some choice in the matter," Malloy said. "Let's start with that mark on your back. Where'd you get it?"

Trevor had a mark on his back that was a tattoo of angel's wings in chains.

"Tattoo artist," Trevor lied.

"Don't think so," Bishop Malloy said. "See, as a man of the cloth, it is my sworn duty to hunt—"

"I know what your kind do," Trevor interrupted.

Malloy, who was clearly annoyed, turned back to Trevor. "Then you will know I'm used to dealing with marks like that. Or at least, those who give out marks like that. You were marked by a witch."

"If you are going to just answer your own questions, can I go?" Trevor asked.

He caught a backhand to the face.

"So, I see you're *that* kind of priest," Trevor said.

Trevor was slapped again. "Bishop," Malloy corrected.

"Yes, I was marked by a witch years ago. Can I leave now?" Trevor asked.

"Let me make one thing clear. You will not be leaving here. You will be executed for consorting with witches. This is—" Malloy started.

"Then kill me, and let me be rid of this boring conversation," Trevor interrupted. "Seriously, this whole damned country is full of you self-righteous bastards who think they are God's chosen emissary. However, you all bleat the same drivel. You have the brain of sheep, with the voice of parrots," Trevor said.

Bishop Malloy lit a fire in his hands.

Trevor let out a small laugh to himself. "I rest my case," Trevor said. The irony of another holy man using fire magic showing his "originality."

"So where is it?" Malloy asked.

Trevor just stared at him.

"The witch," he said.

"Don't know," Trevor said.

Malloy took his hand and put it on Trevor's leg, the heat burning him. Trevor groaned in pain. Malloy let up.

"I know that mark. That mark belongs to the witch Blair. She has haunted these lands for years. She has even killed a few of my own priests, years back. Now, you bear her mark. Where is she?" Malloy asked.

"No idea," Trevor lied.

"I see pain doesn't scare you. By your injuries, you are no doubt used to battle and pain. However, let's see how you enjoy starving to death," Malloy said. He then walked out the door.

"Maybe you still will be the end of me, eh, Hamilton?" Trevor said to himself.

VINCENT HAGLAZ

The company had been marching south for a few days now. It would take another three days to get there based on the size of the company they travelled with. Vincent had taken full control over the company. Ambrose was his theoretical second in command; however, she got the feeling that these religious zealots were not going to listen to a non-believer.

They found themselves just outside of a little village around sundown. Vincent decided that this would be the best place to set up camp for the night. He found a place to sit and pray. He was interrupted by one of the priests, who came by to give a report on their supplies and then left.

The next to visit him was Ambrose.

"Something wrong?" Vincent asked.

"You want me to sit around and sing kumbaya with these guys? Forget it," Ambrose said.

"They're on our side, you know," Vincent told her.

"No, they're on *your* side," Ambrose said pointedly.

"I thought we were on the same side."

"Yes, and so did I," said Ambrose. After a moment, she continued,

"You wanted me to be in a leader position. However, they won't listen to me."

"You haven't exactly inspired them to follow you, you know," Vincent observed. "They want to believe they are following the will of God. It is hard to do that when someone in command turns her nose up at every mention of the word *God*."

"So I have to believe in order to get their respect?" Ambrose asked.

"No. All you have to do is respect their belief," Vincent countered.

Ambrose thought about this. Then she shook it off and sat down next to him. "Do you think they'll be enough to win?"

"I don't know. We still don't even really know what we're up against."

"Are you still thinking about Trevor?" Ambrose asked.

Vincent didn't respond. He simply kept looking up at the sky.

"Well, then, I'm turning in," she said. She left his side and made her way back to her tent. However, on the way back, she walked by a fire pit, where some of the forces saw her.

"Hey there, beautiful, come join us," a soldier called out.

Ambrose thought about lashing out. She was supposed to be a second in command, yet she got no respect from them. But she decided not to take the bait.

"Come on. We don't want a non-believer spoiling our night," said another soldier.

"What? She's a filthy heathen? Why are we fighting with someone like that?" another soldier asked.

Ambrose didn't care about their insults. However, she knew if she ever wanted respect from them, she would have to earn it now. She walked up to the fire pit. There were five soldiers and five priests sitting around it.

Upon her arrival, some of the men whistled and cat-called. She stopped when she had reached the centre of their little circle.

"God or not, I am in command here. You will all apologize at once, and behave like the decent men you claim to be," she said.

One of the priests laughed. "Without God's guidance, how to you plan to lead us? Without his strength, what can you really do?" he teased.

The crowd began to laugh and snicker.

"So you're saying that without God, I'm weak, is that it?" she asked. "Well then, any of you with God's power should easily be able to overpower me."

They all fell quiet, unsure of where she was going with this. Ambrose saw that Vincent had arrived in the background and was watching.

"Come on, I've thrown down the gauntlet," she said. "Anyone feel up for it?"

Again, the crowd just muttered to themselves—until one of the soldiers stood up. He walked to the middle of the circle with her. He was a young man and couldn't be much older than 20. The look on his face was truly insulted.

"I will not let you insult God and his noble subjects. I will take up your challenge for God and for our honour," the young man said.

The others cheered him on. "Get her, Lex!"

"Lex, is it?" Ambrose asked.

"Lexel Just," the young man said. His eyes were full of pride and determination. Ambrose had come into this wanting to hate these men. However, she saw a look in his eyes that she'd once had.

With a standard set of chain mail armour, shield, and sword, he didn't look like the magic type. Ambrose took out Marya.

"I'll make it fair for you. I won't use magic," she said.

He looked a little upset. "I don't need you to go easy on me," he said.

"Trust me, you want me to," she said.

"First you insult my God. Now you insult me by not giving your all. I swear on God I shall defeat you," he said, raising his sword to the sky.

Ambrose felt horrified by the thought that she could have ever been like that.

The two squared off. He made the first move and charged in. He thrust with his sword, followed by a bash with his shield. Ambrose deflected his first strike and avoided the bash. He just didn't let up. He feinted with the shield just to come in with a right swing.

The boy clearly had training. His swings were aimed, and he didn't leave many openings. That was fine. Ambrose only needed one. She swung upward with a full-length Marya, but he was able to avoid it. She then swung down at his head. He was able to block it.

However, he wasn't able to see that when she hit his shield, she split up Marya into two. She used the bottom half to block his sword. This caught him off guard—to see that the weapon could split. She then spun and swept the boy off his feet.

His fall to the ground was fairly ungraceful.

"Is that the full power of your God?" she asked.

This made him mad. He was back on his feet quickly.

Again, he ran in full strength, trying to defend his honour. His stance started off strong and balanced, but he grew angry that he could not land a hit on her. Eventually, she blocked his sword with one hand and the shield with the other, and then slammed his head with both ends of Marya. Ambrose then jumped back.

The boy's ears were ringing and his head ached. Tears came to his eyes. These were not tears of pain. These were tears of anger—ones Ambrose had once shed herself. She looked at him and saw her younger self reflected.

"Damn you!" he yelled, his voice cracking.

He threw his shield to the ground, grasped his sword with both hands, and ran in. He swung upward. Ambrose dodged to the side. However, he did not follow upward all the way through. Midway through, he made a large swing across his body. Ambrose hit up on the blade to parry his strike. However, he had already let go of his sword, and he leaped out to tackle Ambrose. The kid was completely crazy. He was fighting so hard out of pride. His attacks might have been desperate, but they were still effective.

He slammed into her, and the two went to the ground. Ambrose took his force and rolled back. She caught his arm and held him in an arm bar. The boy was caught, yet he still tried to fight out of it. More tears welled in his eyes.

"Come on, kid, the fight's over. You didn't do too bad, but it's over now," Ambrose said. She no longer wanted to humiliate the boy. She dropped him and stood up.

"Damn it," he said, punching his fist into the ground. "What demon gives you strength, foul woman?"

"Years of training," she responded. "Trust me, you don't want to meet an actual demon. You wouldn't win that fight either."

Then, turning to the onlookers, she asked, "So, anyone else?"

The soldiers didn't push the issue further. They seemed relatively satisfied. None of them wanted to be humiliated.

"All right, then. Hopefully there will be no more issues with my command."

Ambrose joined them for food and drink. Vincent looked at this scene happy to see that maybe there was hope for their little expedition. However, this small moment of contentment would be short-lived.

A priest appeared behind Vincent.

"What did you find?" Vincent asked.

"Sir, I talked with the local priests. Turns out a wounded man came through here a day and a half ago. He was armed with knives and two scimitars. They treated him here; however, for some reason, a bishop from a town just west of here requested he be taken there."

Vincent pondered this for a moment. He then walked back to his tent. Ambrose saw Vincent take off with haste, and she followed him. She found Vincent in his tent, packing.

"And just what are you doing?" Ambrose asked.

"I know where Trevor is," Vincent said.

"No, you can't leave now," Ambrose said. "What about the mission?"

"He's a threat to our mission. If he is alive, he'll come back to finish what he started," Vincent said. "I can't lose any more to him."

"If you lead troops to go kill him, he will kill them. These men are no match for him. Even with us there, he could score a couple kills before we brought him down or he got away again," Ambrose said.

"That's why I'm going alone," Vincent said.

"So, you're abandoning your troops?" Ambrose asked.

"No," Vincent said.

"Sounds like it," she said. "So, what, we wait here? For how long? Not to mention, he'll more than likely kill you," Ambrose said.

"Thanks for the vote of confidence," Vincent said.

"Just stop and think!" Ambrose yelled. "If you die, then what does any of this mean? The mission will be a failure. The men will disperse,

I'll be back to square one, and our enemies will get their hands on the most powerful weapon in the world."

"I swore an oath that I would kill him. For vengeance for Hamilton, and for all those I had to cremate. Their burning faces are etched into my memory. I can't simply let him live after that!" Vincent yelled.

Ambrose kneeled down next to him. She put a hand on his shoulder. "Then when we have won, and you rule this country, the two of us can go kill him," Ambrose said. "If you chase him down now, then he will have won, and Hamilton died for nothing."

Vincent was quiet, then said, "All right. We'll see this through. Then we take vengeance for Uppsala," Vincent said.

"Good. Now get some rest," she said.

CHAPTER 7

TREVOR BLACKWELL

TREVOR LAID THERE IN THAT bed. His wrists and ankles were sore from pulling at the restraints. When he would wake, it would be for brief intervals before he would pass out again. Lack of food and water were draining his drive.

However, when he woke this time, he saw that woman by his side. She had a knife in her hand.

"Are you my angel here to free me?" Trevor jested.

"I-I came to kill you," she said weakly.

"Oh great. Please go on telling me how I have wronged you or your family, or—" Trevor began.

"Out of mercy," she said.

"Oh," Trevor said. He could not hide his genuine surprise.

"I can tell by your weapons and armour you're an assassin. Also, the witch's mark on your back means you are not faithful to God. You may be evil, but torture is also evil," she said.

"World's best assassin actually," Trevor threw in. "Worked hard for that."

She looked to all of his wounds and then to the binds. She then gave him a look that told him exactly what she was thinking.

"Times are getting tougher," Trevor said with a smile.

She let slip a giggle and a smile, then went back to trying to be serious. Trevor could tell by the way she held the knife that she had handled one plenty of times. But by the way her hands were shaking, he could tell it was never for combat. He also noticed the cuts that went up her sleeve.

"So, you were putting me out of my misery," Trevor reminded her.

She shakily brought the knife to his neck. She closed her eyes, and then she dropped the knife. She stormed out of the room, wiping her eyes.

Trevor smiled. "Damn, and here I thought I was going to actually get some good rest."

✦✦✦✦✦✦

A day passed, and then Malloy was there to greet Trevor as he woke.

"Feeling like talking yet?" Malloy asked.

Trevor didn't say a word.

"I see you're still clinging to your secrets," Malloy said. "Seems you are not scared of starving to death either. So, if neither pain or starvation will loosen your lips, then I have no more use for you," Malloy said.

Trevor knew the tactic. The man was going to threaten death to make him panic into telling. A useless tactic. Trevor knew either way Malloy was going to kill him. Well, he would try.

Malloy lit his hand ablaze and walked up to Trevor. He leaned in and held the fire to his face.

"Last words?" he asked.

Trevor then slipped his hand up and shoved a knife in Malloy's trachea, before turning it and pulling it out—the same knife that the girl had dropped. He had cut himself free, but kept the restraints on and concealed the knife. Trevor let the blood fall on his face.

"Yes, I'd like a warm bath," Trevor said, bathing in Malloy's blood. Malloy slipped off Trevor and fell to the ground. Trevor began cutting away the other restraints. He had just got the last one off when two priests burst into the room.

Trevor threw the knife, catching one of them right between the eyes. He then ran in with all the speed he could muster, though he was much slower than usual due to being dehydrated. The priest let loose a blast of wind, knocking Trevor to the ground. He rolled out of it and continued his assault. He tackled the other one and the two began a grappling match. Trevor finally got behind the guy and snapped his neck.

Their tussle had spilled out into the hall. Trevor felt weak. Using his speed took a toll on him when he hadn't eaten or had any water. Still, these two weren't too difficult to kill.

Trevor used the wall to help himself stand up. When he looked up, he saw that same girl staring at him.

"Oh, honey, you may want to run. I'm not above killing women," Trevor warned.

"Malloy is dead?" she asked.

"Yeah. It's actually thanks to you." Trevor pulled the knife from the priest's head. He lifted it up to show her.

She looked surprised, now realizing that she had doomed Malloy. Trevor began walking toward her, the knife dripping blood. She stood paralyzed, not knowing what to do. Would he kill her? He had already threatened to.

She wanted to run, but she just couldn't. She could not move at all. She stood still until Trevor walked right by her.

The tension and fear left her body. Trevor just kept walking until he found the stairs. He descended the stairs, having to rely on the railing to stabilize himself.

"Wait!" she yelled after him.

Trevor looked up at her.

"Where are you going?" she asked.

"I need to find my gear. I also need to get some food and water. Still kind of starving after not eating the past several days," Trevor said.

"Your gear is two doors on the right when you reach the bottom floor," she said.

Trevor was surprised by the help. "Well, thank you for another assist," he said.

Trevor went to where she said, and he was able to find his gear. He began to put it on. This was a tricky process, since the armour had hooks that could erect with a string pull, and also hidden blades in the wrists and shoes. Not to mention the daggers strapped all over the place.

As he dressed himself, the girl came around the corner with water and some meat. Trevor looked at her. "You already gave me the tools to escape and told me how to find my armour. You keep helping me out like this, and I'm going to get the wrong idea."

"It's not because I like you that much. Serving with Bishop Malloy has not been the privilege everyone at the nunnery said it would be," she explained. "He doesn't forgive failure. He was abusive, and not just to me. You are not the first man he has tortured looking for that witch. He has had innocent women raped, burned, and hung just because someone accused them of being a witch—in particular, the witch Blair. The church dislikes witches because they give birth to other witches by brewing them from magic, and they stay young forever. The church sees this as unnatural and evil. They aren't seen as real people," she said.

The girl began crying.

"Let me guess: you're a witch," Trevor said.

The girl didn't say anything, but it was written all over her face.

"Well, witch lady, you got a name?" Trevor asked.

"Trinity," she said.

"How did a witch end up serving a bishop?" Trevor asked. He now had all of his gear on, and he began devouring the food that Trinity had laid out for him.

"I ... uh ..." she began.

"Never mind. I don't care," Trevor said.

She was surprised, then a little upset by his dismissal.

"So what ever happened to that witch Blair?" she asked. "Do you really not know where she is?"

"The witch is dead," Trevor said. "I killed her."

Trinity was a little frightened by a man who could kill a witch on his own. "Why do you bear her mark then?"

"I needed power," Trevor said. "I found Blair back when I was younger. I was a talented thief and assassin, but without a lick of magical power. I wasn't 'blessed' with any magical gifts. So while killing thugs or rich assholes was easy, it got more difficult when the targets or their guards had magical gifts. I needed my own edge.

"So I tracked down the witch and bargained for the power. In exchange for power, she said she had claim to my soul. Also, I would be bound to follow any orders she gave. So once she branded me, I killed her, almost instantly," Trevor said.

"So you just kill everyone you meet?" Trinity asked.

"I kill those in my way and when it benefits me," Trevor said. "I told you, I'm the world's best assassin."

"Sounds like that's all there is to you. What kind of life is that?" she asked.

"The life where I'm the strongest, and not with anyone's help. Not even God's."

"But didn't you ever want anything else? Friends? Family?" she asked.

"I was married once, not officially; we were just lovers. When I was younger. She didn't know what I did. She thought I was just a fisherman. That's what excused my disappearances, and why I was scarcely around. So, when I left to find the witch, she thought I was just out on another journey. I didn't find out till I got back that she died. I wasn't even around! That's when I figured out what the witch meant by taking my soul in exchange for power," Trevor said.

Trinity was uncertain what to say here. This was a sad story, but Trevor was trying to pass it off like he didn't care.

"As far as friends, the only friends I ever had have since abandoned me and are now my targets. I learned a long time ago, you can rely on others or yourself. The only thing that's ever worked for me is getting myself as strong as I can be. The only way to justify that I have gotten any stronger is to challenge myself to defeat the strongest enemies," Trevor ranted with some sort of joy.

"But you're an assassin. You deceive, hide, lie, and strike in the dark to kill. How does that prove your strength? Doesn't that make you a coward?" Trinity asked.

"You look at strength like all idiots do. Intelligence, strategy, skill, deception, networks—these are all assets that make up strength," Trevor said. "Now run off. Killing you serves no purpose, unless you want to get in my way."

"If what you said is correct, then why don't you use me to add to your strength?" Trinity asked. "A witch at your side would make for a valuable asset, right?"

"You clearly weren't listening. I only rely on myself. I don't have allies, just those I use," Trevor said.

"You didn't listen to *me* before," Trinity shot back. "I know you don't care about my miserable life, but it's the only life I knew. You took that away from me. Leave me here, and I'm just a witch who has nowhere and no one to go to. I've been used my whole life, that's all I know how to do."

Trevor just glared at Trinity. He wasn't sure if she was being serious. "If you really want to be an asset to me, then know that the minute you're an inconvenience, you're dead."

She made a face that showed she was not happy, but she nodded in acceptance of these terms.

Trevor finished eating. "Come on, we have to leave here. You have 15 minutes to prepare whatever you need to. After that, we need to get moving. Staying here will draw too much attention. Someone will for sure come looking for Malloy."

Trinity left quickly. She had no love in her heart for this place, or Malloy. However, she had never really known any other type of life. She had been living the life of a nun serving a corrupt bishop. Now she would be helping an assassin. Was she forever doomed to serve the wanton and wretched? Still, Malloy was dead; she wouldn't have to suffer his abuses anymore. But had she jumped out of the frying pan just to land in fire? Only time would tell.

VINCENT HAGLAZ

Despite all he had said to Ambrose that night, Vincent knew he couldn't leave Trevor alone. So, in the night, he headed west. He knew he was abandoning his followers, but he couldn't lose anyone else. At least not to Trevor. He was going to finish this and try to redeem himself for the failure of bringing about the death of his oldest and most trusted friend—not to mention for Uppsala and her crew.

Everything his father had built for him was gone. He had lost it all within the first week of being entrusted with it. Vincent knew that one of them had to die. Either Trevor would pay for his sins, or Vincent would.

Vincent spent that night and the first half of the next day making his way to the town one of his priests had mentioned. Vincent knew that he had to find where Trevor was being held, and fast. He didn't expect any place to hold him down for long. If Trevor had gained enough experience and skill to beat Hamilton, then he had gotten even better than he was before. Who knows; maybe Trevor had succumbed to his injuries.

No, not likely. Vincent knew he wasn't that lucky.

This part of Sylvania was very sunny this time of year. He liked the usual overcast and rain he was accustomed to. The sunlight always seemed to give him a headache. Funny, considering that his magic manifested itself as fire. He put on his hood to try and get some shade.

Finally, he arrived at the town, Trautchguard. He dismounted and began looking for someone he could get information out of. There were plenty of people around.

The town was made up of stone houses with wooden supports. Not a lot of forest around here, but enough to supply some lumber. The people went about busy days of haggling in markets, and ... aha, a church.

Vincent tied up his horse to a post outside the church. He opened the doors to the church to find a whole collection of priests standing around three bodies.

The priests looked to Vincent. "Hello there, brother. We're sorry if you have come for our services. We have just lost our bishop and need to prepare for his funeral," one of the priests said.

"How did he die?" Vincent asked, already knowing the answer. There was a fire brewing within him—a fire of rage. Trevor continued to leave a string of bodies in his wake. But now, he'd killed a bishop, a noble and holy figure. Trevor had to be stopped. Vincent didn't want to see any more bodies pile up because of the one he let get away. He wanted no more than was already on his conscience.

The priests showed him the bodies. Two had fatal knife wounds and one a broken neck. There was no mistaking that these kills were the handiwork of Trevor.

"There was a nun under Malloy's care along with a prisoner. Both are missing," the priest said. "Obviously, we suspect the prisoner is involved in the murders. However, did he kidnap the nun?"

Vincent didn't think so. Trevor didn't take things he didn't have use for. Had he somehow brainwashed another soul to follow him? Vincent knew that he had to stay as strong to his conviction as ever. He needed to stop Trevor.

But where would he go? Vincent could only think of one place: Arithia. Trevor would most likely go back to his home in Arithia to prepare for the next attempt on his party.

Vincent left the church and went back to his horse. He was already behind Trevor, and he couldn't afford to fall back any farther. He was off to Arithia.

AMBROSE GAINS

Ambrose awoke that morning and met with the troops that were gathering up camp. She didn't see Vincent, who was usually up before her, praying. His tent was even still pitched. She was starting to worry.

Ambrose went to his tent. "Vincent, the sun is up. We should get moving. Most of the troops are almost ready to go."

There was no answer. This is when she started to realize what had happened. She burst into the tent. No Vincent, none of his gear, nothing. He was gone.

She couldn't believe it. Even after they talked it over, he left anyway. She didn't know what to do. What would she tell everyone? She didn't want to leave the tent; she didn't want to have to face them and tell them that their commander had abandoned them.

For several moments, she stood there with anger and anxiety.

Finally, she begrudgingly walked out to see everyone ready—and somewhat confused as to what was happening.

"What's going on, ma'am?" asked one of the priests.

Ambrose took a long deep breath. "Vincent is gone. He has left. There is something that has required his attention. I'm sorry," Ambrose said.

There was deafening silence. Then one of the soldiers started laughing. There was muttering amongst the ranks. Ambrose could tell this news was not being taken well.

"So now what? Do we just go home? Fuck this," the soldier said, walking off.

"We could wait here," suggested one of the priests.

"No!" came a cry from the crowd. Walking to the front was Lexel Just. "We continue on. Remember what the pope said. He told us that this was a God-given mission. Well, I intend to finish it."

"Who's going to lead us, boy. You?" asked another soldier.

"No. We already have a leader," he said, turning to Ambrose.

Ambrose was shocked to see this change of heart. At first, these troops had wanted nothing to do with her. Now they looked to her. She knew this moment meant everything. She had to show that she was worthy.

"I know we share different beliefs," she began. "I know we may fight for different reasons. But we share a common enemy. We are both fighting for our country, and damn it, we are fighting for our pride. If you want to go home now, go! But if you seek victory, glory, and the safety of our home, follow me! I'll help you find what you seek and more!" she yelled now, breathing heavily.

The troops looked surprised at first, but then they all started to give one another satisfied looks. Lexel thrust his sword into the air. The other soldiers were quick to follow suit. The priests all reached for the holy symbols around their necks and held them close, showing their faith in this mission.

"Let's finish packing up, boys. We're moving out," Ambrose commanded. She would now have to become a leader. She had warned Vincent that if he ever faltered, she would take his place.

Their march resumed, this time under new leadership.

CHAPTER 8

TREVOR BLACKWELL

THE TWO TROTTED WITH HORSES Trever had stolen from Malloy's stables. Trinity was not quite used to riding. She had ridden before, travelling with Malloy, but that seldom happened. She looked over to Trevor, who also looked uncomfortable.

"You look uneasy, sir," she said.

"Don't call me sir," he snapped.

"I'm sorry," she said. "What should I call you?"

"I don't care, just not sir," he said.

"Well, is anything wrong?" she asked.

"No," he said. A quick moment of silence. "I just fucking hate horses."

"Not an animal lover?"

"Animals are fine. It's horses that suck."

"Oh," she said. She couldn't help but let a smile slip. It was in these small moments she could almost forget that she was travelling with a serial killer. Sorry—*the world's best serial killer.*

They saw Arithia in the distance. The sun beginning to set over the horizon.

"Are we going to set up for the night?" Trinity asked.

"No. We will just push on to the town. Arithia may be full of dangerous thugs, but so are these outskirts. I at least know most of the scumbags in town. So stay close," he said.

"Yeah, OK," she agreed.

The two made their way, even in the dark, to town. Once inside, they made their way to the same inn Ambrose and Hamilton had found him in before.

The patrons inside recognized Trevor instantly, though they were unfamiliar with his guest. Trevor made his way up to the bar. Trinity was looking about the inn, seeing all the patrons. They were certainly the urchins of society. These were the kinds of people Trinity would expect to be killers.

"Evening, Jock," Trevor said to the bartender.

"Trevor, we expected you earlier than this. We thought you bought the farm. And where is John?" Jock asked.

Trevor got a grim look on his face.

"I bet he killed the poor bastard to take his share," a voice from the tables chimed in.

Trevor looked back at the poor soul.

"You want to be next?" Trevor asked, putting a hand on one of the scimitars he had stolen from Hamilton.

The thug raised his hands in surrender and went back to his drink.

Trevor looked back to Jock. "I made my kill, John failed to make his own and died because of it. So, the contract is still open."

Jock looked surprised to hear that John had been killed. "Why didn't you kill the target John could not?" Jock asked.

"The target had help. It would have made things quite difficult," Trevor said.

"So where have you been since then?" Jock asked.

"I've been preparing for the next attempt," Trevor said, pointing out the scimitars.

"Those are nice, where'd ... no, *who'd* you steal them from? They clearly have been used," Jock said.

"Trade secret, old man," Trevor said, walking toward the back rooms of the inn.

"How much for the tramp in the nun outfit?" the same thug asked.

Trinity looked horrified, then looked to Trevor to see his response.

"Not for sale," Trevor said.

"So that's what you've been up to all this time? Shacking up with this harlot?" The thug walked up and put his hand on Trinity's shoulder.

Trinity slapped the brute. "Unhand me, you disgusting pig!" she yelled. "I happen to be a nun. It's not a costume."

The thug punched her, sending her into a table, spilling drinks and breaking glass on the floor. The glass cut her hands as she tried to stabilize herself. The other thugs sitting at that table were now angry. Two of them started attacking the first brute, and one of them went to kick Trinity.

Trevor's knife-tipped boot found the groin of this particular man, splitting open his testicles. As he cried out, the others in the inn looked to Trevor.

"You've gone too far this time, you cur," said one of them.

Trinity looked up at Trevor. "I'm sor—," she had begun to say. But then she saw a look of rage-filled ecstasy.

Trevor drew his new scimitars. "I've been waiting to try these out! You better come at me all at once, or this isn't going to be any fun!" he yelled.

The thugs fumbled for the weapons at their hips. Trevor rushed in, slicing the first's throat before he could draw. The next to his left was swinging an axe, coming down at him. Trevor spun, knocking the axe-wielder's hands down and to the left. This left an opening at his throat.

The third, wielding dual knives in reverse grip, went in for a stab coming from his left knife. Trevor spun again, using his increased speed, and slashed an artery in the man's leg. From there, Trevor kept spinning around the man, slicing him up with shallow cuts just to let out his rage.

Two other thugs ran out of the inn. Others, with weapons drawn, started to surround Trevor and Trinity. However, they hung back, too afraid to be the first to draw Trevor's wrath.

Finally, a man rushed in with a shield and axe. Trevor began running toward him at top speed. From the corner of Trevor's eye, he saw something flying toward him. He leaped back, barely dodging a crossbow bolt fired by Jock between the two combatants. Everyone stopped in their tracks.

"Stop this, all of you!" Jock yelled. "I don't want any more damage or mess to clean. All of you sheath your weapons! Trevor, you and the nun are out for the night. You need to cool off!"

Trevor's face scrunched in annoyance. The others waited for him to put his scimitars away before putting their weapons away as well. Without a word, Trevor spun and began walking out. Trinity got up and quickly ran after him.

The two walked the dark streets for a while in silence. Finally, they reached a small house. Trevor opened the door, motioning for her to go in. She quickly did. Trevor had felt the stares of those hiding in the shadows the entire walk. He went in and locked the door.

It was dark inside. No torches were lit, and the place looked deserted.

"Is this your home?" Trinity asked.

"I own the place," Trevor said. He went over to the fireplace and began to start a fire.

The roof was high above their heads, and there were only a couple of rooms. Two chairs were at the table; one looked broken. There was no food or really any personal items. The place seemed almost unlived in.

Trevor had the fire going. He pulled some meat out of his pack and let it sit next to the fire to cook. He sat there just staring into the flames.

Trinity looked at him, wondering how someone could look so calm after killing four people. She began to realize how normal that was for him. She also wondered whether those people in the inn died because of her actions. For so long, she had tried to live life as a good servant to God. Even if she was a witch, she believed in the morality that religion taught.

She knew Malloy was just a bad soul. She knew of the good that religion could bring. Yet the only thing that saved her from her terrible life was a man who had no connection to God and committed atrocious sins. *What did that say about her?* she wondered.

She sat next to him to warm herself by the fire. Trevor was cleaning the scimitars. Even though she thought she should be afraid of him,

Trinity felt safe next to him. She knew how easy it would be for him to kill her at any moment. Still, this was the only place she had.

Back when she was under Malloy's care, she was fearful of being beat over any slight mistake. Trevor had just killed four men for her, and he didn't even seem to see it as an inconvenience—other than the fact that they couldn't stay at the inn.

"Is this where you used to live with your late wife?" Trinity asked.

Trevor said nothing.

"Sorry, that was personal," she said.

Again, Trevor stayed silent, not saying anything.

"Who is this target you're after?" she asked.

"An old friend."

Trinity was stunned by this. "Then why—" she began.

"That's the job," Trevor interrupted. "Someone wants him dead and thinks I have the capabilities to do it."

"And what about this John? Who was he?" she asked.

"Another friend, and an ally. He was supposed to kill the target I'm after now."

"Do you have to?" Trinity asked.

"What?" Trevor asked, now with a little anger.

"Where will it stop? When you are out of friends? When you completely isolate yourself?" Trinity asked.

"It ends when the day comes when someone can kill me. Until then, I'll seek out the strongest and keep hunting. I told you, relying on others will make you weak," Trevor said.

"Not doing so will make you lonely," Trinity replied.

"I thought you agreed you were fine with being used."

"I am," Trinity exclaimed. "Because I always have been. I know nothing else. I'm talking for you. You had a lover, friends, allies. You say you gave that up to become strong. But really, by trying to better yourself, you hurt those you chose to get close to you. You say that was intentional, but I know it's not. You just say that now because you won't accept you didn't mean for those things to happen and they did anyway."

Trevor stood up, the rage back in his eyes. "We leave in the morning, witch. Be ready." He walked off to a room and closed the door, and that was the last they spoke that night.

VINCENT HAGLAZ

Vincent had been riding for hours and hours. Night had fallen, and he had yet to reach Arithia. He wanted to press on but decided to make camp here. He didn't have his tent, just a bed roll. He put a small fire together and ignited a flame.

He thought about what the party was doing right about now. Ambrose had to be furious with him. He knew that much. He wondered if they would wait for his arrival or if they would disperse. He knew he was Trevor's target. He just didn't want any more of his comrades dying for him.

In the night, Vincent heard noises. When he woke, he listened to see if he could discern what they were. It sounded like they were getting closer, slowly.

The sounds were coming from different locations. Vincent could recognize the sound of someone trying to sneak up. He stood up, grabbing his swords. "I'm giving you the chance to leave with your lives," Vincent said.

He still couldn't see who was approaching. They must have been hiding behind the rocks. Finally, a scrawny figure popped out from behind one of the rocks with his hands up.

"You got me," the guy said. "I was looking to nab those swords of yours. They look valuable. Especially the long thin one. Is that actual silver?" the little thug asked.

Vincent didn't respond to that question. "What about your friends. They going to show themselves too?"

This thug gave a nod. "You got us, you got us," he said. "We were going to take your stuff and be gone. Actually, we still are. You can either live through the night and hand us your valuables, or we can take them off your corpse. The choice is yours, my friend," the little one said.

"Please just walk away now, and there will be no need for violence this night," Vincent said.

"I guess you're going for the latter then. Shame," he said.

In total, four thugs came running out at him. They had him on all sides. This didn't worry Vincent too much. He had fire magic; they didn't.

Vincent put his short sword away and used his left hand to hurl a spout of fire at one of them. The man catching ablaze panicked and fell to the ground, trying to douse the flames. Vincent took that man's place, trying to stack up his attackers so he would not be flanked.

The little thug jumped in from the left using two hatchets. Again, a simple fireball was all that was needed to stop him.

Then Vincent took a forward step to make a sideways stance and make himself a small target. He held out his rapier to keep at bay the next attacker, who wielded a sword. The man gave several good swings, but Vincent was a defensive duellist. He loved parrying and dodging his opponents, finally goading them into a mistake, just as he did here. The man finally took a swing that took him off balance, and Vincent ran him through.

The final opponent had simply run off, not wanting to be burned alive as well. Vincent reached out his hand as if he were going to cast a fireball and kill the wretch. He wanted nothing more. But he stopped himself. He knew it was wrong to kill a fleeing man. It would go against the rules of his religion. He was scared of just how close he had come to breaking that code. He was afraid of what this whole ordeal had made him into.

Vincent sat by the fire the rest of the night. The sun would be rising soon, so there was really no point in trying to fall asleep. He wanted to make sure to not lose any time. He couldn't fail now, or Trevor would strike again.

TREVOR BLACKWELL

In the morning, Trinity was the first to rise. She was busy making sure they had everything they needed for a journey. Trevor finally emerged from his room.

"We are low on food," Trinity said.

"Yes, and my stock of knives is a little short. Perhaps I'll need to make a quick run to the market before we go," he said.

"Are you sure we need to?" Trinity asked. "You still certain that you need to kill this old acquaintance of yours?"

"I thought we were done with this topic," Trevor said.

"I know. Just checking, I suppose."

Trevor sighed. "Have everything set to go before I return. I won't be gone long."

Trevor made his way to the centre of town. He ducked into a passageway and behind a curtain to finally come to an alley full of criminals and a bustling market—a black market. Though the market kept up its busy and bustling pace, Trevor could feel eyes penetrating through the crowd and focusing on him.

Trevor started off by gathering the food supplies they needed. Nothing illegal about buying food, except if it's stolen food sold for cheap. Trevor then went over to his favourite weapons vendor.

The tattooed woman saw him approaching and already was giving a devious smile. She motioned to a little dwarf standing next to her, and the dwarf began gathering up weapons from the back.

"Well, well, Mr. Blackwell. I hear that things didn't go so well on your last hit. Hopefully not due to any of my darlings," she said with a wink. She referred to the weapons she sold as her darlings, and knives specifically when it came to Trevor.

"Of course not. They performed beautifully, especially the hook blades in the armour. Smart work as always," Trevor said.

"So even with my babies at peak performance, you still couldn't finish," she said. There was a certain vibe she gave off by leaving that sentence there.

The dwarf came back with a leather wrap full of knives. He unrolled it, displaying the contents to Trevor. There was a large variety to choose from. Trevor picked up some of his usual throwing knives. He noticed some new additions.

"You've been holding out on me," Trevor said.

"And you've been cheating on me," she said, pointing to the scimitars. "And a lady doesn't give everything away. She needs some secrets."

"And here I thought you and I didn't have secrets between us," Trevor said.

"So, you going to tell me about this nun of yours?" she said.

"Tell me about these new ones," Trevor replied.

She held up one of them, with a curved blade. "This one is a bit sensitive. She doesn't like all the blocking and parrying involved in duels. She is made from silver, so a little softer. She has small honeycombed indents in her that ooze a small dose of basilisk venom, just enough to shut off innervation to the site of insertion." She put way too much emphasis on that last word.

Trevor just quickly looked to the next one. A double-sided knife.

"Oh, these are the twins. They have a special connection." She split the knife in the middle of the hilt. Inside was a long coil of piano wire. "Even when they are separated, they are never really alone," she said.

"I'll take the lot," Trevor announced.

"Of course, Mr. Blackwell," she replied.

Trevor paid her and began packing away his new assets. That's when he overheard the conversation.

"Fried 'em, I tell yous," the man said. "We thought he was just a priest that got lost. We were hoping to catch em nappen. That's when he started throwing fire around and cooked the others. Just on those ridges over there," the thug said.

The thugs felt like they were being eavesdropped on and looked over, but Trevor was already gone, happy to have been saved the trouble of hunting down his target.

VINCENT HAGLAZ

Vincent was in Arithia right at first light. He was scoping the streets for his target. He could tell by the looks he was getting that he did not fit in here. Most of the people here looked poor and destitute, not to mention desperate. He could feel the thirst for blood.

He found a local inn, a perfect place for information. Inside he found an innkeeper cleaning up. No patrons this early.

Without looking, the innkeeper said, "No drinks till 10, you all know that."

A small bag of coin landed at the man's feet. "Well, perhaps I can find you a pin—," the man began. Then he looked up at Vincent. "Priest? Needing a pint before prayer this morning, are we?"

"Just looking for information," Vincent told him.

"We have no church in this town. At least not anymore," the man said.

"Trevor Blackwell," Vincent said sternly.

Jock let out a toothy smile. "Oh, I see," he said. "Afraid I can't help you there. You see, I can't go around giving out information on members of the ... the ... the, ah, the *community*," Jock finally said.

"So, is it a matter of money?" Vincent asked.

"Most times, but not for this. However, I can tell you of a nun who came through here last night. She left with a man, and they made their way to a small house on the east side of town. Three houses down from Blazing Glories tavern. My protections do not extend to outsiders, you see. Figure you religious types would want to stick together," Jock said.

Vincent left the inn. He could feel how close he was. This just brought back the feelings of rage that had been stewing within him.

Trevor had taken everything from him. He would not let him take any more. He didn't want to see more lives ruined, not like John's.

However, he couldn't hide his deepest feeling. He wanted to kill Trevor, and he wanted it to hurt. He did not want Trevor to go easy into the night. No; Trevor needed to feel the heat from the flames that were kindling in Vincent's heart. He needed to feel his organs burst like balloons from the pierce of Vincent's rapier. Vincent wanted him to die screaming and choking on his own blood.

CHAPTER 9

VINCENT HAGLAZ

VINCENT STOOD OUTSIDE OF THE house that had been described to him. It was only now he wondered why the man at the inn had given up this information so easily, after saying that Trevor was under certain protections. Did he want to get rid of Trevor? Maybe Trevor was just as much of a thorn in that man's side as he was to Vincent. Or perhaps the man was just trying to lure Vincent into a trap.

Whatever the case, he was here now. At last, he would have his revenge. At last, he believed, he would get to start his mission in earnest. Only one obstacle was standing in his way.

Vincent had a distinct advantage most of Trevor's targets didn't. He knew Trevor's tricks and abilities. They had sparred so many times at Uppsala. However, the same worked in reverse. Trevor knew how Vincent fought. That's why he'd had John attack him. John was clearly a good match against Vincent, with that demon power tucked away for a surprise.

Vincent observed the house. He could smell meat cooking inside. Trevor was home then. All the windows were higher up than Vincent could reach. He wanted to just blast the door down with a fireball and set the place ablaze. It would have served Trevor right after what happened at Uppsala.

However, Trevor had a hostage with him—the nun. Poor girl; did she know who he was and what he was capable of? Vincent just hoped he hadn't hurt her. With no way to observe the inside of the building from here, Vincent would just have to try his luck by going in blind.

He went to open the door, which, to his surprise was unlocked. He opened it up and slipped inside. The view was not quite what he expected. He saw the young woman cooking and packing. She was turned away from him, so she could not see him.

"Just about set. I've cooked and salted us some meat for the road. That way, we don't have to cook every-night—" She stopped abruptly when she saw Vincent standing just past the doorway.

"Who are—" she began.

"Where is he?" Vincent asked.

She was reaching for something in her pocket.

"Don't!" Vincent commanded. "No need for that." Vincent presented his holy symbol. "See, you can trust me," he said.

"How is that supposed to tell me I can trust you?" she asked.

Vincent was walking slowly closer. "I'm also part of the church. I want to help you."

"No, you want to kill Trevor," she replied.

"I'd qualify that as helping you," Vincent said. The two were circling the table.

"Maybe," she said. "And what happens to me when Trevor is gone?"

Vincent stopped and put his hands up. "You are free to go back to your church, or you could come with me," he said.

"Think I'll pass on those."

Vincent was confused that a girl who had been a nun all her life serving a respectable bishop would be turned so easy by Trevor. This just frustrated Vincent even more. He knew he had to help this poor girl. She couldn't see she was making terrible choices.

"Come with me. You don't have to be controlled by him. I'll show you the righteous path," he said.

"I said no," she said.

"He's a murderer. You know that?" Vincent said.

"I know that. Tell me, priest, how many have you killed?"

Vincent was now starting to get a little upset with her. "He's using you, can't you see that!? You're just a—" Vincent began.

"A pawn? A tool?" she said. Vincent was surprised by her answer. "Don't you think I know that?! But that's all I've ever been! I'm just a fucking tool! Not a human being, not a person. I'm someone's possession. A thing. I'm an object for you all to use just because of my birth!"

She unfixed her nun outfit. Below it was a flowy black dress with the back cut away, exposing a witch's symbol. This symbol was a triple helix with a red, blue, and green strand, the colours blending in the connecting strands. She let him see the mark.

"You're a witch?" he asked.

"You want to know the irony?" she asked. "The ones who beat me, the ones who defiled me, the ones who drove me to self-mutilation were not the criminal. It was not the assassin who took every piece of individuality I had and made me conform. No, it was the men who swore to be faithful servants to God and uphold virtue and protect the innocent," she yelled, walking toward him.

Vincent saw the scars on her arms. He could see the anguish and resentment in her weeping eyes. He could tell that this had been a long time coming.

"How many times do I got to tell you? That's *world's best assassin*, actually," Trevor said, standing in the doorway. He had come in without making a sound.

Trevor already had his weapons drawn. Vincent knew if he made a move right now, he would be dead before he could try anything. That's when he made a desperate move. He grabbed Trinity and drew his short sword to her neck.

Trevor didn't even move.

"Trevor, drop your knives or I kill her," Vincent said. He hated doing this. It felt wrong. He just didn't know another way.

Trevor laughed. "Think you missed the point of that little outburst there, Vince," Trevor said.

"You ready to throw her life away, Trevor? She's a witch. I'd be doing my church a service," Vincent said.

"Go ahead. Let's see you do it and prove her point," Trevor said while tossing a knife around in the air.

"You're just trying to call my bluff," Vincent said. "I—" Vincent began.

Trevor laughed. "Vince, after all this time, I thought you were the only one who knew me. Hell, Hamilton thought you knew me," Trevor said.

"You keep his name off your lips, heathen," Vincent said.

"You know, I think that old bat knew me better than you did. Perhaps everyone does. Ambrose knew. You were the only one too blind to see what would happen. Now you've betrayed them both," Trevor said.

Vincent held the blade closer to Trinity's throat, drawing a little bit of blood. "Last chance," he said.

Trevor continued to laugh. "You idiot. There is only one life in this room I care about," Trevor said, releasing both knives and hurling them at the two.

Vincent threw himself down behind the now tipped-over table, the witch falling with him. Vincent didn't need sight; his reactions would just be too slow anyway. He threw a burst of fire on either side of the table, knowing Trevor would now be rushing in.

Trevor was indeed coming in on the right side at breakneck speed. He had to stop dead in his tracks to not be caught in the flame. He turned and jumped up, barrel-rolling in mid-air. He threw two knives at Vincent crouched behind the table.

Vincent was only able to swat away one with his rapier; the other found his right shoulder. Trevor had landed on the left side of the table. Vincent thrust forward his rapier. Trevor deflected with a scimitar. Hamilton's scimitar!

"Those don't belong to you!" Vincent yelled.

"I still remember how he screamed when I flayed his flesh," Trevor said.

Vincent knew that Trevor was baiting him. He knew Trevor just wanted him to make a mistake. Vincent was using all of the training his father had given him. All those times they duelled when he was a boy and in the courtyard of Uppsala. Vincent was always on the defensive, keeping his opponent at bay, waiting for that opening. His father never left an opening.

Trevor left plenty of openings, He just moved so fast that there was no time to riposte. Vincent knew if he thrust his rapier forward, Trevor would rush in and finish it. In that case. Vincent did just that; he thrust the rapier forward. It came close to landing a hit.

Trevor was not expecting an offensive move. Vincent was now anticipating the counter. If Vincent fought reactionarily, he would lose. Trevor was just too fast.

Vincent cast fire with his left hand. Trevor was rushing into Vincent's left side as fire burst forth. Trevor knew he would not escape all of it. He spun to the left, taking a hit from the fire, but as he spun he released the hook blades, cutting into Vincent.

Vincent was cut by those hooks, but the cuts were small. He was not caught by them. Meanwhile, Trevor's right arm and face had burns. As Vincent winced in pain and huffed for air, Trevor smiled and continued the assault.

Vincent had one more trick for him. He blasted a small wall of fire to obscure Trevor's vision.

Trevor quickly bound around the side of the fire and was throwing daggers where Vincent was. However, Vincent wasn't there. Trevor instinctively tried to jump back.

Vincent had jumped up and used a blast of fire and his cape to lift him into the air. Trevor was now just below him. He used fire to propel himself downward, thrusting the rapier in Trevor's right shoulder. Trevor attempted to dodge, and this is why the rapier didn't find his heart. Vincent felt a knife stab into his own right arm.

Vincent and Trevor rolled in opposite directions from each other. The two lay on the ground for a moment. Trevor was beginning to stand up. He pulled the rapier out of his right shoulder, making a noise of both pain and pleasure. He threw it to the side.

Vincent tried to stand. His right arm wasn't moving, so when he tried to stand he fell over on his right side. His breathing was heavy and fast. He tried so desperately to stand, as he knew Trevor would be on the attack again.

He got to a kneeled stance and blasted out fire with his left arm.

But it was too late. Trevor quickly sidestepped the attack, and Vincent was kicked in the face. Vincent fell back into a wall. His hands were quickly wrapped up by a wire, run through by two knives, and pinned to the wall behind them.

Vincent felt the pain in his left hand but had no sensation in his right. Had Trevor cut a nerve or tendon? Why was his arm completely numb and motionless? Vincent struggled but could not get his hand free.

"Well, you certainly saved me the pain of tracking you down," Trevor said finally. He too was breathing hard. The wound on his right side clearly had an effect.

"You'll burn for this, Trevor!" Vincent yelled. "You will die a horrific and meaningless death!"

"You're probably right on that one. This result was inevitable, Vincent. You had to have known that. Admittedly, you definitely have caused me a great deal more pain than expected," he said, holding his right shoulder.

"You took everything from me!" Vincent said. "You have committed crimes against the Church and me. You consort with demons and witches. You kill esteemed members of the Church. And you kill your old friends! You manipulate the weak and frail to work for you. You kill everything you touch, you bastard," Vincent lectured. He knew that these might his final words. Still, these were the reasons he hated Trevor, and he had to let them out.

"Old friends? You don't mean yourself and that old man, do you? Oh Vincent, I figured you were smarter than this. Has the hubris of winning this little contest gone to your head? No, this has always been a contest. We were competitors pit against each other. We still are! Can't you see that? The game is still on!" Trevor said.

Those last words hit hard for Vincent. He had not yet made it to his station of power. Many of the final ten from Uppsala still lived and were involved in this incident. Could the contest really still be going?

It didn't matter right now. Vincent was faced with, most likely, his own death.

"Why, Trevor? Why would someone with so much God-given ability become this? I believed in you, even when no one else did. I thought I saw something in you. But I guess I am the fool you all say that I am."

Trevor took off his tunic, exposing the witch's mark. Vincent stared in disbelief.

"That's right. No God-given talent here. I was born without magic. I had to earn this power. I killed for this power. Sacrificed everything for this power. Look at what praying to God got you! If you want power, get it yourself. Don't borrow it from someone else. Because you're the only person you can ever trust," Trevor said, lifting a scimitar.

"You said the contract was on Hamilton's and my head, yes?" Vincent asked.

"Yes," Trevor agreed.

"There's no need to go after Ambrose and the rest of the party then?" Vincent asked.

"Suppose not."

"Good. Then I hope when this is over, you find what you're looking for and get what you're owed. I have done my part," Vincent said.

"Fair enough."

CHAPTER 10

AMBROSE GAINS

THE MARCH HAD BEEN GOING for about a week or so. They were now nearing the border between Sylvania and Avalon. Ambrose stopped the march just to look on. They were on the precipice of greatness. One step further to achieving their goal.

Ambrose couldn't help but look back. She half expected to see Vincent there. She had been coming into her leadership role well. The troops had really rallied behind her. She inspired them with her confidence and drive. They loved her, even though she was not a believer.

Instead of Vincent behind her, it was Lexel Just. He smiled at her when their eyes met. His blond hair was a bit dishevelled, and sweat was rolling down his face. He had a boyish grin, even though he was a man.

"Something the matter, commander?" Lexel asked.

Her face turned a little red, as she knew she had been caught staring. "Uh, no. Just thinking about how we are going to get through the border. I'm hoping we don't have a problem crossing," she quickly said.

"I've thought the same thing," said Lexel.

"We have a peace with their kingdom, but we still bring such a large force."

"Have faith, commander," Lexel assured her. "We'll make it through."

"Faith, right," she said, laughing.

The company moved on, making its way to the border. They finally made it to their designated border crossing.

There was a checkpoint here that screened all using the road to move through. Ambrose stopped the company a little way from the checkpoint. She didn't want to seem threatening to the guards standing here. She and Lexel made their way to the checkpoint, where they were met by two guards in full armour.

"Hail friends!" Lexel began.

"State your business," the guard said flatly.

"We come hoping to pass with our band of holy followers," Lexel responded.

The guards looked out to the large group of priests and soldiers they had waiting.

"What is the purpose of bringing this many armed men into Avalon?" the guard asked.

"We have orders from high up. We mean no harm to Avalon or her people," Ambrose said.

"Do you have any documentation of this?" the guard asked.

Ambrose's fears were starting to be realized.

"We cannot let such a dangerous band pass through this border. I'm sorry, you'll have to turn around," the guard said.

"Sir, you can't be serious. We have marched all the way from Pavia. We can't turn back now. Our mission is time-sensitive," Lexel said.

"And what would this 'mission' be?" the guard asked.

"For confidentiality reasons, we must keep this secret," Lexel said.

"Yeah, you see, that isn't going to cut it," the guard replied.

"Perhaps I can be of assistance," a priest who had appeared out of nowhere said. This was the same priest who would scout for Vincent. He wore a birdlike mask. He had a magic gift that gave him the ability to teleport.

This priest handed over a document to the guard. The guard examined it and said, "This document, which has been given the pope's seal, defends your statement of such a mission under the command of one Vincent Haglaz. Where is this Vincent Haglaz?"

Ambrose and Lexel looked at each other.

"That would be me," Lexel lied.

"Says here that he is a priest of some esteem. You don't look like any priest. As I've stated. You are denied passage," he said.

The three of the party standing there watched as the guard moved on to the next travellers.

"What now, commander?" Lexel asked.

Ambrose stood in silence. She was trying to think of what to say that would be encouraging and practical in this situation.

"If I may, Commander Gains?" the masked priest asked.

"Go ahead," Ambrose responded.

"There is a way for us to get through without going through the security checkpoint."

"Go on," Ambrose said.

"The Blackwood."

The Blackwood was the huge forest that grew into both territories. In this time of peace, there was little to no security guarding it, as few would risk travelling into a dangerous forest full of magical beasts just to cross the border.

"With our party?" Lexel asked. "We are too large a company to make a voyage through dense forest. Besides, we could lose many within that madness."

The masked priest ignored Lexel and simply looked at Ambrose for her thoughts.

Ambrose took a couple of moments to ponder the huge decision before her. But in the end, she realized there wasn't too much of a choice to make. They were shut down going this way. "To the Blackwood," she proclaimed.

TREVOR BLACKWELL

Trevor had his scimitar raised high. He wanted to swing down and finish the job he had taken on. However, there was something in his way. Or, for that matter, *someone*. Trinity. She stood in the middle between Trevor and Vincent.

"Trinity, what are you doing?" Trevor asked with a frightening and chilling tinge of anger.

Vincent had closed his eyes, resigned to his fate. Now he saw a frightened girl standing before him. No wait, not a girl—a witch. Still, she was the only thing standing between him and death. Between him and the end of his journey and his mission. Why would she defend him?

"I just want to make sure this is what you want," Trinity said.

"He's the target I've been after. Of course it is," Vincent said.

"He's also the only friend you have," she said. "Are you sure you want to go back to taking contracts at that inn where no one likes you? They all want to kill you, and someday there will be a contract with your name on it. Is that the life you want to live? Or do you want to live and die with actual friends?" Her eyes were teary.

Trevor was wondering why this girl cared.

"You might not think it, but you are just as much of a tool to them as I am to you," she said. "I have accepted my fate. I just want to know if you are OK with yours."

Trevor lowered his scimitar and pushed Trinity aside.

"I know there is more to you," she said. "Whether you see it or not."

Trevor was now directly in front of Vincent. "You still on this damn crusade or whatever?" he asked.

"Seems like that's all up to you," Vincent said.

"Still need my help?" asked Trevor. "I have been curious about this Well. I want to see what powers it can grant me."

"It isn't for the likes of you. The whole point of this mission is to protect it from getting *into* hands like yours," Vincent said.

"No. Your mission is to stop it from falling into the hands of this unknown enemy. Besides, we'd be working together, so how can it be the wrong hands? That's my price, Vince. All I ask for at the end of this is just to tap into that power. You can become supreme ruler over whatever you want. That's not really my scene anyway."

Vincent breathed in. He wanted no part of Trevor. He wanted nothing to do with such a criminal. However, he still had a job to do. God had put this mission in his path. If he had to work with Trevor to get it done, then so be it.

"If we do this, you cannot act like a wild animal. We don't kill out of pleasure or for settling rivalries," Vincent said. There was still some disdain in his voice.

"Fine. But I don't work for you. I work *with* you," Trevor said.

Vincent let him have this choice of words. "Also, those swords don't belong to you." Vincent held out his hands.

"How about I return these to you after we finish," Trevor proposed. "I have grown quite attached to them. They fit my style well. So long as I'm using them for you, shouldn't be a problem, yes?"

Vincent begrudgingly agreed to these terms, and Trevor freed him. The two were very injured. "Guess we are pretty self-destructive, aren't we?" Trevor said.

Vincent and Trevor shared a moment of laughter, something the two had not shared in years. Vincent could not believe he was now working with Trevor. After all the hate, after all the bloodshed between these two—friends lost and homes destroyed.

"Come, Trinity, perhaps we can all share a meal before we start on our quest," Trevor said.

Trinity stood and smiled for a moment. She didn't know these two very well yet. But maybe now she belonged to a group as a member. Maybe now she wasn't property. They were an odd bunch, but anything was an improvement over what she had before.

Trinity and Vincent shared an odd and uncomfortable stare, and Trevor still ordered her to make meals. However, this was a step in the right direction.

CHAPTER 11

AMBROSE GAINS

THE GROUP MARCHED ON TO the Blackwood. They took a somewhat scenic route. They wanted to make the guards at the border believe they were heading back to Pavia.

Ambrose had set up her own chain of command in this party. Lexel Just had been serving as her second in command. The two were still a bit awkward with each other—Lexel still coming to terms with the fact that they were on a holy mission led by a non-believer (and the fact that he got beat), Ambrose struggling with her newfound responsibilities. She had to keep a strong face in front of the troops. However, in quiet moments in her tent, she broke down.

Her other leader was the priest who had stepped forward earlier. He acted as a scout. His short-range teleportation made this job especially easy. His name was Father Tal.

The group, after many days' march, was at the edge of the Blackwood. Despite the name, the forest looked quite green and full of life. However, the plant life was thick and the trails narrow. This was not ideal for a group of their size, though it did make things convenient when you wanted to travel undetected.

They all looked in at the huge trees and overgrown vines.

Lexel looked at Ambrose. "You still sure about this?"

Ambrose, not wanting to look indecisive or weak about this decision, took the first steps into the dense forest.

As they trekked through the forest, Lexel spoke with Ambrose. "I hear the elves live in these woods," he said. "Godless creatures."

"I'm godless," she reminded him.

Lexel brushed that comment off. "Come now, you don't feel any connection with the divine spirit? Perhaps you do not realize it, but you have gifts given to you by God. I'm not just talking about magic," he said.

Ambrose spun around and looked at him, her cheeks red.

Lexel threw his hands up in surrender. "I meant like leadership, and … and *charisma*."

Ambrose's cheeks stayed red, and she walked on past him.

Lexel rubbed the back of his head. That was very awkward and was not helping the shaky dynamic they had.

One of the other soldiers came up and put his arm around Lexel's shoulders.

"Our Lord also gave her a nice ass, don't you think?" the soldier asked so only Lexel could hear.

Lexel blushed and brushed off the other soldier.

That night, the group was a bit on edge. The reason it was called the Blackwood was really starting to make sense. Not even the light of the moon was making its way through the dense branches above.

No campfires were lit that night, only small torches. The band was intent on not being discovered by the Avalons, but they also did not want to get the attention of whatever else lived in these woods.

Ambrose had awakened that night to take a shift of watch. They usually had at least five people on a shift. With the dense forest, the tents were more spread out, so there was more ground to cover.

Upon coming out of her tent, Ambrose thought she heard something off in the darkness, so she grabbed Marya and went to investigate. She moved quietly. What she found was Lexel. He was swinging his sword and raising his shield. He seemed to be going through a routine set of exercises. He was making conscious changes in his stances and careful adjustments of how he held his sword and shield.

It was clear to Ambrose that he was trained well. However, the difference between Ambrose and Lexel was not Ambrose's ability to use magic. It was true experience.

Lexel had all the training, all the discipline of a soldier. He simply lacked experience in a true fight. She watched him for a couple of moments. He was no child, but even though he was a soldier, he still had a look of innocence, of optimism. Ambrose couldn't help but see her old self in that. How many years had it been since she'd had that same look of optimism?

Then Lexel had a strange moment where he threw his sword down in almost anger, and he seemed frustrated. *What's wrong?* she wondered. She moved in closer, keeping herself hidden from sight.

Eventually, he picked up the sword again and resumed his training. He moved in a predictable fashion. He would advance with a series of strikes, occasionally reminding himself to keep his shield high. He would then back up and spin to another side, where he would repeat his same set of strokes.

Ambrose got close enough and knew when he would spin around. Right when he spun and swung his sword, Ambrose blocked it with Marya. Lexel jumped in surprise.

"Oh, commander, I … I didn't realize you were watching," he stammered.

Ambrose smiled. "That's the idea of a sneak attack, isn't it?" She spun around, dipping low, and swept his leg. He fell clumsily in a heap. He was still a little rattled.

Ambrose offered him a hand up. Lexel gave her a glare but begrudgingly took her helping hand.

"That's your problem in a fight," Ambrose said. "You are very predictable. You fall into a pattern, and you expect your opponent to do the same. Of course, every fighter has particular tells and patterns. However, the trick is to be a little unpredictable."

She raised up Marya in a readied position, and the two squared off. They began to spar. Ambrose had a clear upper hand in their melee, but all the same, Lexel was a competent fighter. Ambrose could feel the boy's strength in his hits. Clearly, he had trained his muscles too.

Though they did this for training, they enjoyed themselves. In this dance, they felt like they were communicating much better than they did with their words. One spoke in glory and honour for God and country. The other spoke in commands and ambitions. Combat was the language these two shared.

Ambrose could feel his determination to prove himself in every swing. Lexel could sense her cunning, experience, and drive with the way she moved around his advances.

The two finally stopped, both out of breath. They smiled at one another, happy and content. This had been very cathartic for the two of them, breaking down a barrier that had been there since their meeting. However, as the looks lengthened in time, they sunk back into their own. No longer could they feel what the other felt, and the awkward tension rose again.

"I will, uh, go to my post," Ambrose said. "Get some rest."

Lexel wanted to call her back. He wanted more. However, he knew that right now, they would not be able to hear each other's thoughts. They were no longer speaking the same language.

Ambrose made her way around to find the man she was meant to replace—a priest who was standing dutifully at his post, sturdy as a statue. "You are free to take your rest. I'll take it from here," she said.

The priest didn't move. He stood perfectly unmoved. That's when Ambrose got concerned.

"Hey, Father, you doing OK?" Ambrose asked.

She put her hand on his shoulder, and the priest fell over. Ambrose didn't know if he was dead or not.

That's when Ambrose heard a subtle hissing noise. She froze and looked at the ground for snakes. She then heard branches snapping in the distance. She kept her eyes focused on the ground. This wasn't a snake. No, far worse.

Ambrose manifested Marya as a sword and shield. Blasting from the darkness, a large serpent figure rushed her. It slammed into her, sending her backward. The beast was huge, bigger than she'd expected. It was a basilisk.

She had heard about these monsters during her time at Uppsala, but she had never seen one before, let alone faced one. The one rule when you encountered a basilisk was not to look it in the eyes. One look, and you would be petrified.

The beast blew past her and went straight into the camp. Ambrose yelled "Basilisk!" However, the screams from the camp became much louder. The beast was large enough to crush the tents. It weaved its long muscly body around the thick trees of the Blackwood and quickly picked off some of the soldiers.

Some of the priests had emerged from their tents and launched a barrage of spells at it. The scene quickly became utter chaos. Ambrose stood up and ran into the fray. She was trying to keep track of the beast. However, there were bolts of lightning, fire, wind, and other various magic being hurled sporadically.

Ambrose saw the body of the beast, and she ran after it. The head was farther away attacking some of the men.

She shifted Marya into a full spear and thrust it at the beast. The spear just bounced off. No effect whatsoever.

Ambrose looked around. The basilisk seemed almost unharmed. She watched a soldier load a crossbow and fire it. The bolt penetrated the scales, then the beast struck and killed the man.

She realized that the beast's scales were repelling magic. Only physical attacks would work. People were dying left and right. Some were being petrified. Things were going bad.

Ambrose didn't know what to do. Everything was chaos. She wanted to restore some order. "No magic!" she yelled. "Fire your arrows at it! Priests, find cover!" she yelled.

Unfortunately, no one could hear her commands through the screams of death. This battle was looking grim. "*Retreat!*" she yelled.

The command was echoed by many of the soldiers and priests. They were fleeing in all directions, some of them still being picked off.

Ambrose picked up a couple of swords she had found on the ground and charged the beast. She could see the head as it was swallowing another helpless victim. She lifted the sword and slashed it around where she believed the neck was. The cut wasn't deep; still, the beast flailed its body and coiled up.

The body of the serpent knocked Ambrose away. She closed her eyes so as not to meet the gaze. She then rolled to get to her feet. She opened her eyes, keeping them low. She could just see its body.

She could tell when the beast would strike by watching it tense up. She would then dodge. She desperately tried to swing and land a solid hit. However, she would either miss entirely or graze it.

She saw it tense up, and she instinctively rolled. However, the beast waited. It had baited her well. It waited just a moment before launching out.

Ambrose tried to spin away; however, it landed a bite on her right arm. Ambrose stabbed it, which made it release her. She felt a deep pain in her arm, but the pain quickly faded as her arm started to become completely numb. She was barely able to hold it up.

The head of the beast slammed into her, knocking her down. She saw the beast coming, and she tried to get up, but it was a struggle.

She closed her eyes and just braced herself. Then she heard a roar of pain from the beast. She looked up to see Lexel standing before her, his shield raised.

"Guess you don't even like those repugnant eyes of yours, huh?" Lexel yelled at the beast.

"I told you to run, soldier!" Ambrose yelled.

"Not without you!" Lexel replied. He rushed in, shield raised. But the basilisk struck again, its mouth fitting around the shield.

Ambrose could only look on in horror. She had lost Hamilton. Vincent had abandoned her. Many of the lives that were entrusted to her had been devoured and killed in front of her. Now she watched as Lexel rushed off to his death.

"Run, you idiot!" she cried. "I won't lose you too! I can't take this anymore! Let me die!"

"I am of God, of honour, and man. No evil can take that from me!" Lexel yelled.

She could hear him. She could finally hear him! Not only his voice, but she felt the strength of his soul.

This was like when they were sparring. She was seeing who he was, his feelings plain to see. This strength of spirit reminded her of when she was a child, when she had a love for God—that same warmth of protection and safety. The calmness of mind and spirit. She believed again. She finally had not something but someone to believe in.

The beast's jaws began to crush the shield. Lexel spun and slashed the beast, and it released his shield; however, it mainly was just crumpled junk at this point. Lexel knew he had to keep his eyes down. He was faced with the same problem Ambrose was. It's hard to get a solid hit on something you can't look at.

He had to make an opening. So he decided to be a little unpredictable. He rushed in. He knew the beast would strike him. He saw it begin to tense. Once it did, he threw the useless shield at it. The shield smacked the beast straight in the head, throwing it off its rhythm.

It pulled back for a moment, and that was all the time Lexel needed. He was underneath the head of the beast. He hacked upward, slicing the beast throat to jaw. Blood spurted out as the beast waved its head around before finally landing on the ground, dead.

Lexel knelt, breathing hard. He had slayed the beast. He was smiling, happy in his victory. That's when sobering truth came slipping back in: Ambrose was down. Her arm had been bitten. That poison would be taking hold. She could die. He ran over to her.

Ambrose was sitting propped up against a tree. She was sweating heavily and had sharp breaths. Lexel knelt down next to her. "Hey, it's over. The beast is dead," Lexel said.

"Yeah, it is over," she said. "The troops have either died or dispersed. I'm no good like this. The mission is over. We failed. I failed."

"Come on," Lexel said, trying to sound hopeful. "We can rally with everyone who is still alive. We'll get you help and continue on. We aren't done yet." Then he saw the wound on her arm. It was starting to turn black. The poison was spreading.

Ambrose saw his face. "See, even you know it now. This is hopeless." Beginning to tear up, she said, "I tried to make the right decisions. I thought I could do better than Vincent. And then I ended up making a big mistake, just like him. Now it's all gone. Go, Lexel. You should leave. You deserve to make it out of this."

"No! You're not like Vincent! You didn't abandon us. I know you were uncertain when he left. Still, you took that responsibility on. Even if your choices didn't work out, you didn't leave us. You stayed, you chose to lead those who don't share the same beliefs as you. Your actions and confidence inspired all of us. The troops forgot that you were a non-believer, because they believed in you. Damn it, I believe in you!" Lexel proclaimed.

Ambrose looked at him. He was sincere—she could see it. Even through this darkness, he still had faith. He wasn't ready to give up—not on the mission, and not on her.

She unbuckled her belt and took it off. She tied it around her arm, right around her shoulder. She tightened it.

"What are you …?" Lexel asked.

"The poison is spreading. If it continues, I'll die. We have to remove the problem before it gets worse. I need your help," she said.

Lexel caught on to what she was saying, "No, not your arm," he said.

"It's either that or die," she told him.

He took up his sword. Ambrose used the belt to hold out her arm, which could not move on its own. Then Lexel took one decisive swing. The arm came off in one strike. Ambrose couldn't feel a thing. Guess that was the silver lining of losing all sensation to an appendage being dismembered.

Even still, Ambrose cried. Not out of pain; just because of the loss. All of the emotion of this night and the moment hit her. Lexel grabbed her and hugged her.

"Hey, hey, it's all right. We'll get through this," he said, looking at her. But she had already passed out.

CHAPTER 12

VINCENT HAGLAZ

THIS RAGTAG TEAM TREATED THEIR injuries the best they could for now and headed out. Vincent wanted to go back to where he had last seen his old party. However, he didn't know if they were still there. It would at least point him in the right direction of where they went.

Trevor's injuries were the worst, but they didn't even seem to bother him. Still, he most likely wouldn't be at 100 per cent for a while.

Vincent still had doubts. He was unsure how he was supposed to feel about working with Trevor—who had recently killed Hamilton—and also this witch. But he wouldn't be alive if not for Trinity, and also, he needed Trevor's help, now that he was separated from his own party. If he reunited with Ambrose, this would only be worse. She wouldn't be able to accept Trevor back. Still, Vincent still reminded himself that there was still a mission to carry out.

They rode on horseback for two days before arriving at the old campsite. Of course, everyone was gone.

"Guess they gave up on you coming back," Trevor said. "Probably think that you're lying dead in some ditch," Trevor added.

Vincent ignored Trevor's banter. He was too busy looking over the tracks.

"They didn't give up. They went on ahead," Vincent said.

"So you've been replaced. Think Ambrose undermined you?" Trevor continued.

Vincent looked on. He thought they were probably still heading for the border. And they had at least a week's head start.

"Oh man, Ambrose and those damn zealots. Maybe she'll just kill them all," Trevor said.

Trinity was shooting Trevor disappointed looks. Trevor rolled his eyes.

"Not likely. You don't know what she's capable of," Vincent said.

"She has a quick temper just like me, and the same disdain for you religious types," Trevor said.

"We need to find a way to catch up with them. We'll take the horses to the border," Vincent decided.

"Yeah, so that's not going to happen," Trevor stated.

"Damn it, Trevor, are you insistent on being irritating?" Vincent yelled.

"Yes, but that's not the point," Trevor explained. "I don't have a clean slate. My name and face will definitely raise trouble. Not to mention, we have little miss witch over here. Think we stand a chance at making it through border security?"

"Oh, so what was your plan on getting to Avalon?" Vincent asked.

"I'm so happy you asked," Trevor replied. He didn't follow up on that, simply started taking the horse on the east road.

Vincent looked to Trinity. She shrugged and then followed on with him.

Vincent threw his arms up in defeat and remounted his horse. He followed along. He continued to wonder if he was now the follower instead of the other way around. Still, if he wanted any help on this journey, he would just have to go whatever roundabout way Trevor chose. Vincent just hoped that this wouldn't stir up any more trouble.

They headed east for a couple of days. Finally, Vincent's patience started to wear. "All right, I'll bite. Where are we going? Border security will be the same at any checkpoint."

"True. Or at least the ones on land, anyway," Trevor said.

"What, you have a boat?" Vincent asked.

"Nope," Trevor replied.

"So what's your point?"

"I know some folks who operate a small fleet," Trevor explained. "I'll call in some favours, and it will quite literally be smooth sailing from here on out. They should still be in this harbour around this time of year."

"Great idea. One problem. Crew and cargo are subject to search before, during, and after a voyage," Vincent pointed out. "Even if we make it out to sea, we could be subject to search. Then you and the witch will get us into trouble."

"The witch has a name, you know?" Trinity said, frustrated.

"Sorry," Vincent said. The two of them still struggled interacting with one another. Everything in Vincent told him to hate her, but still, he felt she didn't deserve this resentment.

"We won't have to worry so much about being searched prior," said Trevor. "These fellas have a good reputation with the harbourmaster. As for during, they take an unusual route. We won't be seen. Then finally, we will just sneak off once we dock. Not a bad plan, no?"

"These 'fellas'—I trust that they are upstanding, right?" Vincent asked.

Trevor shrugged. "They may be rough around the edges, but they aren't bad guys."

"Trevor, who exactly are they?" Vincent asked.

"Traders."

"They're pirates, aren't they?" Vincent pressed.

"Semantics."

"Damn it, Trevor!" Victor exclaimed. "We aren't doing this. It's bad enough I'm working with you after what you did. I'm not becoming a full-fledged criminal."

"It's the only way we're getting in. Besides, no one's asking you to commit a crime. We are only taking passage. You won't be stealing or murdering. Well, unless you want to," Trevor winked.

"I won't sit by as they murder innocents," Victor insisted. "I should be ridding this land of such scourge."

"Look, as I said, they are traders. They don't go pillaging town to town. They bring in goods that can't be found in Sylvania that you can get in Avalon and vice versa. Sure, this steps outside the bounds of legality, but you still need to get to Avalon with us, don't you?" Trevor asked.

"You say *traders*, but it's smuggling," Vincent said.

"You can call it whatever you want. Still, no one's asking you to commit a crime."

"Yeah, just be an accessory to one," Vincent retorted.

"Not taking me in and killing Trinity already makes you an accessory," Trevor pointed out. "This isn't a scale-up."

"No, it's just adding to the things I'm going to turn a blind eye to. Another thing that will have to weigh on my conscience." Vincent shook his head.

"You know, I'd watch your attitude with them," Trevor said helpfully. "I put up with your self-righteous posturing ..."

"I'm self-righteous?" Vincent snapped. "You're the one who only believes in himself and benefitting himself."

Trevor was now more serious. "I know what I am. I've been OK with that for a long time now. I'm an assassin, the *best* assassin. I have to keep hunting bigger and bigger prey. I accept that I'm not going to be the hero. I accept that I have to hurt others, including the ones around me, to get what I want. It happens time and time and time and time and time again." He paused. "Still, I acknowledge all of these things about myself. What have you accepted about yourself?" Trevor asked. "Think about it during another one of your come-to-God moments."

Vincent had nothing to say to that. Trevor obviously had been tormented by things about himself. Still, he knew what those things were. Vincent had questions about his faith—things he had seen on this journey that made him wonder if his faith was the beacon of light he thought it was. And that made him wonder about himself, what he was, and what he stood for. It only made him want to accomplish this mission even more. Once he was in a position of power, he could make this country and the faith what he wanted, what he needed it to be.

"Fine, so where are these pir ... traders," Vincent asked.

Trevor smiled. "We are heading to the port town of Margaton."

AMBROSE GAINS

Ambrose woke slowly. The light was at first blinding but then opened up a beautiful world of trees with light peering through the canopy. Songbirds chirped lovely songs. The warmth and sweet scents brought a sense of euphoria.

Reality, though, has an awful way of reminding us about the unpleasant. As she went to raise her right hand, nothing happened. That's when the dark memories of the night came flooding back. She felt like crying, but that's when she remembered about Lexel.

She sat up, quickly looking around.

"Hey now, not so fast," Lexel said.

He was sitting next to her. His eyes had dark circles around them. He must have been awake all night, watching over her.

"Lexel, are you all right?" Ambrose asked.

"What? Of course I am. What about you?" he asked.

"Yeah, I guess I'm OK, all things considered," she said. "Have you seen anyone else?"

"No. I haven't seen anyone from the troop," he reported.

"Well, I guess that settles it. This is over."

"No, it can't be," he insisted. "Not while we are still here."

"Lexel, come on. Look at me. I can't fight like this," she told him.

"Then I will be your sword," he replied.

This hurt Ambrose's pride. However, she really couldn't argue. She still couldn't see any possible way to succeed in this suicide mission. Still, Lexel wanted to press on. So maybe she should to.

"What drives this optimism of yours?" she asked, almost laughing.

"Faith," he said.

Ambrose wanted to tease him for this, but it was faith that was keeping hope alive, something that Ambrose didn't think would happen to her again. The two pressed on into the Blackwood. This dense forest was easier to navigate in the light, but less easy to navigate with only one arm. Still, Ambrose continued.

"Silver lining: It will be much easier to sneak into Avalon now," Lexel put forth.

"That's not funny," Ambrose retorted.

"Wasn't meant to be. Just pointing out our situation," said Lexel.

The two heard rustling in the branches above. They immediately drew weapons, ready for what was to come. Ambrose drew half of Marya, making it into the shape of a sword. Lexel brought out his sword, using a two-handed stance now that he had left his broken shield behind.

The rustling above them continued. Something was moving in the branches. Ambrose and Lexel stood back to back. Then, out of the bushes to one side, came a large black panther. Ambrose went to slash at the beast, but Lexel was attacking at the same time. The two were getting in each other's way.

"Damn it, Lexel," she said.

"Sorry," he replied.

The panther swatted Ambrose aside and went to pounce on her. Lexel was about to attack when, from above, another giant panther came leaping out of the branches. It landed on the ground in front of him and then leapt on him.

Ambrose looked up into the yellow eyes of this black beast. The beast was not currently mauling her, simply baring its teeth and growling.

Ambrose just began laughing. Even when they kept faith and kept hope, it all turned out like this anyway.

"Come on, you dumb cat, get it over with. Finish me," Ambrose said.

The beast opened its mouth, still not biting down. Then it stopped, looked up, and looked to its left. The other panther, the one on Lexel, was doing the same. Something had spooked them.

Out from the brush came an equally giant white wolf. The wolf had red markings on its pure white fur. It leapt and tackled the panther on Ambrose. The two, growling and gnarling, turned into a tornado of fur and teeth. The other panther went to help its companion. This wolf now was fighting two giant panthers.

Ambrose looked on in awe. Lexel ran up and grabbed her.

"Come on, we've got to go," Lexel said.

"No, we can't leave it to die. It saved us," she said.

"We got a blessing from God. We've got to take that," he said.

"No, that wolf saved us, not God," Ambrose replied. She took up Marya and ran into the fray.

"Oh, come on!" Lexel said. A minute ago, she had wanted to give up. Now she wanted to fight the two giant cats.

The wolf was holding its own but was certainly on the defensive. One of the panthers was wrestling with the wolf. The other panther was waiting for its moment to jump in. Just as the second panther looked to have found its moment to pounce, Ambrose slid in and slashed at the panthers back legs.

The panther spun around and went to swat at her. She ducked under that swat, then spun and slashed at its nose, which she could just barely reach. This really pissed off the beast. Anther volley of swats followed. Ambrose dodged the first but not the second, and she was again sent flying.

The panther went to pounce on her again, and Lexel swooped in to slash at its head. But the panther was able to move its head with catlike reflexes. Then, it went to bite him.

Lexel went to attack with his sword. The panther bit down on the sword, then started shaking its head, swinging Lexel around. He was thrown upward into the air and came down on the panther's head.

Lexel held on to the beast's ears. The panther continued to shake, trying to shake him off. Lexel pulled out a dagger and tried to stab the panther's head. While he did make a cut, it didn't go through the skull. So he stabbed the panther in the ear to keep his hold.

This made the beast thrash harder, hissing and growling. Then the dagger started cutting. It finally sliced vertically up the ear and tore it. This pulled the beast over onto its right side.

With the big cat's belly now exposed, Ambrose rushed in to stab it. However, before she could get there, a volley of arrows landed in front of her, stopping her in her tracks. She looked up and saw figures standing in the branches above her and all around—dozens of them.

"Elves," she said.

The panthers were no longer attacking. They were now just sitting at attention. *Great, elves that control giant cats*, though Ambrose. *This could only end well.*

Lexel stood up with sword at the ready. "Don't," Ambrose said.

Immediately, a bolas came in and wrapped up his legs, making him fall.

"Damn it," he said.

The wolf and panther were still growling at one another.

"Enough!" came a voice from above.

Down from the trees came two female elves. They seemed more decorated then the others. One was very slender and moved with grace. The other was larger, and she moved abrasively and with much less grace.

"Who are you?" the first elf asked.

"What the fuck did you do to Alabaster and Snow?" the second immediately asked, referring to the panthers.

The first one lifted a hand to calm the second one. The second one huffed and walked off.

"We are in charge of the Blackwood and its inhabitants," the first one said. "There has been quite a stir in the Blackwood lately. My name is Katya, and this is Avaram." She pointed to the second. "I ask again, who are you?"

"Ambrose Gains. We have no hostile intentions towards you or the other elves," Ambrose said.

"Then tell me, Ambrose, why do you come into my woods so armed?"

"We are on a mission to Avalon. These woods are dangerous, so of course we brought weapons," Ambrose said.

"So why go through my woods?" Katya asked.

"Because we have no other way of getting there. We were turned away at the border."

"Why was that?" Katya asked. By the tone in her voice, Ambrose began to suspect that Katya knew all the answers to these questions.

"What do you know, elf?" Ambrose asked.

Avaram growled at that comment but again was waved down by Katya.

"We found the rest of your party fleeing in the woods last night. They were running amok in every which way. We have taken them into our custody for questioning. Some tried to fight back, and I have injured elves because of that. When I questioned them, some refused to give up information; however, some spilled right away. They all said that you were in charge. None of them knew if you were alive or dead after a basilisk attack. So I will ask you now to collect your men and turn back the way you came," Katya said.

"We can't do that, I'm afraid," Ambrose replied.

"The other choice is we kill you and all who refuse to leave," Katya exclaimed.

"We will leave your woods; you have my word on that," Ambrose assured her. "However, we are going to Avalon."

"Yes, we heard a great deal about your mission to find the Well," Katya said. "However, I am not sure I trust you to protect it. Humans are always corrupted by power. Its power may seduce you. I have seen what humans do when they are given great power."

"Humans control the Well now. We seem to be doing OK with it. We are just trying to stop it from falling into the hands of those who would abuse it," Ambrose told her.

"Yes, humans do control the Well now. Do you know who used to control it? We did, until humans came to claim it for their own. Once they had its power, they drove us from our land. Now we only span over these woods. Now you humans cover up its existence and only those in power utilize it in fear others will come and claim it for their own."

She continued, "The Well has great influence over the state of our world. We elves have been dying off quicker. It is not often one of us becomes pregnant anymore. The magical beasts of these lands are also becoming rarer and rarer. Soon it will be all humans that covet this earth. Even then, you all will destroy yourselves fighting over power. There is peace now, but it will not last."

Ambrose felt for them. She knew how humans treated elves. She knew that elves had been driven from the majority of the land. "I cannot change what happened to you. But I can change what will be," Ambrose said.

"Do you think I trust the words of humans?" Katya scoffed. "Of course you believe that once you have the power of the Well you will be responsible. But it will corrupt you, child."

"I'm no child!" Ambrose burst out. Katya was shocked by that outburst. Ambrose then regained control of her emotions, knowing that they would not help her in this situation. "Look, if you don't believe in a human to change the situation of elves, then why not change it yourselves?"

"As I said, we simply do not have the numbers to counter your armies," Katya said.

Ambrose sheathed Marya and extended her one hand. "Then come with us. Join us on our journey. When we succeed, you can be right there with us to hold us good on my promise."

"What are you promising chi—. Excuse me, what are you promising?" Katya asked.

"We can give you access to the lands," Ambrose began. "Like the humans have. Eventually, I would like for elves and humans to get along. I know that will take time and hardship. Hopefully, we can also find a way to reverse your people's fertility problems."

She added, "I need all the help I can get on this journey. We've suffered tragic losses. Also, if you want to find a way to change the state in which your people live without fighting against grand armies, join us."

The giant white wolf came over and sat next to Ambrose. Ambrose looked up at it. The wolf just sat there like a dog coming to its master. The elves looked on in shock.

"The elusive White Wolf has never done this before," Katya told them. "He used to belong to our sister before she disappeared 30 years ago. After that, he ran off into the woods. We tried to track him down and return him home. However, we only saw him a handful of times after that. He would never listen to any of us. How strange he came to your aid, and now sits by your side. Well, human, perhaps your proposal is something worth discussing further." Katya extended her hand to shake Ambrose's.

"Thank you," Ambrose said. "Also, could you release him?" she said, pointing over at Lexel.

Katya laughed. Some of the other elves freed Lexel, and he quickly reunited himself with Ambrose.

Avaram punched him.

"Hey!" Lexel yelled.

"That is for hurting my cats, you dick," Avaram said.

"They attacked us!" Lexel explained. However, Avaram had already left.

The elves led the two to their home. The entire way, the wolf followed closely at Ambrose's side. Ambrose was not sure why this wolf had taken to her. She had never met this wolf before, let alone been in these woods before. However, she was thankful for it. Without it, who knows whether things would have gone so smoothly?

They finally arrived in a settlement. There were homes and various structures built into these giant trees—several layers of homes, one on top of the other. Various connecting branches made up routes for the elves to walk on. There were hundreds of elves running up and down the various levels. It was nothing like Ambrose had ever seen, even in the many missions she undertook for Uppsala. She was blown away. Lexel seemed equally flabbergasted by the sight.

"Welcome to Fairborn," Katya said. "This is one of the largest elf settlements in the Blackwood. It is a safe place. Most humans don't venture into the Blackwood, and the monsters tend to stay away from the main settlements."

"Yes, this is amazing, Katya. However, you said that you were holding our troops," Ambrose reminded.

"Right. I understand," Katya said.

Lexel and Ambrose were led through the settlement. All the while, they were taking in the sights. They were eventually taken to a large tree—large even for this place. They went inside and saw that it had been hollowed out. There they found what looked like prison cells. Inside were some of the soldiers and priests they had thought were lost in the fight with the basilisk. Ambrose took a quick headcount. It looked like there was 28 of them, plus Lexel. So, 11 had died that night.

Some of the men started to notice Ambrose. "Hey, commander! Did they get you too? What happened to your arm?" they asked.

"That's enough," she commanded. "This has all been a misunderstanding. You are all getting out of here. Please try not to hold anything against the elves. We came into their home, not the other way around. The mission shall continue. We will hopefully get some reinforcements provided by the elves. I expect you all to cooperate and work with them. I know we have differences, but that shouldn't divide us when we all have something to gain by working together. I know we have suffered great losses. I ask you to steel yourselves and find the courage to press on."

The cell doors opened. The troops came out and stood around Ambrose. They were all mumbling about having to work with elves.

"Understood, men?!" Ambrose yelled.

"Yes ma'am!" they all said.

"Good," she replied. Then Ambrose turned to Lexel. "I need you to do something for me."

"Sure, what is it?" Lexel asked.

"I need you to look over things with the troops while I go and speak more with Katya and Avaram about what we plan to do next. I need you to make sure no one causes problems—on our side or theirs. If a fight breaks out, I fear any hope of some sort of aid from the elves will be over, and we will be forced to turn back to Sylvania. This cannot happen," she told him.

"Do you believe you'll be OK on your own with them?" Lexel asked.

"Yeah, I do. If they had wanted to kill me, they could have just done so in those woods. I think I've got this handled for now," Ambrose replied.

"Very well then. Still, be careful," he said.

"Thank you, Lexel. I wouldn't have made it this far without you or your spirit."

The two parted ways. Lexel looked over getting the troops back their equipment and making sure everyone stayed in line. Ambrose went to go further the negotiations with Katya and Avaram. Perhaps there was still some hope for this mission after all.

CHAPTER 13

VINCENT HAGLAZ

THE TRIO FINALLY MADE IT to the port town. Vincent was still not sure if this was the best option. He felt like he was betraying his faith by travelling with witches, murderers, and now pirates. Still, he knew the options that were before him, and there weren't many.

This town was full of shady figures too. Everyone he saw he thought might be a pirate. There were either those who were walking up and down the street peacocking, dressing as wild and crazy as they could, trying to show they were unafraid, or those covering their faces and keeping to the shadows. Vincent could see many people making trades and side street deals. He knew to keep his head down and not look too closely, or he could find some trouble. He didn't like being in a place like this.

"Ah, I love this place," Trevor declared. "I really have missed it. It's a whole other world than the usual boring places you find in this country."

"Let's just find your friends and get going. I don't want to stay here long," Vincent said.

"You really are no fun. I was hoping to hit up some of my old friends. If you're looking for a good time, they know how to set you up," Trevor said.

"I don't think either of us is looking for what you consider a good time," Trinity chimed in.

"Fine. Guess I'm outvoted here," Trevor said, leading them to the docks. They walked along the docks for a while. Vincent took in all of the ships that were docked here. He was trying to figure out which one they would be taking.

Trevor then stopped in front of a bar and tied his horse up outside. The others did too.

"Vincent, since you're just going to be a pain in there, why don't you stay with the horses, all right? Make sure no one takes them," Trevor said.

Vincent shot Trevor a look. He still didn't know if he could trust the man yet. "Fine," he said finally.

He stood there waiting for Trinity and Trevor to come back out. Vincent knew he was being stared at just as much as he stared at the folk around here. He was definitely out of his element. What was taking Trevor so long, anyway?

TREVOR BLACKWELL

As Trevor and Trinity entered the Black Flag tavern, Trinity started to have some anxieties about this whole thing. She was wearing a robe over her black dress to hide her witch's mark. The people in this tavern seemed rougher than those in Arithia. While the people in Arithia seemed like the kind to shove a dagger in your back, the vibe she got from these people is that they were looking for any reason to start a fight.

"Relax, Trin. These folks smell fear like sharks smell blood in the water," Trevor said.

"You say *relax*, but you follow that up with a reason to be scared," Trinity pointed out.

"I know that isn't you, Rat!" a large red-haired woman yelled from one of the tables in the bar.

Trevor snapped his attention quickly to this woman, his hands on his weapons.

"Maybe they smelled *your* fear," Trinity said.

The entire bar was now focused on Trevor and the large woman who had stood up and was making her way towards him. She had a very large axe on her back, which she drew to her hands. She also had two smaller hand axes at her hip.

Trevor drew the scimitars.

"Hold it, Titania," another voice chimed in.

The man who said that was referring to the red-haired woman. He was an old man with an eyepatch covering his right eye who was sitting alone smoking his pipe. He had longer slicked-back black hair on the top of his head and grey hairs that were cut short on the sides. His hide was tanned, and he had the look of a veteran sea dog.

"If you and Trevor start a fight," the old man said, "the bar will suffer, and I'm the one who will have to cover that cost. And that will be coming out of your pay."

Titania returned the axe to its position on her back. "Hey, another time then, OK, Rat?" she said.

"Rat?" Trinity asked Trevor.

"Just a nickname she uses for me," Trevor said. The look on his face said he didn't want to talk about that.

"So, you kill someone she cares about too?" Trinity asked.

Trevor was slightly offended by that. However, he figured he deserved that. "No, she is just always itching for a fight. She likes to find strong opponents. As I said, these people are traders. They don't get a lot of action."

"These are your pirate friends?" Trinity asked.

"Boy!" the old man called out. "I assume you have business you wish to discuss. So stop standing there and let's hear it."

Trevormade his way over to the man and sat at the table. Titania stood right behind him.

"Who is your friend here?" the man asked.

"An ally," Trevor said.

"She can't have been your ally for very long. Her skin is so fair, she's been indoors most her life by the look of it. Her wide eyes also tell me she is unfamiliar with such places. She smells like incense and soapy water. Let me guess: a nun?" the man said.

Trinity's eyes opened wider. The way this man was able to read her so easily made her uncomfortable. She hoped that he wouldn't be able to deduce too much.

"By that reaction, I can tell I hit the nail on the head. However, there is something a tad off with you. Something I can't quite lay my finger on. So, you kidnapping nuns now, Trevor?" the man asked.

"Come on, Captain Moulder, you think so little of me?" Trevor asked. Moulder was silent. "Well, I really am getting high-roaded today, aren't I?"

"So what is it, Trevor? You need us to smuggle this nun to Avalon?" Moulder asked.

"Actually, we all need passage," Trevor said.

"All?" Moulder asked.

"The two of us and another acquaintance of mine who waited outside."

"Who is this other acquaintance? Is he as much trouble as you?" Moulder asked.

"No, no, just a priest."

"So, you are travelling with a nun and a priest? Going to Avalon, a kingdom that doesn't follow their religion? What are you up to?" Moulder asked.

"We are going for secrecy on this one, captain," Trevor stated. "You know I can't easily cross a border, and for certain reasons, she can't either."

"And your priest can?" Moulder asked.

"You're full of questions, captain."

"What I need to know is if you are just trying to avoid detection or are actively being pursued. I need to know what risk you are putting to my crew. Just so I know how much to charge you," Moulder said.

"We are just going for discretion on this one," Trevor assured him. "Don't worry, we can pay."

"Ten thousand silver," Moulder said.

"Five thousand," Trevor countered, sounding outraged by ten thousand.

"Eight thousand," Moulder said. "Final offer."

"Fine," Trevor agreed.

"Two days from now, meet here at the docks in the morning," Moulder said. "Bring the money, and keep your head down."

Trevor and Trinity stood up to leave.

"Hey, nun!" Titania asked.

The two looked to her.

"You still promised to God, or you looking to give in to the pleasures of the flesh?" Titania asked, giving a very hungry look.

Trinity's face went bright red. She didn't know how to respond to this.

"Come now, Trinity," Moulder said. "Don't harass our clients."

"Aw, boo," Titania said. "Oh well, we will be spending a lot of time together really soon anyways," she said, winking at Trinity.

Trevor put his arm on Trinity and guided her out of the tavern. Once they were outside, they reunited with Vincent.

"Took you two long enough. What happened in there?" Vincent asked.

"Looks like we got ourselves a ship to Avalon," Trever told him. "However, we are going to have to sell the damn horses."

"You just want rid of them, don't you?" Vincent said.

"Well, I can't say that I'm sad to see them go. Wretched beasts."

CHAPTER 14

AMBROSE GAINS

Ambrose met up with Katya and Avaram inside another large hollowed-out tree. The inside of this one resembled a throne room of sorts. Ambrose was amazed at how these trees survived. They were hollow on the inside; how could such a large tree live with only the outer rims reaching the ground? Guess there was still a lot for her to learn about this world.

The two panthers were with them. One now had prominent scars on its ear and nose. The elves must have used healing magic for the wounds to be repaired so fast.

The wolf was here as well. It perked up and stood by Ambrose when she came in. Ambrose was still unsure why this wolf liked her.

Katya and Avaram were sitting on what looked like thrones that had been cut and shaped into the roots of the tree. Katya was waiting expectantly, stroking one of the large panthers. Avaram was busy smoking from a very long pipe.

"So, you two are royalty, then?" Ambrose asked.

"In a sense," Katya said. "We are in charge of these woods. We have been for a couple centuries now. We have no royal bloodline, but with lives so long, those in charge tend to be so for a long time. So, tell us, Ambrose, how will we see change in our people if we help you on this quest?"

Ambrose had to be careful what information she relinquished here. She needed to let them know she would have some sort of authority but didn't want to let slip that there was a shadow government leading the people.

"As a reward for this mission, I will be granted a seat of power within the government," she explained. "From there, I can work in a way for humans to be more open to elves living in our society. As I've said before, I also intend to help you find a cure for whatever plagues your people."

Katya looked like she was expecting a little bit more. However, she let it go. "What about the Well? Could you return control of it back to the elves?"

"I'm afraid I don't know that much," Ambrose admitted.

"Ambrose, I do not doubt your sincerity," Katya began. "I wonder about how much influence you will hold and if you can really prove good on your word."

"Do we really even want to interact with the humans? I don't like them, and I don't like change," Avaram said.

"I understand. However, our people need this." Katya returned her gaze to Ambrose. "We will be there with you when you reach the Well and upon completion of your mission. Be warned, however. We mean to keep you good to your word."

"Of course," Ambrose said.

"You know, we have medics that could take a look at that arm," Katya said.

Ambrose looked up. "What can they do for a missing arm?"

"Unsure. Were you elven born, our magic could easily replace a missing limb. However, they may be able to help with the phantom pains, or at least clean up the end," she said.

Ambrose was escorted to one of the healers in Fairborn. The healer pulled out what looked to be a seed of a tree, almost walnut-shaped.

"This is a seed that gives rise to the trees you see in Fairborn. The trees here have magic within them. They have regenerative properties. A tree can lose branches or be cut and regrow. For us elves, these seeds can help regrow limbs. However, for humans, all they seem to do is repair small wounds. Still, better than nothing," the healer said.

Ambrose took the seed. She looked at it for a while, examining it. She then swallowed it. She could feel something happening to her—a rush of feeling like pins and needles swarming around her stubbed arm. The wound, which was scabbed and still a little bloody, was now shedding the scab, and skin was forming.

It didn't stop there, however. Before Ambrose's eyes, the stump seemed to be pushing out. Like pulling out a sleeve from a coat, an arm began to form. After about 20 minutes, Ambrose's full arm was returned. She looked at it in absolute amazement. She couldn't believe what she was seeing.

She couldn't move the arm, though. It just kind of sat there, dangling at her side. It was numb, with no feeling. It didn't even really feel like part of her. Rather, it seemed like someone else's arm.

She felt it with her left hand, expecting it to be soft. However, it was hard. It felt almost like wood.

Even the healer looked on in disbelief. "Oh my, I've never seen this kind of response in humans before. This will require further investigation and study," she said.

"I can't move it," Ambrose noted.

"Yes, that sometimes happens," the healer said. "But you should regain mobility slowly."

"Why does it feel like wood?" Ambrose asked.

"Well, it is supposed to grow trees. Unfortunately, that part is a bit more permanent. Still, I would count yourself lucky that you have two arms again."

Ambrose left the healer's feeling quite strange. In the span of a couple of days, she had gained formidable allies and lost and regained an arm. Well, right now, it was more for show. She put her arm in a sling for the time being while she tried to get feeling and mobility back into it.

The white wolf was sitting outside of the healer's waiting patiently for Ambrose to come out. The wolf then came up and started licking her. She at first pulled away. He was huge, and his tongue was wet. But then she leaned into his fur.

Ambrose knew the road ahead would require strength. She had to be strong to make it this far. In this moment, she could be vulnerable. She didn't cry, though. She just melted into his coat, trying to hide from the world.

The wolf sat down, allowing for Ambrose to do so as well.

She looked up at him. "Why me?" she asked.

The wolf, of course, did not respond to her, but still looked concerned. Ambrose just shook her head, not knowing why she expected a response.

She began heading back to where her troops were. She stood out easily in this place with a giant wolf following her through the paths woven in the trees.

She finally made it back to where everyone was still gathered. Lexel was the first to see her return. He was the only one among them who recognized the giant wolf. He smiled when she finally was close. That's when he noticed her arm in the sling.

All of the troops now surrounded her, surprised and astounded by the large creature. "Shit, commander, this is one hell of a dog. It's not surprising after you were able to defeat that snake, even after you lost your arm," one of the soldiers commented.

Ambrose was confused as to where he came up with that one. She looked over to Lexel, who just winked. He had lied to the troops. Why? They would obviously look up to him if he told them the truth that *he* killed the basilisk.

Still, she awkwardly went along with his story. The troops were sitting at wooden tables inside another tree building. The elves had provided food and drink.

"Here's to the commander, slayer of monsters and master of the white wolf. Ambrose the beast tamer!" the soldiers yelled. The priests among the group couldn't help but also cheer for her. They were usually the more reserved of the group.

Now Ambrose understood the lie. Lexel had told it so they wouldn't lose faith in her.

"Thank you, men," she began. "You all should know that starting tomorrow, we are going to be working with the elves. I know this may be difficult for some of you. I know humans and elves don't usually trust each other, and especially since you were all just held prisoner by them."

Ambrose could hear some of the quiet scoff and disparagements in the crowd.

"That being said!" she shouted to silence the crowd. "We need the extra hands. Especially after we lost many friends, comrades, and brothers just the other night. We are fighting to maintain our way of life. You are fighting to uphold the values of your God. They wish to join us to help fight for a better life. They are willing to fight and die beside you to have a life like we have. I ask only that you let them do so. Without them, we won't leave the Blackwood alive. With them, you will do God proud by protecting the country that you love," Ambrose concluded.

There was silence in the crowd. Ambrose really thought she was getting good at these speeches. However, there was a hesitation here. She hoped that her words would take.

Finally, there were claps in the audience. Then all of them were clapping for her. Ambrose raised her glass high, and a night of drinking and celebrating began.

✦✦✦✦✦

Later that night, Ambrose was watching from a distant table at the soldiers hooting and hollering. She looked down at her right arm. She could just barely twitch it. Her fingers would barely curl as she strained to make a fist.

"So, how did they do that?" Lexel asked as he sat down next to her.

"Not sure. They said their magic could only help me clean the wound, since I'm just a human. But clearly it completely restored my arm. Well, kind of. It doesn't feel like my hand. It feels more like a piece of wood than anything," she said.

"What a miracle God has granted you," he said.

Ambrose gave him a look.

"You don't see this as a miracle?" he asked.

"I call it extremely lucky," she told him.

136

"It saddens me to see someone so gifted dismiss the faith so quickly," Lexel said.

"It saddens me to see someone so able attribute all his strength to God," Ambrose countered.

The two sat in silence again. They were not meant for conversation. Ambrose represented what Lexel did not want to become, and Lexel was someone she didn't want to be again.

"So, you told them that I killed the basilisk," she said.

"Of course. You should know that they need something to believe in. Since you don't believe in God, we have to make them continue to believe in you," he said.

"I think that you might be the one more fit to lead them. You share their faith and have an optimism so strong it can be overbearing at times," Ambrose said.

"You find me overbearing?" Lexel asked.

"Sometimes," she admitted. "But it's kept us going, so thank you."

The two shared a small chuckle.

"Well, tomorrow's another day closer to completing the mission, so I'm going to hit the hay," Lexel said.

"All right then," Ambrose replied.

"You should get some rest too, commander. You need it."

"I'll do that."

And with that, Lexel left. Ambrose still didn't know how to talk to him. It was as if when they didn't talk, she had an infinite amount she wanted to say. But when they actually began talking, she couldn't come up with anything.

She now knew a little of what Marya felt. Ambrose had had to be strong for herself. Being strong for others was much harder. She understood now the strength of her late older sister, who had to be strong for the both of them, even around their father.

Ambrose went outside. She had no intention of sleeping this night. There was just too much on her mind. She looked up at the sky above. It was amazing. Unlike the rest of the forest, here she could see through the canopy revealing the endless sea of stars. She wanted to be up there, away from all her problems.

Ambrose caught an unfamiliar scent. She spun around to see Avaram leaning against the side of the tree the troops were in. She was smoking something in her pipe, which Ambrose assumed was creating the smell.

"Relax, human. We're friends now, remember?" Avaram said.

"Still, you're here spying on us, I presume?" Ambrose asked.

Avaram shrugged and continued to smoke. She took in a deep inhale and let out a huge puff of smoke. It seemed to also double as a sigh. She looked up into the stars above. She reached out the pipe to Ambrose. Ambrose waved it away. Avaram shrugged.

The white wolf made a huge yawn. He was sleeping just outside of the tree. Ambrose looked to him and smiled.

"His name's Fenrir," Avaram said.

Ambrose looked back to Avaram.

"At least that is what our sister called him before she disappeared. But I guess he belongs to you now," Avaram said with only a small amount of resentment.

"I do apologize for hurting your cat …" Ambrose tried to say.

"Alabaster!" Avaram said.

"Right … Alabaster. I apologize for hurting Alabaster," Ambrose said uncomfortably. She could bring up the argument that she had been attacked first again, but Ambrose didn't think that was worth it.

"You should be. He's my beautiful baby boy. He is very sensitive, you know?" Avaram said, letting out more smoke.

Ambrose laughed. "Sorry," she said. Ambrose just found it slightly comical that someone was referring to that massive beast as *sensitive*.

"You really want to help elves?" Avaram asked.

"Yes," Ambrose replied.

"Why? You didn't know of our situation until now."

"I want to change a lot of things about our country," Ambrose began. "We are too blinded by 'God.' Faith helps those in hard times. It gives the people a purpose. The Church provides support to our orphans and elderly, and the priests even fend off bandits and monsters. However, there is a darkness to it too. The Church can put those in power who abuse it. When the weak look to them for support, the corrupt abuse them, and they feel like they deserve it. The Church also fills us humans with such pride that it justifies atrocities we do to others—even to other humans."

She added, "I used to believe in the Church too. So I know first-hand the temptation of it. No more. I won't let others use faith to justify wicked deeds. I'm going to make things right because they are the right things to do, not because some old book says they are."

"Wow, that's some serious shit," Avaram said as she coughed on some smoke.

Ambrose felt like she was being dismissed a bit.

"So, why travel with priests and Sylvania's holy soldiers?" Avaram asked.

Ambrose looked down, thinking about all that had happened. "Things just kind of worked out like that," she said, trying to fake happiness.

Avaram didn't seem to buy it.

"You know, I think I do need some," Ambrose said.

Avaram handed her the pipe. Ambrose held the pipe in her mouth as Avaram touched her fingers to the pipe and it lit. Ambrose took a long deep inhale and let out a huge stream of smoke. She sat down, leaning against the wooden railing. She began to feel the tension she held in all parts of her body begin to sink away.

Avaram sat next to her, cuing up the next hit. "Katya wants us all to meet out in the training fields tomorrow," she said. "She wants our units to go over joint training exercises."

"That's tomorrow's problem," Ambrose replied.

"Maybe we can be friends after all," Avaram said.

The two smoked late into that night, Ambrose taking a much needed break from her troubles.

VINCENT HAGLAZ

It was the morning before they were to depart for the open sea. The trio had found an inn to stay at. When Vincent awoke this morning, he found Trevor sharpening knives on a whetstone and working on the mechanisms in his armour. Vincent thought that Trevor should work on taking a bath. His smell might ruin his angle as a stealthy assassin.

Trinity was also hard at work at a small desk. *On what?* Vincent wondered. He walked over to her. She had a variety of vials and flasks and was brewing some concoctions.

"What are you up to?" Vincent asked.

"I don't like the judgement in your tone," she replied.

Well, someone is picking up Trevor's attitude. "I apologize. What are you working on?"

"Potions," she said.

"What kind of potions?"

"Ones that will keep us from getting sick at sea," she explained. "Also, the two of you are still nursing wounds from trying to kill each other. These should speed up that healing process. Also, potions that can entrap magic."

"Entrap magic?" Vincent asked.

"Yes. For example ..." She pulled over a small pot of clear liquid. "Cast your fire into this," she said.

"It's not going to explode, right?" he asked.

"Just trust me," she said, rolling her eyes.

Vincent didn't ignore the fact that she didn't say it wouldn't explode. Still, he went along with it. He tried to cast fire. Nothing happened.

"C'mon," she said.

"I'm trying," he said. Strange; his magic had never behaved like this before.

"Technical difficulties?" Trevor laughed.

"Not helping," Trinity said in a quite annoyed tone. Trevor threw his hands up in surrender.

Vincent touched his holy symbol, and finally the fire began to flow from his hand into the pot of water. The colour of the water changed to bright orange. Trinity took a small vial and scooped up some of the liquid.

"And there you go: instant firebomb," she said.

"Where did you learn to do this?" Vincent asked.

"I learned this at the church. Some of the other nuns made potions— mostly medicines for the sick. However, sometimes the priests needed a little ... oomph, you know," she said.

"You know, with the technical difficulties," Trevor chimed in again.

"These potions can either be medicine or poison, and trust me, poison is easier to make," Trinity said.

"Speaking of, how are those potions coming along?" Trevor asked, also walking over to the table. His armour was off, so his chest was exposed. Vincent saw the prominent mark of the witch he had stolen power from. Not only that, Trevor's body was covered in old wounds and scars—not to mention the newest one in his left shoulder. He still had that one wrapped up in bandages.

Vincent wondered what he would be doing had he been able to kill Trevor. Definitely not out hiring pirates to smuggle him. Still, with Trevor here on his side, not many would be able to get the better of them.

Trinity handed Trevor a small flask, and Trevor swallowed it down. "Not much for taste," he said.

"You're welcome," she replied. "Here, Vincent, have some too."

Vincent went to take it. He hesitated, but finally drank. The instinct in him was telling him not to trust the witch. However, she had given him no reason to distrust her. She looked a little hurt that he had hesitated like that.

"Where did you get this stuff, anyway?" Vincent asked.

"Trevor and I went to town this morning. They have a surprising amount of ingredients and materials. Guess it is a trading town of sorts," she said.

"Yeah, most likely stolen. Can we afford this?" Vincent asked.

"Yeah, we did decent selling the damn horses. Not to mention, I had a little on myself. Would have had more too if you were dead," Trevor quipped.

Vincent glared at him. Trevor rolled his eyes and went back to his own project.

"Well, I'm going to get some fresh air," Vincent said.

He left the inn and wandered around town for a bit. He was looking for a church but was hard-pressed to find one. It made Vincent upset to find no church in such a large town.

He finally did end up finding one towards the edge of town. It looked run-down. When he entered, he found that it was totally abandoned—and looked like it had been so for a while. He sighed. What had he done to end up here?

Vincent walked up to the altar and knelt down. He began his morning prayers. However, he felt no connection—like he had been cut off somehow. Was this why his magic wasn't working earlier?

Vincent heard someone entering the church. He stood up, hands on his swords.

"Easy," came the voice. It was Captain Moulder, and he had someone else with him: a boy of maybe 17 or 20, who was shorter, wore black robes, and had long black hair. His were the garments of an Avalon alchemist.

"We aren't going to hurt you. Just curious is all," Moulder finished.

Vincent took his hands off his swords. "Who are you?" Vincent asked.

"Right. Guess I should introduce myself. I'm Captain Moulder, leader of the crew escorting you to Avalon."

"What are you curious about, captain?" Vincent asked.

"Well, about you, for one," Moulder said. "Why is a priest running away to Avalon with a nun and a notorious murderer? It almost sounds like the opening of a bad joke. I'm just waiting to hear the punchline."

"I have business in Avalon," Vincent said.

"So why take my route?" Moulder asked. "There is a peace. The border is open."

"Were I alone, I could do so."

"Alone?" Moulder asked. "I'm well aware of why Trevor would have trouble getting through the border. What about the nun? She wanted too?" Moulder asked.

Vincent kept quiet. Moulder was smart. He was picking up on the vernacular quickly.

"I see. She also didn't answer that question. Which means I'm on to something there. Let's move on. You all seem to move about freely, which means that Trevor isn't turning either of you for a bounty. So, Father, why travel with such a man? Don't tell me he is just a bodyguard," Moulder cautioned.

"We all have business in Avalon. We all have something to gain, so it is convenient to travel together. Also, yes, having Trevor along does provide a little extra security," Vincent said.

"Those wounds—are they knife wounds?" Moulder asked.

Vincent kept quiet.

"Interesting," Moulder said. "The last thing I will ask you is this: Is there anyone hunting you?"

"No," Vincent said.

Moulder seemed unsure of that answer. "Very well then. We should be heading back."

"Who is he?" Vincent asked, motioning to the younger man.

"Oh, sorry about that. This is Soren," Moulder said. "He is my assistant. Someday, he will run the ships."

Soren simply bowed his head, and the two of them walked away. Vincent was now a little more concerned about who he would be sailing with. The captain seemed quite cautious, but perhaps a little too perceptive. Vincent didn't like the man poking around his business.

Vincent decided to head back to the inn where the others were. He started to think that maybe Trevor and Trinity would be the ones he could trust the most on that boat. When Vincent returned to the inn, he told the other two about his encounter with Captain Moulder.

"Nothing to get spooked about, Vincent," Trevor assured him. "Moulder just likes to make sure no one is bringing too much heat on the crew. He'd still transport us even if we did. He might charge us more for that, though. In all honesty, he is doing it to protect his crew."

AMBROSE GAINS

Ambrose woke the next morning still sitting against the railing where she had fallen asleep. Avaram was gone now. Instead, kneeling in front of her was Lexel.

"Long night, commander?" he asked.

"Something like that." She wiped both her eyes.

Lexel looked at her in amazement.

"What?" she asked.

"You're using both arms," he pointed out.

Ambrose looked at her right arm. It was now working. She opened and closed her fingers several times. "Still doesn't feel like my arm," she said.

"Everyone's heading to the training fields for these joint exercises. You good?" Lexel asked.

"Yes, I'm ready to go." Ambrose stood and put her hair up. Lexel couldn't help but smile.

"What is it now?" she asked.

"You finally look as confident as you were the day you whooped my ass," he said.

They shared a genuine smile.

＊＊＊＊＊＊＊

Everyone headed to the training grounds. The fields were not flat and open. While there were open patches of grass, there were also hills and large trees mixed in.

"Welcome to the training fields," Katya said. Behind her was a proper battalion of elves, armed head to toe in armour that looked to be made out of the wood of the trees of the Blackwood. Also, there were elves who seemed to be in robes and gowns decorated with jewellery. These appeared to be more of the magic types. Both elves and humans seemed a little anxious about working together.

"The grounds here can be altered via magic to change the landscape. For example, we are standing on a grassy field, but ..." She motioned to an elf looking on from above. He waved his hands, and the ground turned into a rocky landscape.

"This might make for a better representation of the conditions we will see at Mount Bors," Katya said. "Now, just like your army, some of us elves have become quite attuned to magic, while others have better physical prowess. Then, even within those divisions, there are many types of magical affinities. Some become accustomed to long-range magical attacks, some focus on healing, and some have magic that amplifies their abilities or grants them new ones.

"The reason I bring up these basic facts," she went on, "is because from what I understand of our situation, we are quite unaware of who our enemies are or what they are capable of. So we will be running through many different scenarios and types of battle. Our fighters of both magical and physical standing will practice one-on-one sparring and also battalion-versus-battalion combat. Our long-range magic users will practice launching attacks and also trying to counter other long-range users.

"Finally, the leaders and captains will collaborate on coming up with clear concise orders and battle strategies. A formal chain of command will be implemented so we can be one organized and unified force. Does this sound agreeable, Commander Gains?" Katya asked.

"Couldn't have said it better myself," Ambrose replied. The two shook hands.

Ambrose, Lexel, and Father Tal gathered as the human leaders. Avaram and Katya were the leaders of the elves. Ambrose appointed a captain for her fighters and for the priests. The same was done for the elves. These captains would be leading the drills. The leaders went over in their own area. They were going to come up with battle strategies to best utilize their armies.

"I know you said before that we were unsure of our enemies, but do you have any idea of what we're up against?" Katya asked Ambrose.

"Not really," Ambrose admitted. "The only interaction we have had is that they sent a couple of assassins."

"Assassins? What kind of assassins?" Katya asked.

"They actually were old acquaintances. Somehow our enemy knows of myself and my old comrades. This meant these assassins were not just simple cut-throats. They had magical powers beyond what normal mages use. One of them even had a demon sealed inside in case he failed."

"A demon, my word," said Katya. "The fact that they used old acquaintances against you, and that these individuals were powerful, indicates that our enemy has intel on you—and has money. Anything else?"

"We were able to defeat one of the assassins after he turned into a demon. Once defeated, he told us that they had been hired by some woman. I have no idea who that might be, though. It really doesn't narrow down the list of suspects," Ambrose admitted.

"Only one of the assassins?" Avaram quickly asked.

"Yes. Unfortunately, one got away. He is still out there, and even though the one who was killed had a demon in him, the other is the real monster."

"Well, this means that we will have to be vigilant if this capable assassin is still out there," Katya said solemnly.

"Oh, who cares. This bitch failed before when he had the element of surprise. Do you think he'll do any better now that we can see him coming?" Avaram said.

"He didn't fail, though," Ambrose said. She could feel the rage and tears boiling to the surface. She was able to keep herself in check, though. "He killed my best friend in this world," Ambrose said.

Avaram looked shocked.

"I'm sorry," Katya said for Avaram.

"Well, now you know you just got to get stronger and kill that rat bastard!" Avaram said.

"All I care about is our goal. I won't let anything distract me," Ambrose said. Lexel put his hand on her shoulder, knowing exactly what she meant.

"Well now, before we get to the battle planning, I want a more in-depth look at what your abilities are. Of course, we shall show you ours once you show us yours," Katya said.

Ambrose brought out Marya in two pieces, making her usual sword and shield. "Who's first?" Ambrose said.

"Me!" Avaram yelled.

"No weapon? You're a mage then?" Ambrose asked.

"Not quite," Avaram replied.

Avaram threw her huge fist toward Ambrose. Ambrose instinctively blocked it with her shield, but a second fist was coming in fast. Ambrose dodged and went for a swing of her sword. Then a huge cloud of smoke appeared where Avaram stood. When Ambrose struck it, the sword passed right through. She was gone!

Ambrose took a defensive stance, waiting for the counter from Avaram.

"Maybe the rest of us should give these two some room," Katya said. This match had started very unceremoniously. Avaram was quite impatient. The others backed up to keep safe. They didn't want to get mixed up in this.

Lexel looked at Ambrose. She was right at home in a sparring match. He was happy to see her in her element. She seemed so alive and vibrant in these situations. He also felt saddened by this—to see a girl who was so comfortable with battle.

A couple of nights ago, they had faced the only time in Lexel's life when he had been truly in danger. He had been in sparring rings and drills from a young age. How many times had she been in fights that could have so easily been her last? She had a lot to prove. That was the sheer drive pushing her forward. Lexel knew she carried a burden within her. What that was exactly, he didn't know.

Ambrose was looking around to see where Avaram would come from. The elf had to be using magic to make herself invisible, but Ambrose didn't hear a sound—no footsteps, no breathing, nothing. Could she have erased her presence completely?

Ambrose turned the shield into a sword. She kept the blades dull; she didn't want to cause any uncurable injuries. She turned around.

From behind her, the smoke started to take form and condense again. When it finished, it materialized Avaram. Avaram went to grab Ambrose in a huge bear hug to throw her. However, Ambrose ducked down out of the grab and swept at Avaram's legs with Marya. When Avaram was on the ground, Ambrose pointed the sword to her. Avaram couldn't hide the annoyance in her face.

"How did you dodge that?" Avaram asked.

"I intentionally gave you an opening too tempting to turn down. Figured you'd turn up if I did that. I simply anticipated you would be behind me. Plus, when you reappeared, I could hear your loud breathing," Ambrose said.

Ambrose extended a hand to help her up. But Avaram simply laid back, content with being down there.

"Wonderful! So you're an artefact manipulator?" Katya asked.

"We call them relics in Sylvania," Ambrose explained.

"Well, it's all the same," Katya said. "Next, I'll spar with you," she said, pointing to Tal.

"No, I think not," Tal said. "I may be blessed with gifts of our Lord, but I'm no combatant. I can only teleport. Hopefully, that gives you a sufficient synopsis of my usefulness."

"Guess that means you'll have to fight me," Lexel said. He was already drawing his sword. He had a fire in his eyes and was eager to prove himself to Ambrose and the elves.

"You've got some spunk," Katya said. "All right, come now, attack when ready."

Ambrose saw Lexel studying Katya. Her flowing robes with wooden bracers and shin guards indicated she was no heavy fighter. No doubt a mage. This left Lexel at the disadvantage of not knowing her methods of combat.

Katya was not backing up. She was only a few paces away from the tip of Lexel's blade, so she must not be a long-range fighter. She seemed wide open for an elf who had lived hundreds of years and was clearly used to battle. The fact that Katya was standing so still was unnerving. Even Ambrose was not sure she would tackle this one.

Wait, that was it: Katya wasn't moving at all. Ambrose could only hope Lexel noticed the same thing. She could call it out, but that would be a dishonour to Katya and also to Lexel. If he won because of that, he wouldn't ever know if that was why.

Finally, Lexel attacked. He had been holding his sword two-handed, his arms up by his head and the blade angled downward as he stood sideways. He pushed off his backfoot and slashed downward. At that moment, the image of Katya shattered like glass that floated past Lexel. Then, from behind, Katya came slicing with a katana.

Lexel felt the attack coming and blocked it with his sword. When the swords clashed, there was a flash of light, and Katya and Lexel got knocked back.

"Since when did you have a sword?" Lexel asked.

"Since when did you have magic?" Katya countered.

"Magic?" Lexel asked. "I was not blessed with any gifts of magic."

"Your sword?" Katya asked.

Lexel and Ambrose looked at the sword. It had a yellow aura about it. He looked at it in amazement.

"This isn't your doing, elf?" Lexel asked.

"No, it is all you," Katya assured him.

His sword's aura continued to grow more vibrant, and the sword vibrated.

"What do I do?!" he yelled.

"Swing it!" Katya said.

He did, aiming the slice upwards, and a burst of energy from the base of the strike to the top released a light that chopped through the canopy. All stared in awe at what had just happened. A boy never known for any magical gifts released a burst so powerful, it cracked the ground and sliced through thick branches—which came crashing down to earth, barely missing the sleeping Avaram.

Ambrose looked to Lexel. He had collapsed on the ground, fully unconscious. Of course, he'd never used magic before, so releasing something this big drained him.

"Well, that was surprising. Guess we'll call this one my win. I can imagine the boy will want a rematch. Still, a little late to start teaching him how to control mana," Katya commented. "Let's get him inside and rested. We will take a lunch, and then we can start making battle preparations."

CHAPTER 15

VINCENT HAGLAZ

VINCENT CAST HIS GAZE OUT towards the sea. He looked out from the docks at the early dawn horizon. He had come here to pray. Lately, he had been feeling lost in his connection to his faith. He felt his magic was failing because of this. Of course, right when he needed to beat his best, his gifts were taken away.

He felt angry but didn't want to feed into that feeling. Doing so would mean that he was angry at God. So instead, he tried to find patience. But all that seemed to come was anxiety.

"You done with your sulk session?" Trevor asked as he carried crates onto the ship. "Just because you're a priest doesn't mean you skimp on manual labour."

"And should you be hauling such heavy burdens with your injuries?" Vincent asked.

"Aww, I didn't know you cared," Trevor mocked. "Move your ass or I'll leave you here."

Vincent looked at his hands, which had been injured in his bout with Trevor. The wounds were closed and just scars remained. Whatever concoction Trinity had given him seemed to work. This meant Trevor would be back up to fighting form too.

With Trinity's potions and Trevor's battle skill, Vincent wondered if he would be a liability with his fire seeming to be failing. He still had his blades, and he was plenty useful with those, but nowhere near as potent without his magic.

They boarded one of the five ships in this crew—one of the smaller vessels. On the off chance that they were stopped, the captain's flagship would be the most thoroughly investigated.

They were kept in the cargo hold. Notably, on this ship was Titania, who acted as captain of this boat. Still, Moulder was captain of the fleet. Vincent felt like she was there to keep them in check just as much as she was there to guard them.

·✦✦✦·

The ships took off and began heading west. They needed to swing a long wide route to avoid the usual checkpoints along the coasts.

Vincent again felt his anxiety build. He had never felt like this before. He'd always had his faith to keep him grounded. Now that he was losing his grip on it, he didn't feel confident in anything he was doing.

Was he no longer doing this mission for God? Was he no longer doing this mission for his country? Was he just doing this for himself? The fact that he could no longer answer these questions upset him greatly.

Trevor and Trinity couldn't be any more different from him. Trevor, like always, was going about sharpening his blades, filling one with poison, and adjusting the mechanisms in his armour. Trinity, who had started to come out of her shell, was working on more potions. She had a smile on her face. When Vincent had first met her, she'd seemed so timid. No longer. She even would talk back to Trevor.

Why did she feel so safe around him? Vincent knew the man better than most, and he knew to be on guard around Trevor. Where had she come from that this was a better life? She had no stake in this. The zealot in Vincent felt as if there was some hidden plot being brewed by this witch.

Trevor began to sense Vincent's anxieties. "You should try to relax. We will be at sea for a couple weeks."

"You could do well with a little more concern," Vincent said.

A week passed. They spent most of their time in the cargo hold. While Trevor and Trinity would speak to one another. Vincent would sit alone. Many times, he would try to pray, but he just felt so lost.

Crew members would bring them down meals, and they would occasionally go on deck to stretch their legs once the scouts saw no ships approaching. The intense light in the open sea gave Vincent a headache, so he preferred to stretch his legs at night.

One night, Trevor had chosen to go up top to get some fresh air. Vincent was keeping to himself. Trinity was peeling some of the apples that had been brought down for them.

Then Titania strolled in. She did not come down very often, just to make sure everything was going all right. This time, however, she actually sat down next to Trinity. Trinity felt uncomfortable next to this huge brute, but she continued to peel her apples. And Titania continued to stare her down.

Trinity offered up an apple to Titania in the hope that this might ease some of the tension. It didn't. Titania just shoved it in her mouth and crushed it with her huge jaws.

Trinity's eyes went wide, and she tried to keep her face from going red. She felt beads of sweat forming on her forehead.

"So come on, are you and Trevor an item or what?" Titania asked.

"N–no," Trinity said. She was talking in her old timid way.

"So, you're available," Titania said very directly.

"Available?" Trinity asked.

"You know, sexually," Titania clarified.

Trinity's face went bright red. Vincent was curled up in the corner trying his best to pretend he was not here and could not hear any of this.

"I … uh … believe that I belong to Trevor," Trinity said.

"Belong to? You said that you weren't—" Titania began.

"He is my master for the time being," Trinity said.

"Master? How does Trevor own a nun? What is he holding over you?" Titania asked.

"Nothing. I owe him my life. He does not keep me hostage but does require I am useful to him while we travel," said Trinity, still terrified of Titania.

Titania now looked a bit calmer and more serious. "He's always so practical. Won't let anyone look down on him. He respects strength. He wants to be the strongest, the best. He's willing to cut down anyone for that dream. What he wants to do with all that power is a mystery to me. He doesn't want for anything but to get stronger; he doesn't want to protect anybody. Hell, he doesn't even seem that concerned with staying alive, for that matter.

"But there is something else to him," she continued. "He doesn't show it or talk about it. He has another side to him, but he won't let that out in fear it dulls his edge. So he takes on this persona of a beast. He can be quite a bastard too. Also, he makes for quite the terrifying foe in battle. That's why when he ran with our crew, I called him *Rat*. The vermin creep me out. There are few men that terrify me, especially skinny ones like him, but he for one reminds me of a rat running around in the shadows to find its next meal."

"If all he respects is strength, then he must not think much of me," Trinity said.

Titania laughed. "That's not true at all. If Trevor thought you were useless, he wouldn't bring you along. Plus, remember what I said: there is some other side of him. I have barely seen it. But when you two stumbled into that bar, it was there. He was protective of you. You mean something to him."

Trinity smiled. "I've seen it too," she said.

The two laughed. Titania pulled over a crate and pried it open. Inside were bottles of wine. "Aw, piss, I thought it was rum," she said.

Still, the two began drinking down the bottles. Titania did so in a very crude and rapid fashion. The two continued to laugh and drink.

Vincent, still pretending to be asleep, was taking in what they had said about Trevor. There where others who saw him as more than just a murdering psychopath. Even though these two were criminals of the state and heathens, they seemed to have good spirits. As much as he felt he should loathe them, he didn't. They were his allies and perhaps even friends.

He took a look at the holy symbol around his neck. What did it mean to him?

TREVOR BLACKWELL

Trevor was peering off the bow of the boat. The wind had been whipping hard all day but was now much tamer. The cold air didn't bother Trevor at all.

It had been days since the crew had seen another ship. This meant that in the morning, they would start going south towards Avalon. Trevor thought about what he could do with whatever power the Well contained. He didn't mind letting Vincent save the day and become whatever. He just wanted a taste of this hidden power.

"Oi!" a voice from behind him called. It was one of the crew members—one of the scouts. Trevor just looked at him.

"I've got some ale, if you're keen on sharing a drink?" the scout said.

"Don't you have a job to be doing? Looking out for other ships?" Trevor asked.

"Oh, come on. We haven't seen ships in days. Captain is just being a little extra cautious. Trust me, there ain't nothin' out here," he said.

"No?" Trevor asked sarcastically. For in the distance behind them, he saw a light.

"Shit, you better go below. I'll signal Moulder a ship is coming," the scout said. He was beginning to leave when Trevor put his hand out to stop him. They looked in front of them. There in the distance was another light from the lamps on the ship.

"Signal that we are about to be attacked," Trevor said.

The scout looked terrified and ran to raise a flag that would signal the other boats in the fleet.

Trevor ran down to the cargo hold where the others were. "Get ready. We have friends coming," Trevor said.

"What are you talking about?" Titania asked.

"We got two ships trying to cut us off from in front and behind. They are going to attack," Trevor said.

Vincent was now standing. "How can you know that?" he asked.

"Not my first ambush," he explained. "I've done many myself."

The bell from the flagship started tolling. Three tolls. "The navy!" Titania exclaimed.

"We're in Avalon's waters. Why is the Avalon Navy coming for us way out here?" Vincent asked.

"Either they want to haul in some pirates, or they want us. With our luck, what do you reckon?" Trevor asked.

"Stay down here!" Titania ordered.

"No ma'am. I don't intend to sink to the ocean's depth with such poor company," Trevor replied. "Besides, looking at the crew you got up there? You'll need some competent fighters."

"Fine. Don't blame me if you get killed, though," Titania shot back.

Trevor ran up to the deck. The first bits of daylight were peering over the horizon. Trinity began to race up towards him, but Titania stopped her.

"Let me go. I can help!" Trinity said.

"I know. However, I feel like by the end of this, we will need the old Trevor. We need the Rat. I don't want him distracted with worrying about your safety," Titania said, more serious than usual.

Trinity backed down begrudgingly. She hated the idea of being a hindrance to them.

Titania put her hand on Trinity's shoulder. "You bring out the best in him. I need him at his worst," she said, smiling.

Trinity wasn't sure this comforted her at all. She hated what Trevor becomes. She didn't mind that he killed; he had to. But seeing him kill gratuitously, with pure malice, was a sight she was happy not to see.

Vincent also made his way topside, blowing right passed Titania while she was talking to Trinity. He no longer wanted to sit down here and sulk. He needed to be of use to someone, at the very least himself.

Titania rushed to the deck and began barking orders for the other sailors to get to their positions. She was looking around for Trevor, but she didn't see him—until she looked up to see him standing on one of the sails.

Trevor felt wind on his skin. The cold morning air only stimulated him. He began to feel that rush that came during an intense fight. He could smell it. He could smell the blood of those coming to kill them. He wouldn't be a helpless doe. No—he was just as Titania described, a cornered rat. Small, seemingly insignificant in size compared to the wolves that hunted it. But his fangs were sharp, and his lust for the kill compensated.

The ships began to close in: two large frigates, one from the west and one from the east, along with several smaller clippers. The clippers began their charge on the fleet. The frigates were staying back, carefully waiting for their time to strike.

Moulder's fleet assumed battle positions. The ships had mounted catapults on board. The flagship even had a couple of ballistas primed. The sailors manned their positions and started loading catapult balls. They waited for the clippers to be in range, then they fired off their volley. Only two of the five met their mark, but this meant that two of the clippers were sinking. There were six more.

Trevor's lust for blood was festering within him. He knew he was useless in this kind of long-range naval battle, so he waited—waited for those frigates to start closing in. There could be over a hundred Avalon soldiers on those ships. He couldn't wait.

More of the clippers started going down. There were now four left. Catapult balls were starting to run low. There had been no plan for a battle on this route, and they were really only prepared to scare off other pirate crews trying to rob them.

They began loading random items from the cargo hold in the catapults. These were mostly crates, bottles, and random weapons. They began firing, hoping the debris would shred the ships' sails. There seemed to be injuries on board their ships as well.

Another two were effectively disabled. Morale was high among Moulder's fleet. They, for the moment, had been quite successful in dealing with the enemy. Then a huge catapult ball came and crushed one of the fleet's ships, and it start sinking. This was a shock. The frigates had slowly been closing their distance, coming into range.

Vincent looked to Titania. "We should try to rescue those men who are sinking to their doom! Hurry!" he said.

Titania backhanded him, knocking him on his ass. "You don't call the shots, priest. Those men are goners. We will be too if we don't keep fighting. So go be useless somewhere else," she barked.

"Get me closer!" Trevor yelled down to Titania.

Titania growled, "Unbelievable. They come onto my ship and think they can bark orders." She was mainly speaking to herself but didn't care who heard her.

Vincent stood and ran over to the catapult crew. They were loading their next volley of random debris. He approached them and said, "Let me help."

They looked at him, bewildered to see a priest trying to help them. Finally, one barked, "Grab something then!"

"I got a better idea," Vincent said.

He began trying to cast his fire. Again, no good. The crew just looked at him and went back to loading. They fired off a shot. No good; miss.

The flagship, which still had proper ammunition, sunk another clipper. There was one left. The crew of Titania's ship began to load the next shot.

Vincent held out his holy symbol and, with great effort, was able to produce a small burst of flame, setting the heap on the catapult ablaze. The crew looked quite pleased and fired off the shot. This hit the last ship. The fire caught on this last clipper, but it still moved. The vessel was going to sink, but for the time being, it still was charging into Moulder's fleet.

"Hard to starboard," Titania yelled.

The ship creaked as the crew desperately turned it about. The sailors on the engulfed clipper were jumping into the ocean. The clipper blew right past Titania's ship, and the crew let out huge cheers. That was, until they saw it smack into one of their own ships.

This silenced the crew. They saved themselves, but this meant that some of their friends would die. Vincent especially watched as his flames burned the very men charged to protect him. His enemies were the Avalon soldiers. These were good men, even though his enemies in this case. His allies were pirates he should be working to capture. He felt like he was fighting on the wrong side in this battle. This meant he didn't like to see any side take losses.

So he finally did as Titania said and went below deck. He couldn't watch this anymore—or at least he would no longer take part in this. He would pray for the scores of men he had doomed to a tortured death, even the pirates. None of these men deserved to die this day. His actions had led to this. His choices had resulted in the events that had and would transpire this day. Every one of the hundreds who would die this morning were on his conscience.

If he had been questioning his faith before, now he was sure that he had severed his last connection. There was a part of him who hoped he would be killed so he could suffer the punishment he deserved for this.

Trevor, on the other hand, was nearly vibrating from sheer anticipation as he watched them close in on the western frigate. The crew continued to load more random cargo. However, supplies were running low. Soon the only thing that would be left for them to hurl would be their food supplies which they would need to get back to shore. That Is, if they were going to make it out of this.

The next catapult shot from the frigate landed far too close to Titania's ship. The ship was rocked by the wake it made.

"Fire back!" Titania yelled. The ship fired off its own shot, which seemed to be on target. Then it was shot down by a bolt of lightning.

"Damn mages," Titania growled to herself. "Trevor, are you—," she began to ask, only to see that Trevor had already leapt from the sail and was manoeuvring and leaping on the floating bits of debris and crippled ships. Finally, he gained enough speed to jump through one of the portholes. He looked up to see soldiers stunned to see a man leap through the opening. They were backing up but trying to form a line.

"Hello, prey," Trevor grinned.

The soldiers charged halberds first, hoping that having him surrounded and outnumbered meant victory or anything at all. It was all futile. Like moving in slow motion, they closed in on him.

This is where Trevor was most himself, where he had been born. This was how he had been baptized, in blood and anguish. The thrashing of enemies before they left this world. Their screams and the clang of metal made his symphony. The base of a heart beating, beating, beating, beating, building to a climax before fading.

This is why he had to be alone. No one was safe from the performance he would put on, because after living in a colourless world there was finally a colour, one colour, the most vibrant and vivacious colour …

RED

As their halberds came thrusting in, it seemed as if Trevor would not move, defiant to acknowledge them. Not until the moment before impact did he slip under them in one motion, simultaneously liberating their tips. The first soldier, finding a knife lodged in his throat, could not utter a cry but could only choke. The next had his jugular hacked. Two more had daggers so carefully aimed between their eyes, and the last one found the severed metal of a broken halberd shoved in the weak point of his armour. The bodies of the soldiers fell at about the same time as the tips of the severed halberds. *RED.*

Trevor moved to the next hallway, lined with more prey. Twelve more men. The first two did not knowing anything was amiss until their heads were removed. The rest fumbled helplessly for their weapons. Systematically were their aortas punctured and their throats slashed.

Two tried to run from the whirling dervish massacring them. As all experienced trailsmen will tell you, in the face of a predator, never run. It only makes the hunt more thrilling. Their bodies would not be so clean. Their entrails were so mangled one would not be able to distinguish where one left off and the other began. *RED.*

The victims in the next room were not even soldiers—cooks, servants, ship hands. Coming on a ship bound for battle and not having a weapon? Foolish. Blood and sinew would be tonight's broth, and the deckhands would not be able to wash their own blood out of the deck. *RED.*

Room by room, hallway by hallway, level by level, more kept coming. More prey. But the hunt wasn't over. No beast would be content hunting such measly morsels. No, there were true quarries to be found. The nest just needed a little more shaking. More screams. More *RED*.

Finally, he reached the top deck. The scene was already a battlefield, with archers firing off the sides of the decks and arrows being returned. A mage was firing his bolts of lightning.

In a herd, it is best to make yourself anonymous, like the rest. Be one more face in the crowd, a zebra that blends with the rest. Those who stick out are the ones who get battered down and hunted first. Now, without the confines of an enclosed space, the hunt could get more intense. From rail to rail, on each side of the boat, Trevor sliced and separated souls from their bodies.

The mage began to catch on. He started casting bolts of lightning in every direction, trying to catch the demon slicing up the crew. But the bolts only hit after-images. The demon got closer, closer, closer. No predicting if the beast would zig or zag.

So, in a desperate attempt, the mage cast a wave of lightning that spread across the entirety of the deck, causing onboard fires and killing scores of men. The mage sighed out, horrified by what he had done.

From above, like a hawk, Trevor came, lobotomizing the mage. Then he spun around to see a man on an upper deck, his uniform more ornate then the rest. *A captain. The quarry.*

The man simply spun and walked inside a cabin on the upper deck. Not in fear, not in a hurry. The confidence really stood out to Trevor, making him thirst for this kill all the more. Trevor had to sink his fangs into such a beast. *RED.*

He burst into this upper cabin, chomping at the bit and salivating. Inside stood the captain. His dark purple uniform signified his importance. No weapons. A mage? Mattered little. Trevor threw five small daggers. They all missed their mark. That was fine; they were merely distractions to make an opening.

Trevor leapt and spun sideways with the scimitars, but again, the attack missed. The captain just sidestepped.

Trevor bounced off the backwall, launching at the captain. The man seemed to move in slow motion. Still, none of Trevor's attacks landed. His scimitars got lodged into the back wall.

"Oh, Trevor, that won't work," the man said.

Trevor couldn't hear him. The bloodlust drowned out everything. He dislodged the scimitars and kept slicing away. It didn't matter. None of his attacks landed.

"You think this state makes you strong? No, Trevor. I know you. You are far more lethal when you are coherent. This lust for blood dulls your edge," the man said.

Again and again, Trevor threw knives and dived about the room. The walls and floor were being torn up. Finally, Trevor was struck in the face by a metal object: a pocket watch, a *very heavy* pocket watch. The man standing in front of Trevor was the one swinging the pocket watch. He was swinging it side to side like an old grandfather clock.

"C'mon, Trevor, listen. I know you're in there."

Trevor's nose was bleeding and broken. He came again this time, sliding low. Again, like the man knew what would happen, he was kicked in the head. This time, the kick seemed to start sobering him up. He shook his head slowly.

"Oh, coming to?" the man asked. "That's good."

It wasn't till then that Trevor began to recognize that voice.

"Zachariah?!" Trevor exclaimed.

"Look who is finally awake," Zachariah replied. He swung his pocket watch again; it barely missed Trevor and smashed the floorboards. Trevor had narrowly dodged it.

"So, after you left Uppsala, you got a cushy officer job?" Trevor asked

"My brother and I both did. We are both Avalon natives. We were just petty officers when we got the call. Thought it would be a good résumé builder. Turns out it was," Zachariah said. "Even though we were removed from the program, we still learned the skills we needed to climb the ladder in the military. That was easy. What we didn't realize is that we weren't out of the competition."

"What are you talking about?" Trevor asked.

"Oh, come now, Trevor. You must know."

Trevor kept quiet, and the two were in a staredown full of tension. Trevor knew exactly what Zachariah was talking about. He just didn't like the idea that the others were starting to catch on. Zachariah was one person Trevor did not want to still contest with. He and his brother,

Klein, were about the smartest tactical minds in the program—the Uppsalans, as the final ten had started to call themselves.

The brothers' talents in magic were related and polar opposites. Zachariah's magic altered his own perception of time. Each second could feel like a minute, each minute an hour. This made it seem like he had superior reflexes. Some even thought his power was speed, like Trevor's. But he had no such gift. It was a simple trick of altering his perception. This gave him the clarity to make decisions not only in a fight but in giving orders to troops. With his perception of the world so slow, he had time, lots of time, to think. He could turn this on at will.

His brother, on the other hand, affected others. His power gave his enemies an accelerated perception of time. Those targeted by his magic would feel as if time was moving twice as fast. Their reflexes would not be as fast, and this usually ended up fatal for them. The only downside was that this drained mana quickly, and it only affected one person.

"We were there when you were kicked out of this little race," Zachariah said. "You tried to attack Hamilton. Didn't go well. By the looks of those scimitars, thought, seems like you finally got your man. So why are you here?"

"Initially, a job to hunt Vincent," Trevor said.

"Uh huh. Yeah, my brother and I received orders from a mysterious source. Someone up top. Told us that there was a small group of individuals being smuggled into Avalon. They are dangerous and most certainly armed. When I saw your names on that ledger, it got me thinking. Who is trying to get the old Uppsalans killed? Clearly, this is another test. Only this time, we are the obstacle. They want to be rid of loose ends, Trevor, since in the end there can only be one winner."

He continued, "The game is most certainly still on. It just made me ask, who of the ten are left? We were told at least about you and Vincent. We heard about how John killed Morgana. Gregor died while we were at Uppsala. John, Piers, and Lilith are still a mystery," Zachariah listed off, trying to see if he could read any reaction from Trevor. "My brother and I get sent to take out two other Uppsalans, and now I hear you had been sent before us. You must see this as the final test. Vincent has been their 'final candidate,' hasn't he?"

Trevor tried not to react.

"Thought so. So come on, let's get this game back on," Zachariah said. "They will need a new final candidate once Vincent is out of the picture. You want to seek the strongest and fight the strongest. Well, Uppsala thinks Vincent is the strongest. There's your target!"

Trevor's gaze didn't shift. No ease in his tense persona.

"Oh, Trevor, you see, this calm and clear version of you, that's the version that truly inspires fear. Not the wild animal."

"I'll kill you!" Trevor screamed.

"I see. Too bad," Zachariah said.

Trevor launched himself at Zachariah, coming down with a slash of the scimitar. The attack barely missing. Zachariah grabbed his arm, only Trevor had now pulled the string releasing the hooked blades. These cutting into Zachariah making him release quickly.

Trevor swiped his left arm in a backhand, the blades catching Zachariah. When Trevor went to sweep his leg, Zachariah jumped. The pocket watch swung at Trevor's face, barely missing. However, this was a ruse. The chain of the pocket watch wrapped around Trevor's arm. This way, Zachariah could catch the rat without getting bit.

Trevor tried to stand up and catch him with a hidden wrist blade. But of course, Zachariah saw it coming. He was pulling on Trevor's arm, which spun him around. With his back now to Zachariah and one arm in a chain, the other held by Zachariah, the trap was fully sprung.

"So falls one of the mighty Uppsalans. You were a fearsome candidate. Yet your rage and impatience were your fatal flaws," Zachariah preached.

Trevor shot Zachariah one last deathly gaze. The crunch of bones was audible.

VINCENT HAGLAZ

"Damn mages," Titania growled to herself. "Trevor, are you—"

Vincent could hear Titania yelling from above deck. He collapsed in the cargo hold. He no longer wanted to keep going. He was ready to accept any fate that came now.

He opened his eyes to see Trinity standing in front of him. She had lost the nun costume and was in her black dress, with a pack and belts full of potions.

"Are you hurt?" Trinity asked.

"My soul has been torn," Vincent said. "There is no point in this fight anymore."

"What are you talking about? We can still win," Trinity said.

"It doesn't matter even if we do. Who would be winning? Some pirates and criminals, not to mention a witch? Despite the victory today, I doubt that this will be a victory for God."

"Then win this fight for yourself!" Trinity said.

"If I do, I'm no better than the rest of you," Vincent said, sitting up in anger. He had been tiptoeing around this before but didn't care anymore. "I've been able to keep going with this heresy for this long because I told myself that it needed to be done for God. God would forgive me so long as my cause was holy. But is it? Can I say that anymore?"

Trinity kept silent. Her face gave away that she could not answer.

"Good men have died for my cause!" declared Vincent. "Friends have died for my cause! Good men are currently burning and dying because of what I've done! I've shouldered those burdens and kept true to this path this long because I had God with me. What do I do now, huh? Tell me, witch! What's the right thing? Tell me how you justify such wanton bloodshed with no purpose?" he yelled, now on his feet.

"You think God makes you good?" Trinity asked.

"Watch your tongue, witch!" Vincent snapped.

"Your character makes you good," said Trinity. "I can see that."

Vincent was confused by what seemed like a compliment.

"I've lived my whole life around 'holy' men, some good, some bad," she continued. "They lived under the same tenets as you, but that didn't stop them from being murderers, rapists, and greedy mongers. You, on the other hand, have tried at every turn to be a good man. You want to see the ideal world come to pass. You have tried to protect what you believe in. You have a good moral compass. Sometimes, you let your faith blind that."

She concluded, "I know you hate me and think me an enemy. However, I don't see you as one. I've seen you on your worst day, and it doesn't make me happy; it makes me sad. So, can I really call you an enemy? Ask yourself. If you watched all of us die, would that make you happy?"

Vincent's anger quelled.

"Now, I don't know about you but I'm going to go save my friends. Because they aren't perfect, but they're the best I've had," Trinity said as she began to leave.

"Wait!" Vincent said.

Trinity stopped.

"I'll come too," Vincent said. He had found some reason to keep going.

Trinity smiled. The two made it to the top deck, which was being bombarded by a hail of arrows and lightning bolts. Then the bolts of lightning abruptly came to a stop, and the deck of the enemy's frigate was set alight by a wave of lightning.

"Rat's done it!" Titania yelled. "Helmsman! We are boarding them. Ram those ripe cunts!" she roared in delight.

The boat began a beeline for the starboard side of the frigate. "Brace for impact, ladies!" Titania yelled.

The boat slammed into the frigate, rocking the entire boat. Vincent, stumbling over, was making his way to the front of the boat. Those of the crew who hadn't been taken out by the arrows or the lightning began to line up at the bow. They were all ready to go and take this boat by storm. Ready to go for death and glory.

Vincent had caught up to Trinity, who was standing with the rest of the crew. She seemed eager to board this ship, but perhaps for different reasons than the others.

"Hey wit ..., um, Trinity?" Vincent piped up.

She spun to look at him.

"You may not want to see what's up there. Trevor, he ... well, he has a tendency to get a little unhinged."

Trinity looked down in sorrow. Then she looked back at Vincent. "It doesn't matter. He is still the one who saved me from my terrible fate. I'll follow him anywhere."

"You may come to regret that," Vincent said. "I know I did." His words were no longer meant as lectures but merely as a friendly warning. He had been hurt and did not wish to see her get hurt in the same way.

Trinity didn't care that Vincent disliked her. She had been accustomed to being looked down on for being a witch. She had suffered much worse before. Besides, she truly did see the good that was in Vincent.

The charge began. The crew leaped onto the opposing ship, swords and axes brandished. The top deck, however, was a graveyard. Bodies were cut to ribbons by blades and charred by lightning. The deck had several small fires burning.

This place was not the battlefield the crew expected it would be. This was a graveyard. Actually, more like a slaughterhouse, as the bodies were flayed and cut to ribbons. The crew was a little stunned.

Trinity started running to the top deck—to the cabin Trevor had entered just moments earlier. Vincent was confused at first, but as began to hear the sounds of fighting, Vincent thought to chase after her. Then he thought against it. He wanted her to see what Trevor was.

TREVOR BLACKWELL

Trevor felt a large pop in the arm caught by the chain of the stopwatch. His left shoulder had been dislocated. Yet he felt no pain. He just kept snarling at Zachariah, who met him with cold eyes. There was no joy in Zachariah's eyes, no hate, no satisfaction, not even sadness. It was a completely blank stare.

Zachariah threw Trevor to the ground, still keeping hold of his left arm by the chain. He then produced a sword and prepared to give his coup de grace to Trevor, ready to put down the rabid beast.

The fight in Trevor's eyes began to fade. He almost seemed ready to accept this fate. Finally, he would be free from his pain—the pain of losing those he cared about. Free of his obsession with power that led to the death of countless friends.

"You really are just a disappointment, Trevor. It's truly just a sha ..."

As he said that, he turned upon hearing the door to the cabin burst open behind him. Zachariah spun around quickly, activating his power.

Directly in front of his face was a vial full of liquid being launched at him. He tried to sidestep, but it was still too late. The vial was already making impact and caught the left side of his face.

There was an explosion in the cabin—a flash of fire and a forceful blast, blowing out the back part of the cabin. Trevor was thrown to another wall, freeing him of the chain. He staggered and struggled to get to his feet.

Trevor coughed on some smoke. The cabin was engulfed in flames and filling with smoke. He looked to see Trinity lying near the door of the cabin. She must have thrown one of the flasks using Vincent's fire magic. She must have been caught in the blast.

The fire was creeping towards her. He took a step towards her, and then, looking to his left, saw Zachariah hobbling over to the back of the cabin, which had a new opening. He was grasping the left side of his face, which was burnt and bleeding. The two locked eyes. Zachariah then looked at Trinity. He laughed.

"Another ally foolishly trusting you? Throwing her life away for you? So, what do you do in this moment? Save her, or come claim your kill?" Zachariah said before coughing.

Trevor took one step towards Zachariah. Then he saw the image of the flames engulfing Trinity in his mind. For a brief second, he even saw her with the face of his ex-lover.

He closed his eyes and doubled back for Trinity. He grabbed her with his one good arm and tossed her over his right shoulder.

VINCENT HAGLAZ

Trinity disappeared into that cabin, and Vincent instantly heard the explosion and saw the fire. He began to run up to the cabin, but he was stopped by Titania.

"What are you doing?" he asked her.

She responded by pointing her finger. Coming up to the back of the frigate was the other frigate that had engaged them. While the ship they were on was heavily damaged, this other frigate seemed just fine. Its hull only had a couple of dents.

The crew that had charged onto this frigate was backing up, afraid that the other frigate's crew would try to board to take them out. However, it just made a pass, the left side brushing dangerously close—close enough to let someone from the cabin on this frigate leap onto the new frigate as it began to sail off.

Then, emerging from the cabin's door, came Trevor carrying Trinity on his right shoulder. Trinity didn't appear conscious.

Vincent now rushed past Titania up towards the cabin. These flames would soon spread, and he had to do something. He passed by Trevor, who didn't even look at him. His eyes held inner torment—something Vincent had never seen in him before.

Vincent held out his hand, pointing it at the flames. He was attempting to use his gift to extinguish the flame. He knew his powers had been failing him as of late, but he had to try.

Nothing. The fire still raged.

"*Come on,*" he said.

The fire grew larger.

"*Come on!*" Vincent yelled out.

Titania yelled to him, "Vincent, we got to go. That fire is going to get out of hand."

Vincent didn't move. This was something he had to do to prove he wasn't so lost. If he couldn't do this, then he didn't know if he should continue this quest.

"Come on, come on, come on, come on, come on!" he yelled. The fire was drawing closer.

"Please ..." he asked. The heat was becoming too much to stand ... however, it was dissipating. The flames were being extinguished. His gifts were working. The flames were gone. In the face of this smouldering cabin and the blue sky above, he felt something of a connection for the first time in so long.

There was a cheer from the crew below. Vincent spun around and looked out at them. He barely knew them, yet they were cheering for him. Cheering the loudest was Titania. She walked up to him and threw her arm around him.

"I didn't know you were holding out on us. Where were those powers before, huh?" Titania asked.

"Trust me, it's a bit of a surprise to me too," Vincent said with a sigh of relief.

The crew watched the other frigate disappear into the horizon. They must have had enough for one day. However, only two ships from Moulder's fleet were left: Titania's ship and the flagship. The flagship seemed damaged, and Titania's ship was in bad repair. There could not be another battle.

Trinity was finally awake, and Trevor was tending to her, even though he had serious injuries himself. Vincent was starting to believe Trinity could be right about him.

"All right, ladies," Titania yelled, "take anything of value on this ship and let's get the hell out of here. I don't want that frigate coming back with reinforcements!"

The men got to work. It was then that, from the lower cabin, sprung a child with a loaded crossbow.

"Don't move, I'll shoot!" the kid yelled. "I know how to use this thing."

The crew backed up a little, as they knew that a shot from the crossbow could kill. They could easily swarm the child and take him out, but no one wanted to be the first to take the bolt.

The boy spotted Trevor and pointed the crossbow at him. Trevor had his back turned to the kid and was taking care of Trinity.

"You! You killed my mom and dad!" the child screamed, sobbing while trying to sound tough. "They didn't do anything! They were just cooks! You killed them, you bastard!"

Trevor wasn't even acknowledging him.

"Hey now, let's take a moment to relax, all right?" Vincent said. He had his hands up and was slowly making his way down the stairs to the main deck. The boy glanced over but kept his crossbow fixed on Trevor. The boy was no more than 12, red-haired and freckled. Tears were streaming down his face, which was bright as a tomato.

"He killed my mom and dad. He has to die!" the boy yelled.

"I understand. I know where you're coming from. I've lost people too, even my mother," Vincent continued, trying to strike some sort of common ground with with the boy.

"But he killed them! He's evil! They weren't even soldiers. They surrendered. He carved them up like pigs!" the boy cried.

"It's not fair, I know," Vincent said. "Fights usually have a lot of unintended consequences. You could shoot him. He deserves it for sure. But if you do that, then the crew will have to take revenge and kill you. If you just lower the crossbow, though, we won't hurt you. I swear," Vincent said.

The deck was silent. None of the crew made a sound. The boy kept his crossbow raised, but he looked down, clearly wrestling with a dilemma.

"Come on. I know you don't want to die. Don't be a killer like him. Be better," Vincent pleaded.

The boy looked up at Vincent, still with tears in his eyes. Vincent could see the hate fading. Then the boy wrenched back, with a newly placed knife in his forehead. Vincent's heart sank as he watched the boy's knees give out. The boy fell in a heap with the crossbow.

"Looks like I got sloppy and missed one. I am losing my edge," Trevor said.

Titania sighed and shook her head. "All right, get to work, boys. You know your orders."

The crew quickly went below deck, looting all they could find. Vincent had gone to his knees. This one good thing he tried to do, to save an innocent child, right when he thought he was re-finding his connection to God, and look what happened. This world was not meant for pure souls. Vincent could see that.

He heard Trinity cough. She was coming to. She had just missed seeing her hero murder an innocent child who was going to surrender.

"You bastard!" Vincent yelled. It had been years since he had cursed. The faith frowned upon this language. He didn't care. The atrocities he had taken part in today and this entire endeavour would null any chance for salvation. He knew he was damned. "He was just a boy. A child! He was giving up! You know he was! Are you so hungry for blood that you have to kill an innocent!"

"He's no innocent," Trevor countered. "Man, woman, or child, if you're able to raise a weapon to someone, you're ready to die. I was younger than him when I killed. Younger still when I got beat within an inch of my life."

Vincent went over and grabbed Trevor's collar. "No one should ever be like you. No one like you should even exist. You corrupt everyone and everything around you before you kill it or let it die," Vincent whispered to him angrily.

Trevor wasn't even listening. His mind was clearly elsewhere.

"Listen to me, damn it!" Vincent yelled.

"It was Zachariah," Trever muttered.

"What are you on about?" Vincent asked.

"Zachariah," Trevor repeated. "He was in charge of this attack. Just like me, someone mysteriously gave him a mission to kill us. He said that the game was still on."

Vincent shook his head. He let go of Trevor.

"He's right," Trevor said. "This contest *is* still on. Someone who knows all the Uppsalans is pitting the last of us against each other. They tried with John and me. Now it's Zachariah and Klein's turn. Only this time, they have the Avalon military. You're fucked! We're fucked! I had the chance to kill Zachariah. One chance to save us, and now that's gone," Trevor said.

"Why didn't you?" Vincent asked, still bewildered by this information.

Trevor looked to Trinity.

Vincent understood. He now understood the conflict that had been in Trevor's eyes. Still, Vincent couldn't forgive him.

"You'll never be half as good as she thinks you are," Vincent said.

"I know," Trevor whispered, mostly to himself.

CHAPTER 16

AMBROSE GAINS

IT HAD BEEN SEVERAL WEEKS of hard training for all. The troops had been running different formations and strategies. It had been rough at first. The priests were a little hesitant to work with the elves. In their minds, elves could easily be the enemy. Also, the elves had initially arrested them.

However, the elves had shared some of the berries they ate to help them replenish their mana, while the priests eventually showed the elves how their holy symbols could be used to amplify the potency of their magic. In the end, it really came down to survival. Both groups knew that they might have to depend on the other to survive. Better a friend with a shield at your back than an enemy with a dagger.

Ambrose and Lexel had also been training hard. Ambrose had been training with Fenrir. Avaram had taught Ambrose the commands they used for the panthers. Fenrir seemed to already know these commands. The sister they lost must have already taught them to him. She even learned how to mount and ride him. She felt a little awkward riding a giant white wolf, but it was still thrilling.

Meanwhile, Lexel was training with Katya on how to harness his newfound power. In the past few weeks, he had learned how to reinforce his blade with magic and release the energy in a large slicing wave. He wondered how long he'd had this power. Was it new or simply lying dormant within him all this time? Why had it appeared now?

On one of the nights after a long day's training, Ambrose was looking over the balcony of the tree they were staying in. She looked out at this vast forest honeycombed with houses and various other establishments. Lexel was behind her. She had been almost happy these past weeks, but now she looked anxious.

"Patience thinning?" he asked.

She turned around and looked at him for a moment before turning her gaze back off the balcony. "I want us to be ready, but we can't wait forever. We should move out soon."

"Then give the word," he said.

"What of the elves?" she asked.

"Avaram and Katya respect you. They'll go along with what you decide."

"And if I lead us all to death?" Ambrose asked.

"You won't," Lexel said with a smile she didn't even turn to see.

"You don't know that! How could you?! I don't, that's for sure. You would follow someone who doesn't have the slightest clue what will happen?" She was now facing him. She was very animated, using her arms to emphasize as she did her tone.

"To my death," Lexel said without missing a beat.

"Why? I don't even fight for your beliefs. That goes for the troops and priests as well."

"We believe in you," he said simply. "The woman who fights better than any soldier or priest in the whole damn army. The woman who fights to better her country despite having a difference of opinion. The woman who led us when we were abandoned. Some of those priests respected you because they knew your father. They stayed out of respect for him. However, they didn't follow you into this forest because of that.

They all see what I see. The woman that fought and killed a basilisk to save them," he said.

"Only I couldn't save all of them, nor was I the one to kill it."

"I really think you're missing the point there," he said. "That being one of your less appealing qualities."

"Oh yeah? And what other 'less appealing' qualities do I possess, Lexel?" she snapped.

"That temper, for one," he laughed.

Her cheeks turned red in embarrassment, but then she too laughed. Then the two were back to silence. No longer was it such an awkward silence, however; it was almost comforting. She went to staring and leaning on the balcony. Lexel joined her, standing right beside her.

"Tomorrow, I'll tell Katya and Avaram we are to head out. I'll give the order," she said.

"Yes ma'am," said Lexel.

Ambrose slumped over, resting her head in his chest.

"Ambrose?" he asked.

"Shut up," she replied. There was a pause. "It's *commander*, by the way," she corrected.

"Yes, commander," he said softly.

◆◆◆◆◆◆

Morning came, and Ambrose was ready to give the order. She spoke with Katya and Avaram. They agreed. Avaram had been not so patiently waiting for this order, in fact. Katya, more cautious, agreed due to Ambrose believing it to be the right time.

They agreed to move the following morning at first light. They would need the day to get everyone ready to move. The finale Ambrose had been waiting for was soon to come. She couldn't help but think of Vincent at this time. She dismissed it, though. She no longer wanted to linger on those ideas.

That night, like the last, she sat in her quarters. She had been cleaning Marya and her leather armour. Now she was yet again looking out amongst the trees. She felt her anxieties creeping in again. However, she chose not to give in to them. She looked at Marya, which gave her strength. She looked to her new arm, which felt natural now, though still tough as bark.

Then she heard the door open.

"Lexel, you can't keep coming by. You're going to start rumours with the other troops," Ambrose said, almost laughing.

Then she looked back and saw no one. She quickly grabbed Marya and produced a spear.

"Trevor?" she asked with hate on her voice.

"Ooh, swing and a miss. But good guess," came a voice from her right. She jumped and quickly adjusted her stance to face the stranger. He was adorned in a officer's uniform—an Avalon uniform. This uniform was golden. It put her off slightly; she couldn't see the man's face, as he kept his hat tilted down.

"Who are you?" she asked.

"That hurts, Brosie," the voice said. "We went through so much together."

That nickname struck her. Only one person used the nickname she was not fond of.

"Klein?" she asked incredulously.

"Give the good lady a prize!" he said. He tipped his hat up. "How's it going, Brosie?"

"What are you doing here?" she asked, spitting in anger.

"Checking up on an old friend," he replied.

She kept staring at him, her eyes meeting his in a glare that could kill.

Klein was unflinching. He wasn't intimidated by her.

"As you can see, I'm fine, Klein. Now leave," she hissed.

"So hostile. And after I came here with some information you might find appetizing," he said. He began walking to the door.

Ambrose sighed deeply. "Fine, I'll bite," she said, knowing she might soon regret that decision.

Klein spun on his heel, almost as if he'd anticipated this decision. "Oh, Brosie, I'm so glad," he said.

"Stop calling me that."

"Aw, gonna make that boyfriend of yours jealous?" Klein asked in a cute voice.

She said nothing, but her face got red.

"Fine," he said, shrugging. "We can make this all business. What if I told you that one of us could still win the spot for the last Uppsalan?" he asked.

"What do you know?"

"Well, I'm pretty sure that Vincent is the last Uppsalan," he said.

"Then that would mean that he has been chosen, and we have lost," Ambrose said.

"Does it?" he asked.

Ambrose kept her gaze.

"I can tell you feel the same. Tell me, Ambrose, what are you doing right now, in this place, with a sizable force of elves no less? Tell me why you've been running military drills with plans to march on Mount Bors. Are you not planning to take the position away from Vincent? If not, where is he? Do you know?" Klein asked.

Ambrose didn't like where this was going. Klein had obviously been keeping tabs on her. She didn't even like that he was here right now. If a fight broke out, she was unsure if she could win. She knew very well what Klein could do. He could manipulate her perception of time, messing with her reflexes. A fighter such as herself would be handicapped without good reflexes.

She knew Klein thrived in one-on-one combat but was less effective in group battles. Even still, Klein might act like a fool but had a great mind for combat. His body was not as hardened as hers, but he was smart. She really wanted to avoid a fight here. She had to keep her own emotions in check. Though she wanted to avoid a fight, she would love to run him through.

"I'll take your silence as you know exactly what I mean," he said. He began walking around her, keeping distance between them. "I could tell you where Vincent is," Klein proposed.

"Why should I care?" Ambrose asked.

"Don't you want to know where another competitor is?" Klein asked.

"We're not competitors anymore," Ambrose tried to insist again.

"Please stop pretending that you're not trying to get to Mount

Bors to take this position you've coveted so long," Klein said. His tone implied he had lost his patience.

Ambrose fell silent again.

"What if I told you that Vincent is now travelling with Trevor and a witch and has hired a pirate gang?" Klein asked slyly.

"Bullshit!" she yelled.

Klein held his finger to his lips to signal her to be quiet. "You don't have to believe me, but what I say is the truth."

"Trevor murdered Hamilton and everyone at Uppsala. Trevor led John to his death in the hopes of completing a hit. Now Uppsala is completely destroyed, and everyone Vincent knows is dead. He betrayed Vincent's trust, and this almost ended in Vincent dying! He wouldn't do that," Ambrose said.

"Just like he wouldn't abandon your party, right?" Klein asked.

Ambrose was silent again. Her ability to keep her emotions in check was thinning.

"You said Trevor did all this on a hit?" Klein asked.

"That's what John told us," Ambrose answered.

"I see. Did he say who gave the order for the hit?"

Ambrose tried to remember what John's last words were. "He said that some woman had approached them or something," she said.

"Yeah, something similar happened with my brother and me," Klein said. "We were given orders from up top to hunt down the remaining Uppsalans. In particular, Vincent and Trevor. However, in our search, I also discovered you were still around. Doing a little more digging, I find you have this whole operation."

Ambrose was tensing up at the idea that he might be hunting her.

"Oh, relax. I wouldn't bother with this rambling if I had come here to kill you," he said.

"Then why are you here?" Ambrose asked.

Klein smiled. "Well, we all knew one fact about this competition from the very beginning: there can only be one winner. Currently, Vincent is the front runner. He has Trevor with him, which makes him a significant threat. Not to mention, he has a witch and pirates with him. You have an army of elves, priests, and soldiers who are devoted to you. This makes you a sizable threat for sure.

"Now, my brother and I have a significant amount of our own troops at our command. By this point, Vincent and Trevor will be aware that my brother and I are still in this fight. They also know of you. So, the players seem to be set.

"There is going to be a three-way struggle," he concluded. "We both need to get rid of Vincent and Trevor. I'm sure you have no love for those two—especially Trevor." Klein let that last comment sink in.

Ambrose fully understood the situation now. Klein and Zachariah were looking for their leg up against Trevor and Vincent. They wanted rid of those two first. She couldn't blame them for that. However, this meant that they thought their best chance was trying to get rid of her last. She was the least threatening to them. This was insulting, but she was happy to hear she wasn't on the top of their list of to be removed.

"So, what happens when it comes down to you and Zachariah?" she asked. "Will you kill your own brother?"

"No." He was very serious now. "When it's just the two of us, he will take the seat. I have given up on this game. I found something else. I am content with leading the men and women under my command. I can't leave them for some cushy office job or whatever this is. However, I want someone I trust in that seat. So, Zachariah is the man to do it. No offense to you; that's just how I feel. Do you really want Trevor on that seat?" he asked. "No. No one wants that. I mean, Vincent is a good man, but perhaps a little too much of a zealot, no? So join the winning team." Klein extended his hand.

"And when Vincent and Trevor are dead, you and Zachariah will turn all your attention to killing me and my troops?" Ambrose asked.

"It doesn't have to be that way," he suggested. "You can join us. Fight for Zachariah and me. We don't need to kill each other. However, the same cannot be said for Vincent and Trevor."

"Thought you said Vincent was a good guy?" Ambrose asked, though she was unsure why. In her mind, Vincent was dead to her. Why did she care? She decided she didn't. *What a dumb question*, she thought.

"Vincent is their chosen for the moment. We need to kill him so there is an empty seat. I'm sure you can understand that. Plus, I'm sure you wouldn't mind seeing Trevor gone. So, what will it be, Brosie?" Klein asked.

"I've promised the elves here sanctuary and a different life for their help," said Ambrose. "I won't abandon them."

"Zachariah and I are from Avalon. We're a bit more tolerant than those of Sylvania. So perhaps we can work something out."

Ambrose was silent, this time for contemplation. What would everyone think about this? Would they want to side with the Avalon army? Or would they rather fight? Could she really be talked out of her ambition so easily? Was that a good enough reason for lives to be thrown away? What was the right answer? She didn't know.

"I can see you're having some trouble with this," Klein said finally. "Look, our men will be stationed at the base of Mount Bors. They will be ready for whatever decision you make. You can have your revenge on those two. I know they hurt you." He put his hand on her cheek.

She slapped his hand away as she turned and looked over her balcony.

"You know where to find me then, Brosie," he said. And after that, he left, leaving Ambrose in her room alone.

She was now left with a hard choice: give up on her ambition and settle for Zachariah winning, or fight a battle they might not win so she could achieve her goal. Even worse, there was the possibility of Vincent or Trevor claiming the spot. She felt horrible for weighing the cost of lives versus her ambition. Moments ago, she had been eager for the battle between her and some mysterious foe. Now, she knew it was part of the Avalon army, along with familiar faces from Uppsala.

Also, how the hell were Vincent and Trevor a team? She'd figured that since she never heard from Vincent again, he had simply died in his attempt to kill Trevor. Trevor did always have an uncanny ability to draw people to him, though, getting them involved in his nefarious plots.

She had been worried about fighting a foe she did not know. Somehow, fighting foes she did know was worse. Killing faceless and nameless enemies is always preferable.

Tackling this problem alone seemed overwhelming. She didn't realize that Lexel had been outside the door and had heard their conversation. He had in fact meant to visit her that night and he held a bouquet of flowers, wanting a sweet night before they might die. He hadn't known this would happen, and now he didn't know how to help. In the end, he left her on her own.

CHAPTER 17

VINCENT HAGLAZ

VINCENT AND THE REST OF the crew believed that they had won this day. They thought the fight had been theirs. However, they had lost more than they thought.

Moulder's ship had been attacked by the frigate. The ship had taken some damage but was still in working condition. The crew, however, had taken heavy losses. About half remained from the flagship.

Moulder was among the casualties. He had been right there with the rest of the crew on the deck, fighting. However, in the melee, he was killed. Notable among the crew to survive was Soren, Moulder's understudy.

The two remaining ships in this pirate fleet were currently anchored near some islands. There was a meeting among the notable figures remaining of the crew. This included Soren, Titania, and Trevor. Vincent and Trinity were on the outside of this conversation.

"Time to turn back," Soren said up front.

"Sorry, ass wipe, that's not an option," Trevor replied.

"Last I heard, you left this crew to become an assassin. You really shouldn't get a say here," Soren argued.

"Soren, please," Titania broke in. "Trevor may have been gone a while, but he was aboard these vessels longer then you. Besides, he's our client now. We already accepted the silver."

"A lot of silver, mind you," Trevor added.

"He lied," Soren protested. "We didn't know the Avalon Navy was after him. We were to protect him from random sweeps and patrols, not a targeted assault. We lost the captain, so I'd say that contract is over now."

"All right then, squirt, you want to be tough?" Trevor challenged, drawing a dagger. "Let's see it."

"Rat!" Titania growled. "I'd love to watch that any day, but we do have a significant problem here. We don't have a captain to lead the fleet. Plus, I'm not sure we could get you into Avalon if they are looking for you, and especially—"

"But who's hiding?" Trevor cut her off. "Let's hunt them down and kill them."

"Rat, I love the enthusiasm, but we don't have the manpower. Especially if they got reinforcements. Also, you kind of got your ass kicked the last time. We may have to reassess our situation here," Titania said in a calmer tone than usual for her.

Trevor stormed off. On his way to below deck, he passed by Vincent and muttered something like, "Do what you all want. I'm getting that bastard no matter what."

Trinity chased after him.

Vincent saw Titania and Soren still talking. He stood up and made his way over to them.

"Well, fireman, what can I do for you?" Titania asked. Her tone made it sound like he might just be another problem to throw on top of their already precarious position.

Vincent went ahead and explained part of the objective of their true mission—that this was a test for political power in Sylvania. Also, that they were on their way to secure a power source known as the Well. He explained that Trevor was in this for a chance to tap into that power, and thus their unusual pairing made sense in this case.

He may have also hinted that he might be able to replace the ships they lost once he was granted his position. Vincent didn't like the idea of negotiating with pirates, but at this point, it wasn't the worst thing.

"So now they admit to lying to us," Soren said.

"We preferred to keep all of this private. We had no idea Avalon's navy was after us," Vincent said.

"This changes nothing," Soren said firmly. "We still don't have the appropriate force to take on something like this. I'm sorry, but this is game over."

Vincent looked to Titania, who seemed frustrated and annoyed with the whole thing. "We have connections in Avalon," she said. "We can gather up a group of spies and get some information. We will have to move stealthily for this one."

"You can't be serious," Soren said.

"This is for the captain. This was his last mission. Let's see it through."

TREVOR BLACKWELL

Trinity found Trevor below deck, aggressively sharpening his knives. She could tell he was in a foul mood. This wouldn't be a fun conversation.

"How are you f—" she began.

"I would have killed him if it weren't for you," Trevor interrupted.

"Excuse me," Trinity said. She expected no thanks for saving him back there, but she in no way felt that she was to blame. After all, *she* saved *him*.

"What's the point of an ally?" Trevor asked.

Trinity didn't answer, knowing full well that any answer she gave would be wrong.

"Allies make us stronger. They are a tool like any other," Trevor said.

"Did I not save you?" Trinity asked.

"Yes, but you also almost got yourself killed doing so. I had a choice, you know. In the flames, I could have run down Zachariah. But you would've gotten yourself killed. I can't have someone holding me back like that."

"I didn't ask to be saved," Trinity pointed out.

"And yet, I could not leave you there. Why? Why couldn't I just do the job I was meant to? You're holding me back," Trevor repeated.

"I thought when we started this, you said you would use me until I wasn't useful," she countered. "I saved you in the only way I could think of. I asked for no help, and if I became a hindrance, you could have let me die. I thought I was being useful to you."

There was a pause as neither said anything.

"I don't care how you use me," Trinity went on, tears in her eyes. "Just don't leave me. Don't leave me alone. I can't go back to that darkness. Not again. I don't know where I'd go or what I'd do. It doesn't matter who you are or what you're involved with. You gave me a place to belong where I wasn't in hell every day. This band of misfits we formed gave me the closest thing to friends and family I've ever known. I don't care if I die doing this, since my life never meant anything to begin with. Just let me go out helping a friend instead of alone in the streets!" Trinity was yelling now, bawling.

Trevor stood up and pulled her head into his chest. "Don't say you're life never meant anything. It means something to me," he said.

The two shared a quiet moment. Then they heard cheers coming from the upper deck.

"Sounds like the crew is back on mission," Trevor said.

"Then let's brew up some trump cards for the next time we find that bastard," Trinity said with a treacherous grin.

Trevor had never been so turned on.

183

CHAPTER 18

AMBROSE GAINS

THE FOLLOWING DAY, THE LEADERS met before heading out. There was one exception: Father Tal was missing. There was a search, but upon inspecting his bunk, they found that all his belongings were gone—meaning he left on his own. Given his ability of teleportation, it would have been easy for him to slip out unnoticed.

Not only this, but Ambrose had some news of her own to give them. She told them that she had met with an officer of the Avalon Army. She told them that the army was onto them. If they did not work with the army, they would definitely lose. Theirs was a sizeable force, but not large enough to take on a full-scale army. Besides, there was a worse enemy to fight.

Ambrose was telling them the truth. However, Lexel knew that she was leaving some of that conversation out.

"What of the future you promised?" Katya asked angrily.

"They are of Avalon. They don't share the same prejudice as Sylvanians. Besides, I have been given their word that they will try to come to some arrangement."

"I do not know them. I cannot trust them. How could you come to such a decision without us?" Katya asked.

"I will still be around. I will ensure that my promise is kept. Besides, it will look good for the elves if they help in this battle," Ambrose assured her.

"What of your missing man. What if he was a spy?" Katya asked.

"He very well could have been. I did not know. I thought he was with us."

"This is bullcrap! You've deceived us!" Avaram yelled. She walked up and struck Ambrose, knocking her to the ground.

Lexel and Fenrir jumped in front of Avaram to protect Ambrose. Snow and Alabaster jumped to Avaram's side.

"Stop it! We are still on the same side," Lexel said.

"Screw that!" Avaram yelled.

"No, he's right," Katya said. "While this is an un-ideal change in fate, we can still hold this human to her word."

Ambrose sat up and wiped some blood off her check.

"Still. Betray us, and consider that a warning shot," Katya said.

Lexel extended a hand for Ambrose. He had that same honest smile he always did. She took his hand and stood beside him. He whispered into her ear, "I hope you know what you're doing. Also, you don't need to bear these burdens alone. We can help."

Ambrose was shocked by his words. As Lexel walked away, she looked on. What did he know? Why did he continue to trust her so much? She had no way of knowing whether what she was doing was right. But she now knew what she had to fight for was to live up to the expectations everyone had for her.

She decided there and then that she would make a world where the elves could find acceptance. Along with that, she would be as strong and noble as Lexel believed her to be.

This meant that Trevor had to die, along with Vincent. She had to be ready for that.

Fenrir stood beside her. She petted his stark white fur. *That's right. I have to be all I can, for everyone.*

They made the three-day march to the base of Mount Bors. Waiting for them was an encampment of Avalon's soldiers, looking to be at least 500 strong. Not enough men for a war amongst armies, but their number far exceeded Ambrose's.

Klein, of course, was there to greet them. Ambrose went forth to speak with him, and Lexel joined her.

"So, the fact that you didn't attack us on sight must mean that you have decided to join us," Klein said.

Ambrose said nothing.

"Oh, this is fantastic, Brosie. We surely do appreciate it. Zachariah arrived just the other day—although I wouldn't bother him right now. Looks like his encounter with Trevor and Vincent didn't go well. Glad you and I could be more civil."

"Zachariah met them, together?" Ambrose asked.

"See, I wasn't lying. They are coming. We expect them any day, really. Their numbers are nothing to worry about. Still, we know far better than to underestimate former Uppsalans. Heard Trevor wiped out almost a hundred men by himself in their last encounter," Klein said with a laugh.

"You lose a hundred men and laugh about it?" Lexel asked.

"Oh, and you must be the boyfriend, right? So serious. I see how you two work so well," Klein said.

Lexel went red in the face.

"So, how do you plan to stop Trevor this time?" Ambrose said, getting back to the topic. "Not to mention, he has Vincent with him. I'm not the kind willing to throw away my troops so easily."

"One thing to make clear: I didn't lose any men," Klein pointed out. "My brother did. My men are my brothers, and I mourn every single time one of them falls. My brother is a good man but perhaps a tad bit more detached."

"So where is this brother of yours?" Lexel asked.

"He's up there," Klein said, pointing to a stone lookout tower that was built into the mountainside. It was overhanging the encampment so the occupant could oversee the forces. "Yeah, we call it the nest. We can observe the entire north side of this mountain."

"Are there camps around the rest of the mountain?" Ambrose asked.

"No need. We found a trail that leads to a set of doors. These doors have markings matching those we have seen in Uppsala. Best guess says that's where this Well is," Klein told her.

Ambrose's eyes widened. "If you've found the Well, then why haven't you—" she began.

"Now, now, be patient, Brosie," Klein cut her off. "We can't get in. The door won't open. We can't get it to budge at all. Seems like we are missing whatever opens it. For now, though, that isn't the problem. The problem is Vincent and Trevor. Once we take care of them, we'll get some of our greatest minds to help us with those doors."

"So about them? What's the plan?" Ambrose asked. "As we've discussed, no one is interested in unnecessary loss of life."

"Oh, Brosie, I'm so glad you asked."

CHAPTER 19

VINCENT HAGLAZ

AFTER ANOTHER WEEK OF SAILING, the ship reached Avalon's borders. It pulled up on a bank and anchored just offshore. They were not in any port or city, just a deserted bank near the edge of a forest.

The pirates set up camp in the forest. If the ships were discovered, they would be destroyed. For the time being, the best idea was to abandon them.

Mount Bors was a day's journey ahead of them. Everyone was on edge. The crew had never taken such a hit, and a lot of those they knew had died in the attack a week ago. Now the plan was to strike back with an even smaller force. Most felt that this was just a hopeless suicide mission.

Trevor was packing for something, and Vincent had to figure out what he was planning.

"You don't intend to abandon us now, do you?" Vincent asked.

"You aren't rid of me that easily, fool," Trevor said. "I just want to see what's waiting for us on the other side of these woods. I'll be back tomorrow with a report."

"I'm going with you," Vincent insisted.

"Thanks, but I move faster on my own."

Vincent knew this was true. He would only be a hindrance for Trevor's little scouting mission. He wouldn't be able to keep up with Trevor's speed. "Promise that this is only a recon mission," Vincent said.

"That's what I said, isn't it?" Trevor retorted while still packing.

"And what if you see Zachariah?" Vincent asked.

There was a silent moment.

"I'll be back," Trevor said.

"Trevor!" Vincent shouted. "There are people counting on you now. You're going to throw everyone's life away for reve—" Vincent began.

"You don't think I know that?" Trevor said. "You know, despite what you think of me, I feel for those who die around me. I don't ask anyone to follow me, because they always end up dead. Doesn't matter how I distance myself. It never gets easier to watch an ally die. I tried to make myself strong so I could protect the most important person in the world to me. But she died because of it. So I surrounded myself with lowlifes and criminals so it wouldn't matter who died. But they just ended up being a family, and in that line of work, death is common.

"Then I got a summons to enter some competition to hunt enemies of the state. I thought in a competition of killers, we would all be too busy killing each other to care for one another. But we grew close over the years. Though everyone was strong, I thought we were strong enough to live forever. But no; we still lost lives.

"So I shut off. Became the one thing that doesn't have to worry about seeing a friend die: an assassin, a lone killer only interested in the next score. Never thought a guy like John would find the same line of work. When we got our mission to hunt you down, I thought I had prepared myself for his death. I still see his face when I close my eyes.

"Then there was you. You came to kill me for killing Hamilton. Part of me wanted you to get your revenge. I understood. Trust me, I did. But a zealot like you would have put Trinity to the stake. Somehow, another life worth something had clung to me. Another reason to fight. I couldn't let her die for me too.

"So there you were, caught in my trap, your life in my hands. I had denied you your revenge and my rest. I could have killed you, but that would mean seeing another friend haunt me. So yes, fool, I know what's at stake. See you tomorrow," Trevor said as he walked away.

Vincent had never spoken so plainly with Trevor. Never had he heard Trevor express feeling for anyone besides himself. Never had Trevor called him *friend*.

Trinity ran up to see what was happening, but Vincent stopped her, telling her of Trevor's mission and promising he would come back. It was a promise he hoped he would not see broken. Vincent kept thinking he had nailed down who Trevor was and what Trevor would do next. He was never right.

TREVOR BLACKWELL

Trevor moved through the forest with the speed of a jungle cat. There had been so much clouding his thoughts lately—his loss, Vincent, Titania, the crew, Trinity. But here, he was focused. When mistakes meant death, it gave him a rush that let him send those thoughts to the back of his mind. He could focus. Nothing like looming death to make one see one's priorities.

At last, he had reached the edge of the forest. It let out to a clearing that was the base of Mount Bors.

In the clearing, he saw the army that awaited them. He had liberated a telescope from the ship and could see the full might the enemy, the gold signifying the army and the purple marking the navy. Seemed like 500 army and 100 navy troops.

This meant that Zachariah wasn't the only commander here. No doubt his brother was in on this too. Trevor saw the tower built into the side of the mountain. There was an opening at the top, and there he was—Zachariah, with a new eye patch and burnt left side, looking over the troops. Perhaps Klein waited for them below. Trevor couldn't see him. There was no tent signifying a high-ranking officer or anything.

Trevor also surveyed the mountain and its trails. Then, a quarter of the way up, he saw it: a set of large doors made from stone. The doors led inside the mountain. If the Well was here, that's where it would be.

Trevor was gathering more information on guard movement patterns and positions when he heard the snapping of branches. Guards in the forest? No, sounded bigger.

Trevor tried to hide in the tree's branches. He knew how to sneak around, being an assassin. He stayed perfectly still. Below him were two giant panthers, about twelve feet tall, standing on all fours. They might be cats, but they were clearly too big for these woods. They were not from around here.

Had Zachariah brought in monsters to guard the woods? Trevor began to think he had underestimated his opponent. The cats sniffed around, following Trevor's scent. They were hunting. Trevor, not quite used to being prey, found himself afraid—another feeling he was not used to. He pulled a dagger, ready to kill, fight, or run.

The cats were getting closer, closer. They were right at the base of the tree Trevor was in. Then their ears perked up, and they ran back the way they came. Did something startle them? What startles beasts like that?

That's when Trevor heard voices calling in the distance. Someone really did control these monsters. The upcoming fight would not be easy.

He wanted to track down those monsters, find who was calling to them. He wanted to climb up to the tower and kill Zachariah. These were things that called to the nature of Trevor. However, he had something to fight for now—*someone* to fight for. His failure here would mean they would die. He decided the info he'd gathered would have to be sufficient.

VINCENT HAGLAZ

Waiting for Trevor to return felt like waiting for something that would never come. Vincent was a man of faith, but it was hard to have faith in someone like Trevor. He'd had faith in the man before and was let down. However, Vincent hadn't really known Trevor then, didn't know his feelings.

But do I know him any better now? Vincent wondered. *Or do I know him less?*

As bad as the wait was for him, he could see the anxiety building in Trinity. He could tell she was running through the same cycle.

Vincent had struggled to talk with Trinity. Their differences—well, the differences he believed—prevented them from speaking as equals. However, she had reached out to him when he was in a low moment, and now it was time for him to return the same kindness.

He moved over to where she was sitting next to Titania. Trinity was cooking up some potions in a cauldron, while Titania was sharpening her axe and giving sideways glances to Trinity. Trinity didn't seem to even notice those stares.

Vincent sat next to her and said, confidently, "He will come back."

"I know, but that doesn't mean he won't eventually have to fight this Zachariah character. We both know he can't leave that score unsettled."

Vincent knew that all too well.

"So, uh, what are you cooking up?" he asked.

"Our trump card against Zachariah," Trinity exclaimed.

Vincent made a quite-intrigued face.

She pulled out some blue vials. "These will amplify one's magic." She pulled out some cloudy white ones. "These will give one resistance to magic, in case we run into other mages." She then pulled out the familiar orange ones. "Of course, you will remember these that are imbued with your own fire magic. They have quite the explosive burst to them too. Not sure why they have that effect, but at least I learned that now," she added with a devilish spark in her eyes. She was truly the right match for Trevor.

Vincent nodded his head and was about to stand up.

"He does see you as a friend. You know that, right?" Trinity asked.

Vincent didn't say anything.

"I think he dislikes you because he wants something like you have," Trinity said.

Vincent turned around, unsure what she meant.

"I think he would like to have a set of rules to guide him. A creed. I think he's grasping at straws for what his values are. That's why his actions don't match his words. He thinks he has to be the unfeeling tough guy. But he cares more than he lets on. Showing that, though, would mean showing how much his own actions pain him. In his line of work, showing that weakness is death. I know you can't forgive him, but maybe you could just try to understand him?" Trinity asked with sincerity.

"I think in the month you've known Trevor, you might have him more figured out than in the years I've known him," Vincent answered.

"Oh, come now," Titania butted in. "Rat's just a wild spirit who's taken a fondness for you, girlie, and so have I, you know. But I understand, you and Rat got a little thing going."

Trinity blushed. Vincent shook his head. He had believed that to be the case in the beginning. But he was beginning to believe Titania might be right here.

✦✦✦✦✦✦

Later that night, Trevor returned. Vincent was the first to greet him. Trinity was also awake. Neither could sleep until his return. Trinity got up immediately and ran to him.

"So, what are we up against?" Vincent asked.

Trevor, unusually serious, looked into Vincent's eyes and shook his head. He explained to the group what he'd discovered, including the beasts in the forest. The others listened in sober silence. The odds were stacked against them. It was a fight so unwinnable that retreat seemed the only route.

"So, Rat, seems like you might have bit off more than you can chew on this one," Titania observed.

"No. There is a way. Pretty boy here," he pointed to Vincent, "will follow me up the mountain. From there, we separate. I'll go take out Zachariah; Vincent makes his way to the door. Once Zachariah is dead, I'll cause some chaos. They'll be without a commander with death awaiting them. The rest of you conceal yourselves a safe distant in the woods. If those beasts find you, be ready. Spread out; use arrows and torches. If you're ready for them, they'll be at the disadvantage. Once they're dealt with and all hell breaks loose on the ground, our archers can pick off runners. Once their army is sufficiently scattered, rush in and take 'em out."

Not even Soren could argue against the logic of the strategy, but he tried. "While a decent plan, this does depend on you defeating Zachariah. What if you lose ... you know, like last time?" he asked with a hint of sarcasm.

Trevor shot a nasty look but composed himself. "I won't. But should the plan fail and their army still stands strong, flee. We'll have what we need. Vincent will have made it to his destination, and I'm most likely dead. At that point, your contract will be fulfilled."

Everyone seemed in agreement. All dispersed to prepare for the coming morning's battle. Trinity came up to Trevor and said, "I'm coming with you."

"Trinity, you ..." he began.

"You promised not to leave me," she pointed out. "I won't let you go off on some suicide mission alone. We go ... we go out together."

Trevor didn't respond. Trinity began explaining the effects of her potions to him, and Trevor listened with great enthusiasm.

CHAPTER 20

TREVOR BLACKWELL

THE CREW WAS READY. The archers were armed with bows, torches, and a lot of rope. Their plan was to trap the beasts before cutting them down. Trevor stored some of Trinity's potions on his person, plotting their best use. Trinity, Trevor, and Vincent were about to depart for a head start to begin their covert operation. Then Trevor brought out three cups with some wine in them.

"Would have used harder stuff, but pretty boy here is a little bit of a pussy," Trevor said.

"Religious," Vincent corrected.

"Yeah, that's what I said," Trevor teased.

Vincent rolled his eyes. The three took their drinks and cheered. They were turning to leave when Trinity fell to her knees.

"Trinity?!" Vincent yelled.

Trevor didn't turn around at all.

"What's going on? Someone help," Vincent said, kneeling down beside her. She was trying to stand but couldn't. "Trevor what are you doing, she's … oh." Vincent realized, as no one was moving, that Trevor had put something in her drink. How heartless.

"You … you … bastard … you promised …" Trinity said.

Trevor turned and knelt down. "I'll be back, my wicked witch. I won't lose to that bastard. But I can't fight while having to worry about you. This way, you also won't have to sit around worrying about me. You'll be asleep the whole time. I'll be back before you know it," Trevor said, closing his eyes and smiling.

"Don't leave … me …" she cried, fighting off sleep.

Trevor planted a kiss on her lips, and the twisted anger and pain on her face relaxed. Vincent thought this could have been from the kiss. More likely the drugs though.

Once Trinity had passed out, Titania picked her up and passed her to one of the pirates. "Hide this one well," she said.

Trevor took Trinity's satchel of potions that had dropped onto the ground.

"All right, everyone, you know your jobs," he said curtly. "Don't die out there."

Trevor and Vincent travelled for a long time before they spoke to one another.

"Do you think what you did to Trinity was right?" Vincent asked.

"Thought your kind didn't care about witches," Trevor replied.

"She's not like the witches I was told about. She has a soul. Anyone can see that."

"Trinity will live because of what I did. That's the right call. If she would have come, I could not guarantee her safety, and she might have tried to sacrifice herself for my sake. These aren't outcomes I agree with," Trevor said.

"Are you sacrificing yourself?" Vincent asked.

"No. I won't lose," Trevor declared.

"What if your prediction is right and Klein is there. Can you take the both of them?"

"They'll be cocky and sure of their victory, just as I was. This will be their downfall."

Vincent realized the hypocrisy of that statement. If Trevor truly felt this way, he must mean that he didn't know if he could win. However,

Trevor wasn't betting the operation on his success. There were still a lot of unknowns that could ultimately be the reason they lost this upcoming battle.

They made it to the edge of the forest just before dark. No sign of the terrible cats. They checked the coast and set out in the cover of darkness. Ideally, they would have waited for complete darkness, but they couldn't risk being discovered by the beasts in the forest.

It wasn't hard for two competent and well-trained individuals to slip by undetected to the base of the mountain. They wouldn't take the main trail: too many guards. They would have to do a little bouldering to get up to the doorway. Trevor would have much more to do to get to the tower.

They used an animal trail to make their way up about halfway to the doors, then found a small cave they would rest in for the night. They couldn't start this gambit in the middle of the night, as the crew wouldn't be able to tell when the operation was a go. They would have to do without a fire to avoid detection. Neither of them would sleep well this night.

✦✦✦✦✦✦

Just before first light, the two began their climb. Trevor would have been able to move much faster without Vincent but had to get him to his destination. Once they had the doorway in sight, Trevor would leave.

There were guards surrounding the door. "Once all hell breaks loose, you storm the guards and get in," Trevor said.

"Good luck," Vincent told Trevor.

Trevor seemed a little caught off guard by this. "Uh, yeah, don't fuck this up, OK?"

The two went their separate ways. Trevor looked back and realized in that moment that Vincent was most likely the last friend he would see. He had no guarantee he would come back. In fact, he bet more on the fact that he wouldn't.

He scaled the rocky surface like an ibex, moving with unrealistic grace and speed. He was climbing up in a diagonal direction, with his target a second-level balcony of the tower. The guards on that balcony couldn't see him, as he was crawling underneath them. He was right under them now, ready to choose his moment.

The guards were in the midst of a conversation, and Trevor took the distraction. He leaped up and placed daggers between their eyes. If all the kills were this easy, Trevor would have nothing to worry about.

He spiralled his way up the tower, removing guards as he found them. He also was placing vials of the orange potion about in various locations.

Finally, he was at the door leading into the main overhang. Zachariah was surely inside. Trevor pulled out one of the potions of enhance magic and took a sip. Immediately, he could feel the power rushing through him. It felt like a rubber band pulling to its longest length, being stretched farther and farther, desperate to be released.

Trinity had warned him that if he took too much, it could cause his magic to go wild. She also warned that taking more than one potion at a time would cause adverse effects. Trevor took out his dagger with the basilisk venom. He then took out the cartridge and spilled it out. He filled it full of the magic enhancing potion. He had plans for this.

Trevor made his way to the door, which was slightly ajar. It seemed too perfect, like he was being invited. He wouldn't have any element of surprise here.

He slowly pushed open the door and inside, waiting by the far window, were Zachariah and Klein.

"Oh, Trevor, you've finally made it," Zachariah said.

Trevor didn't like this. He hadn't expected to have to fight the two of them together. But he couldn't run now.

"Trevor, I offer you one last chance to give up Vincent, and we don't have to do this," Zachariah said.

Trevor pulled out the cloudy white vial and took a sip. He would need magical resistance if he was to fight Klein. "I'm done with killing friends," Trevor said. He felt a burning pain all over; the mixture of these two potions was causing waves of immense pain. Trevor was now all but sure this fight would end poorly. He tried to hide the pain on his face, but it must have shown a little.

"Oh, you take a bad hit of something?" Zachariah asked. "Looks like you've lost this fight before it's begun. Trevor, you really have chosen the wrong day to gain a moral compass."

Klein shook his head. "There was a day, Trevor, we would have called you friend too."

"I know," Trevor said. "But I have to fight for those who need me today."

Trevor threw five daggers. Two went for Zachariah and three for Klein. Zachariah easily dodged them. Klein blocked one with a sword, one missed, and the third landed in his thigh.

"Klein! Now!" Zachariah yelled.

"He's dead!" Klein yelled in anger.

Trevor was already blitzing for Zachariah. He could feel his sense of time speeding up. Klein's movements seemed blurry, but he was resisting it with the aid of the potion. He could still see Klein.

Klein's sword came in to cut down and intercept Trevor. Trevor pretended not to see it till the last second. He had been following Zachariah's right eye as it watched Klein come in. Zachariah was able to see both of them due to his slowed perception of time. He used that to time when he pulled the cord releasing the hooked razors on his armour to flip up and slice up Klein.

Klein fell in front of Trevor, for a split-second obscuring Zachariah's vision. Trevor leapt up in that split second and tried for an aerial attack. He kicked out with the blade in his boot. While Zachariah was able to see Trevor, he was struggling to keep up with his increased speed. He barely avoided the kick.

Zachariah quickly evaded the other incoming attacks before catching Trevor with his chained pocket watch. He had caught him by the leg and threw him to the edge of the overhang. Trevor was tipping over the edge, looking down at hundreds of feet between him and the ground. When Zachariah ran in, Trevor threw one of the orange vials, but this was all too familiar to Zachariah, and he instinctively dodged it.

Realizing immediately the repercussions of doing this, Zachariah turned to see the vials hit the back wall, and a fiery explosion followed. Zachariah felt a sharp pain in his leg—a poison dagger thrown by Trevor that was full of a potion that would send Zachariah's magic into a frenzy. Zachariah's internal time was slowing, slowing, slowing. The seconds were feeling like hours or days; he couldn't tell.

He watched in every agonizing moment as the explosion caused by Trevor created a chain reaction in the tower thanks to the individual vials sprinkled throughout. Zachariah couldn't shut off the power. He had no idea what was happening. He watched for what felt like months as the fire of the explosion burnt and scorched his little brother. It would be an eternity yet until he would hit the ground.

The explosion sent Trevor flying over the overhang. The tower was exploding in sections as each of the vials was triggered. Trevor was falling towards a rocky wall face, and he reached out, trying to grab it. He then slammed into it, breaking several ribs, and continued to slide down. He tried to sink his hooked blades into the rock face. They scraped and sparked, some breaking and snapping off.

His left arm finally caught on a surface. The force of his body snapping to a halt dislocated his shoulder yet again, but he clung to this rocky face. He looked back as the tower collapsed and the snow and rock above it came tumbling down on the hundreds of soldiers below.

"Guess that will do for a signal," Trevor said, laughing and spitting blood.

CHAPTER 21

AMBROSE GAINS

AMBROSE'S ARMY HAD BEEN GIVEN orders to lie in wait in the woods. They would wait until the battle started and then aid Avalon in a pincer attack. They were also to survey the woods for the enemy force.

The elves were used to fighting in the forest. Their nimble and agile bodies would give them the advantage if the fighting was to start in here. However, it had been three days. The scouts kept reporting back that everything was quiet. Alabaster and Snow also found nothing in the woods. No trace of any forces.

Ambrose felt like she had been sidelined for this. After all that training, she'd ended up as some glorified guard. Part of her wished she had fought back—fought for a last charge against Avalon, against Klein and Zachariah. Maybe she could have won. But she just couldn't throw all of these lives away for her sake.

Lexel had been slightly distant from her. His smile had also started to come around less and less. They'd started to find out how to be around each other when not in combat, but everything had changed the night Klein came to visit. Had she been acting different? Or did he resent her for giving up?

Part of her wanted run out there right now and take on Avalon. Another part wanted to run away—run away and hide out for the rest of her days. No one would expect anything of her. She wouldn't fail anyone, and no one's life would hang on her shoulders.

There was a sharp crack in the air. Then another and another. Birds flew away as fast as they could. A thunderous sound followed. Ambrose and Lexel looked at each other, then ran to the forest edge. There they saw an avalanche falling upon the Avalon force. The tower Zachariah and Klein had been perched in was destroyed.

"They're here," Ambrose said incredulously.

Avaram and Katya joined them at the forest's edge. Avalon's forces were in shambles, and most were running. Some looked to try to help those caught in the avalanche. Then the cries of men from the forest emerged. *These must be the thugs Klein talked about*, thought Ambrose. The attack had begun, and it had started off just about as badly as it possibly could.

"Katya, Avaram, Lexel—command our forces. Kill these brigands! I have to stop them from reaching that door."

"I'm coming with you!" Lexel said.

Ambrose wanted to argue, but there was no time. She whistled for Fenrir, and her giant white wolf appeared from the woods. Lexel and Ambrose got on board and darted towards the mountain.

They moved with the speed of a hurricane. Ambrose knew this was her moment. This would be the moment that decided what this journey had amounted to. No—what all these years had amounted to. Was she a failure or a success?

⁘⁘⁘⁘⁘

Within the hour, they had made it to the trail and were bounding up the mountainside. It didn't take long to reach the door.

"It's ... it's *open*," Lexel said.

Indeed it was. The giant stone doors had been opened. Surrounding the doors were corpses with stab wounds and scorch marks. The snow around them had been melted, and there were burn marks upon the ground.

"Vincent …" Ambrose said. She'd known she would be faced with Vincent once again. After all this time. After his betrayal, after leaving her behind for a vendetta he wouldn't even carry out. Now he was associated with criminals and murderers—namely Trevor. He'd left her behind for *him*. She hated Vincent for all of this.

"Stay here, Lexel," Ambrose said, walking in with weapon drawn.

"Wait!" Lexel said, getting in front of her. "I can't let you go in there alone. Whatever or whoever is in there is strong enough to cause all this. I know you're strong, but I won't sit out here and do nothing."

Ambrose hugged and kissed him. Lexel was tense at first and then relaxed. This moment had been a long time coming. It was a tension that hung in the air, a truth they didn't speak. Now there was an easiness between them.

"Thank you, Lexel. I mean it when I say I couldn't have come this far without your smile. I have to do this next part alone—not because I don't need you, but because I do. I do need you. But please stand guard and don't let anyone in. I'm counting on you," Ambrose said.

"Uh … yeah …" he said.

"Excuse me?" she teased.

"Yes, commander!" he played along, drawing his sword, which was glowing bright. "I will guard my station with my life!"

"I know you will perform your duty faithfully," she said.

"I love you, Ambrose," Lexel said. "I know that because I have loved my church. My faith has inspired me to have courage and bravery. To do the right thing and be my best self. I never have seen that embodied by one person. But you do. You inspired all of us that way. That's why we didn't care if you believed; you remind us of why we love in the first place."

He continued, "If you need a rock to be sturdy for you, I'll be here. You don't need to worry about failing me. I love you for you. If we fail, I did it with love in my heart. But with you with us, I know we'll win!" he said, his boyish smile as radiant as ever.

She smiled with tears running down her cheeks, "Dumb soldier boy," she said, walking away. Fenrir followed close by her.

Oh, and the dog gets to go? Lexel said to himself.

CHAPTER 22

AMBROSE GAINS

SHE WALKED THROUGH THE DARKNESS and stone. It wasn't cold in here like it was outside. Here it was warm. Not hot, but warm.

She had Marya drawn and ready. Where was Vincent? Was Trevor hiding in the shadows? She was so unsure.

Then, ahead, there was a light—a light coming from above and centring itself on something. There was a silhouette as well. She recognized that silhouette.

"Vincent!" she yelled at him.

All of a sudden, light filled the entire cavern. Where was the light coming from? She and Vincent, and Fenrir, were in a giant circle. The walls were rock, but the ground was marble, with engravings carved into it.

Vincent spun around. "Ambrose?" he asked incredulously, then backed away as he saw the large wolf. "Why are you here?"

"What did you want me to do? Wait around for you never to return? Or just give up?" she asked. He seemed like he was going to respond, but then he didn't. "How did you open the door?" she added.

"What?" Vincent asked.

"Zachariah and Klein couldn't get the door to budge. How did you do it?"

"It just opened as I approached it," Vincent said.

Ambrose figured that Vincent must have somehow been the key. Even if she had fought her way up here, it would have ended when she couldn't open the door. But now she had him here all to herself. She could finish him and take what was hers.

She manifested a twin blade on Marya and took a step towards him. She then stopped. All the hate she had for him—or at least thought she had for him—didn't equate to her killing him in cold blood.

"Is it true you're with Trevor?" she asked, deactivating Marya.

Vincent had already drawn his swords and was ready to defend himself. But he was at ease to see Ambrose wasn't going to attack him. "It's a bit complicated. How did you know that?"

"*Why?!*" she screamed. "He killed Hamilton! He destroyed our home! I thought you were going to kill him when you abandoned us. Guess you thought you'd be better off with him? Well, I guess it worked out for you. You're here now. Do you even know how many of our troops died trying to get here? Do you care? Right now, those thugs you brought here are being cut down by those very men you brought here—along with a band of elves and beasts like him," she said, pointing at Fenrir.

"What are you …?" Vincent said in a horrified realization that the pirates were being ambushed. "You're the ones pulling the strings of those cats?"

Ambrose was now the one shocked to hear Vincent knew about her army. "So we brought two armies here just so they could kill each other," Ambrose said. "Damn it. This is all so pointless!"

Fenrir barked. The two turned to see Umbra and a woman standing opposite them in the circle. Umbra was wearing a large black bearskin coat, his hair in long black curly waves. The woman looked elven. She wore a long white dress with golden armour decorating her. Her hair was silky and almost floated as she moved.

"Well done to both of you," Umbra spoke.

"Father?" Vincent asked.

"Yes, Vincent, it's me. You made it. You completed your quest. You made it to the Well. You are our champion," Umbra said.

"This is the Well?" Vincent asked, looking around.

"Yes. Sorry if it is not what you were expecting," Umbra said. "But yes, this is the Well."

"I thought this was supposed to be some source of power. I expected to see shrines of God. Instead, all I see are these engravings," Vincent said.

"Look familiar?" Umbra asked.

Vincent looked again. He then realized the markings were the same as those at Uppsala. "I see. So there was never any real threat to the Well, was there?" he asked.

"Not necessarily. There is a threat coming. You were trained to be prepared to handle it. However, currently, no, the Well is safely under our control."

"Our?" Vincent asked.

"Yes, sorry. I guess it's safe to tell you now," Umbra began. "As you know, the King of Avalon and the Pope of Sylvania are mere figureheads. Both countries are secretly under the rule of a council. I had told you before there were secret leaders of each country, and that you would be contending for a lone title of a country. That wasn't entirely correct. We try to let this information out to as few as possible. There is really a council of seven who oversee things. We are but two sitting members of that council."

"That reminds me," Ambrose chimed in, gesturing towards the woman standing next to Umbra. "Who is she?"

The woman lifted up her hand, and Fenrir ran over to her. Fenrir was excited, not hostile. He licked her when he got over to her. Ambrose could see the joy in his eyes.

"You're the sister of Katya and Avaram," Ambrose said.

"Indeed, my child," she said. "Hopefully they don't resent me too much for my disappearance. But I couldn't let them know about the council."

"My name's Ambrose. I'm not your child," Ambrose replied.

"Oh, but you are, dear. In quite the literal sense," the woman said.

Ambrose was stunned, as she had never known her mother. Vincent was looking back and forth between the two. This moment was big for both of them.

"You can't be. You're an elf," Ambrose said.

"Yes, making you and Marya half-elves," she said. "That fact was hidden, as your father's reputation would be ruined if he was discovered with an elf."

"Why did you leave us?!" Ambrose cried "Why did you leave us with that man?"

"Again, I had a calling to come here—to help both human and elven kind. I heard about what happened all those years ago, so I asked Umbra to take you in. You've proven stronger and more resourceful than I could ever have imagined."

Ambrose was taking time to absorb this.

"The council holds these tournaments once in a while to replace members that either die or retire," she continued, "and that's why we have held this little tournament to decide who would be fit for seats. Vincent, you are our victor."

"Excuse me, but what happens to me now?" Ambrose said.

"You, dear child, will stand by in reserve. If and when we lose another council member, you will be our replacement. You have been adequately trained and have the wherewithal for the position," the elf said.

"Excuse me, elf?" Vincent asked, with a hostile voice.

She glared at him for his obvious disrespect. "The name is Elara," she said.

"You're on the council, so you knew us Uppsalans?" Vincent asked.

"Yes, I did," Elara replied.

"Were you the one who sent Trevor and John after us?" Vincent asked.

She smiled. "Well, technically, they were sent after *you*. They failed, and you succeeded. Most likely since Trevor got distracted by his own personal vendetta."

"Why?" Ambrose asked.

"Don't take offense, you two," Umbra said. "This was Vincent's final trial. We had to put obstacles in his path to test him. Trevor happened to be one of those obstacles."

"Yes, but Hamilton died!" Ambrose yelled.

"Again, not the intention. That was Trevor's doing. Though we did not say he couldn't kill anyone else, he was only after Vincent. I did warn the both of you in the beginning not to seek out the other Uppsalans, as we were going to set you against them. Klein and Zachariah got orders from 'above.' Orders I gave."

Both Vincent and Ambrose were starting to feel uneasy regarding just how much control this council had. Everything had gone according to the test. This is how they had wanted it to go from the start. Hundreds had died in this endeavour. How could that be acceptable?

"So back to the Well," Vincent said. "Exactly what is it if not a holy relic?"

Elara giggled. "Why, it is the source of all the magic in this world!" she said.

"Impossible," Vincent declared. "We priests derive magic from God through prayer. Others, such as those in Avalon, derive their magical strength from nature. Some, like witches—and Trevor—are abominations that utilize their own magical cores."

"Vincent, these are the beliefs of the masses," Umbra said. "I know it must be difficult for you, but this is where magic is derived from. The Well is where souls return when they die. Souls hold quite potent energy. This energy is passed through this mountain into the Well, and that gets seeded into the earth. This is how magic flows though the land."

He continued, "This is what the magicians and alchemists of Avalon refer to as *nature energy*—which is partly right. Meanwhile, in Sylvania, the priests believe it to be a blessing given to righteous souls. Again, souls are the fuel for magic, so I guess both parties are partly of right in this sense. Of course there are exceptions to this rule. Witches have their own unique magical cores. This is why we label them a scourge. Also there are weapons and various other relics that have been imbued with magic after being exposed to the Well. This is how your weapons functions Ambrose. So while it still used human souls to power it. It is not using your own connection to the Well." Umbra said.

"That's unbelievable," Ambrose said with amazement.

"No, that's heresy!" Vincent said.

"Oh, no. I was afraid of this," Elara said.

"Vincent, learn your place!" Umbra shouted.

"Like hell I will!" Vincent yelled back. "You mean to tell me that the church is just a lie? That when we use magic, we are consuming human souls? If that's true, we are worse than witches! We're the monsters! So you're telling me we're just baser creatures drawing power from human souls?"

"I figured your child might act up like this," Elara said to Umbra. "I always knew he was a bit overzealous. Hate to break it to you, kiddo. This is the very council that invented your God."

"You lying bitch!" Vincent yelled, sending the biggest wave of fire he'd ever had at Elara.

"Vincent!" Ambrose yelled.

Elara ducked out of the way and snapped her fingers. Immediately, the fire disappeared and stopped erupting from Vincent's palm.

"Sorry, boy, but I can shut off someone's connection to the well," she snapped. "Now, grow up! You're on the council now. These are facts you'll have to live with."

Vincent went down to his knees. He was shaking. Everything he ever knew was a lie. Everything he had based himself on, all his values, his actions, everything. If there was no God guiding him, who made the tenants he followed? Who decided what or who was evil? How many had he put to death in the name of this false God? "I don't want it," Vincent said.

"Vincent!" Umbra exclaimed. "Stop this foolishness. You've passed all the tests. You've fought and killed for this. We trained you to be the best. Stop moping!"

Vincent began speaking in a mantra:

"Tenant number 1: Those who want salvation and paradise must act in accordance to God.

"Tenant number 2: To harm the innocent and defenceless is a sin.

"Tenant number 3: Those with power should protect the weak and the will of God.

"Tenant number 4: Creatures based upon unnatural and ungodly sources are the work of demons and devils and should be purged.

"And Tenant number 5: Those that speak or commit heresy shall be purged from the earth!"

Vincent put emphasis on this last point. He stood up with his swords drawn and charged at Elara. He knew it was suicide. With no magic, and against two council members and this wolf, he knew he would die. But in this godless world, he was OK with that.

Stepping in front of him was Ambrose.

"Move, Ambrose," Vincent said with defeat already in his voice.

"I told you back then: If you ever falter in this path, I will take it from you," Ambrose said, activating Marya with twin blades.

The two began an intense melee. Ambrose was the aggressor. Vincent was on the defensive.

"Fight back, you coward!" Ambrose yelled. She didn't let up. Still, Vincent had no fire in his eyes. He seemed so lost, so ambivalent to all that was happening. He was only fighting out of reflex. Meanwhile, Ambrose was going all in, but she was still not trying to kill him.

Finally she spun, and her blade connected with Vincent's. Vincent had to use both his blades to block. As he did, she released her weapon and tackled him—a move once used on her. She landed on top and started letting Vincent have it. She beat him again and again, which was especially painful for Vincent with her new arm.

"You come all this way just to give up?" she cried. "How many fought for you? How many died for you? Do their lives matter to you? Or are we all just so insignificant to you? Where's your God? Not here? Did he abandon you? How does that feel?" she asked, pounding away at him.

Her knuckles were bloody, and so was Vincent's face. He wasn't even resisting. He had just given in.

Ambrose rose a fist to slam into him when she felt a piercing pain in her hand—a dagger.

"No!" she yelled as the speed demon rushed in and knocked her over, his boot on her chest.

"Careful—one flick of my boot, and the blade inside the tip will cut your throat," Trevor said.

She looked up at him. His face bruised and burned. His right eye was red and full of blood. He had soot and blood all over his armour.

"What did you do to Lexel?" Ambrose asked, tears in her eyes.

"Who?" Trevor asked in genuine confusion.

"The man outside. What did you do to him?!" Ambrose asked, fearing she knew the answer.

"The boy with the glowing sword?" Trevor asked devilishly.

Trevor drew a scimitar with blood on it. Fresh blood. "I didn't know you liked blonds."

Ambrose saw the scimitar and recognized it.

"Oh, this?" Trevor teased. "Got it off some old guy. He wasn't using it anymore. How rich that he would give me this to use on golden boy out there. Sorry, if I knew he meant something to you, I would have taken my time," Trevor laughed.

"*I'll kill you!*" Ambrose screamed.

"Sorry, you won't get the chance," Trevor said. He was lifting the sword.

"Tre-trevor," Vincent said with all the strength he could.

Trevor looked back. "N-no more," Vincent said.

"What? What about …?" Trevor looked down at Ambrose. "I hope you're worth it. I'm breaking a promise for you," he whispered to her.

Ambrose didn't know what he meant by that.

"Well, the failed assassin returns," Elara said.

"Well, well, the gang really is all here," Trevor replied, stepping off Ambrose.

"Trevor, you are the one standing before us. Technically, the seat belongs to you, as Vincent no longer is deemed fit," Umbra said.

"Pass," Trevor said.

"Figured that was the case," Umbra nodded. Black forms began appearing around Trevor. They were wolves made from shadows.

"So this is what you've been hiding, big papa? Kind of a let-down, really," Trevor teased.

Umbra said nothing. The shadow dogs surrounded Trevor.

Trevor sprinted out, faster than the hounds could track.

"Oh, sorry, no magic," Elara said.

Trevor's speed was unaffected. His magic was based off a witch's power, not the Well.

Elara's eyes widened. She had to put her arms up in a last-second defence, and Trevor leaped onto her and stabbed through her hands, barely piercing the left eye. She screamed.

"Oh, wow, and that was just the tip!" Trevor taunted. He would have continued to stab into her, but the shadow dogs finally caught up. All his limbs had a beast biting into them, pulling him away.

Elara was mostly fine. Her hands were pierced and her left eye was gone, but she'd live.

A black hole opened in the ground. The beasts drew Trevor towards it. Trevor laughed and screamed in pain as they ripped away at him and dragged him into the pit.

Ambrose heard Trevor's last words: "Sorry, Trinity."

This meant nothing to her. For all she hated him for, it was still a brutal end. She didn't pity him, but who was Trinity?

Ambrose looked around and saw that Vincent was gone. A trail of blood led outside. He must have used the distraction.

Umbra walked up to Ambrose. "Well, looks like we have an opening. Interested?"

ACKNOWLEDGMENTS

Alexander Stokes, for some character inspirations

Kate Brown, for initial edits

Matthew Turner, for inspiring me to publish

Many other friends and family members for their continued support.